Niki Mackay studied Performing Arts at the BRIT School. She holds a BA (Hons) in English Literature and Drama, won a full scholarship for her MA in Journalism. Under Niki Mackay, she is the author of *I, Witness* and *The Lies We Tell*, as well as the gangland thrillers *Loaded* and *Taken*. Under NJ Mackay she has published two standalone psychological thrillers, *Found Her* and *The Girls Inside*.

Also by NJ Mackay

A DI Sebastian Locke Mystery

The Quiet Dead
The Sweetheart Killer
The Vanished

NJ MACKAY
THE
VANISHED

hera

First published in the United Kingdom in 2025 by

Hera Books, an imprint of
Canelo Digital Publishing Limited,
20 Vauxhall Bridge Road,
London SW1V 2SA
United Kingdom

A Penguin Random House Company

The authorised representative in the EEA is Dorling Kindersley Verlag GmbH. Arnulfstr. 124, 80636 Munich, Germany

Copyright © NJ Mackay 2025

The moral right of NJ Mackay to be identified as the creator of this work has been asserted in accordance with the Copyright, Designs and Patents Act, 1988.

All rights reserved. No part of this publication may be reproduced or transmitted in any form or by any means, electronic or mechanical, including photocopy, recording, or any information storage and retrieval system, without permission in writing from the publisher.

No part of this book may be used or reproduced in any manner for the purpose of training artificial intelligence technologies or systems. In accordance with Article 4(3) of the DSM Directive 2019/790, Canelo expressly reserves this work from the text and data mining exception.

A CIP catalogue record for this book is available from the British Library.

Print ISBN 978 1 80436 491 8
Ebook ISBN 978 1 80436 490 1

This book is a work of fiction. Names, characters, businesses, organizations, places and events are either the product of the author's imagination or are used fictitiously. Any resemblance to actual persons, living or dead, events or locales is entirely coincidental.

Printed and bound in Great Britain by Clays Ltd, Elcograf S.p.A.

Look for more great books at
www.herabooks.com
www.dk.com

For our Mimi – furry little mewer. You were the best big girl and we miss you.

PROLOGUE

CHARLIE

I wake up to the sound of my own coughing.

My whole body is involved, shoulders shaking, chest rattling. Eventually it turns into an extended episode of dry heaving. I lean sideways, but it's unproductive, just exhausting. I shut my eyes just for a second, and pull myself upright, one arm under my head because I've learnt that's the best way to keep the acid down. The bile sits in my chest, a hard, fiery ball, and I swallow thickly. Once, twice. Breathe in, exhale. That's when I notice that I'm lying on what smells like clean sheets. I open my eyes, only a little bit because light is gonna fuck up my delicate situation almost as hard as a punch in the face.

Yup. Fresh, white cotton.

Maybe I am in a hotel? I roll the other way – no one there, just a blank wall. I shut my eyes again.

If last night me had any sense, and that bitch usually does, I'll have left a little something somewhere I can reach it.

I must drift off on this thought though because I find myself waking up all over again.

This time the heaves come straight away and are accompanied by the kind of sweat that lets me know I need to sort myself out and fast.

Fuck.

I open my eyes properly and find the light isn't too bad. It's also artificial.

I'm in a windowless room.

I frown and the use of face muscles sends all kind of raggedy jagged pain through my head. I swing my legs off the bed, my bare feet meeting with a hard floor. I lean forward, over my knees, head sinking into my hands. I press my fingers into my eyes, willing the pain to stop. The thump-thump-thumping inside my head is a terrible foreboding drumbeat.

What I need is a fix or a drink. I force myself up. There is a table next to what is an actual bed. I can't remember the last time I slept in anything other than an uncovered mattress on the floor. I guess last night I got lucky. Maybe some guy was so fucked up himself he could overlook the state of me.

Maybe Sid came up with some cash and booked us into a hotel.

Whatever.

On the table, there is a small white container made of paper, and inside are two white pills; my first thought is hospital. Next to it is a glass of what appears to be water, which is a disappointment on a level I can barely comprehend. I have all the rage at past-me right now. I reach for it though, the water, just in case. And sniff. It *is* water. My stomach won't cope with that but my mouth is like sandpaper so I take a teeny tiny sip then put it back down. It shakes as I do, my hand wobbly and unreliable.

There is a piece of paper on the table. Folded over. Plain white. I wrack my brains trying to think what it might be but I can't even grip my last memory and until the pounding in my head subsides, I'm not going to try.

Time isn't how it once was, that's for sure, trying to keep track of it gives me a headache on good days. Plus – what's the point?

Maybe it's a man's piece of paper. A faceless unremembered man who must have brought me here.

I glance at it and although it hurts my eyes to look at anything and try to keep it in focus, I see my name on the folded side.

My full name, which no one calls me anymore.

Charlotte.

It says in neat typed letters.

I shut my eyes, a flutter of panic in my chest. My mother? My husband? The thoughts are fleeting. Neither scenario is likely, though both of them have been on my mind of course.

I open the note, read the rest of the message.

Take the pills. Use the bathroom – through the little door. Get rest.

What the actual fuck.

I look. A little door and a big door.

I do need to piss and I propel myself on towards the little door, leaning on it and almost losing my balance. My legs are like cotton wool.

It is a tiny bathroom, illuminated by the faint light in the bedroom. Like the room I'd come to in, there are no windows. When I pull the light cord, a burring fan starts up and makes me jump out of my skin. The noise seems to expand and join forces with the thump-thump of my head. I stand, one hand holding on to a sink in front of me.

There is a toilet, a shower cubicle and the sink.

I head to the toilet, lurching forward as the cacophony of noise and pain comes to a mighty crescendo, yanking deep nausea from inside me and making the room spin. I catch myself just in time, hands reaching for the seat, knees buckling as I sink to the floor where there is a welcome coolness on my legs.

A moment's pleasure. Short lived. I'm going to throw up.

I lift the lid just in time and lean forward. A thick stream of bright yellow liquid hurls out from my body. Once. Twice. Three times.

My stomach cramps and I lean back, slope sideways, pressing my cheek against gloriously cool tiles. White in here too.

I shut my eyes. Focus on breathing for a bit and trying not to piss myself.

When I can, I get up, turn around and lower my arse onto the bowl. I'm wearing some kind of gown and pants made of paper, which slide off and down to my feet.

A moment's relief before another wave of nausea hits me and my skin itches like ants crawling at pace.

Am I in a hospital? Am I hurt? Like wounded hurt, not just sick.

I sit after I'm finished for a bit. Mainly because I know that any movement is going to cause me a fair amount of pain, though I'm so thin now that sitting itself is uncomfortable.

Eventually, I pull up the paper knickers and look down at my legs. Bruises cover them, old and new. At varying stages a mottled mess. My pale skin is a patchwork pattern of blues, greens and yellows, scratches, scrapes, little nicks and cuts. No unusual ones, nothing unduly alarming. I check over my arms my eyes quickly moving on from the badly tattooed letter T on the inside of my wrist. I think I attempted that one myself. I'm always grateful it was just one letter, though that is reminder enough. A permanent inky punishment. An image flashes in my mind. A chubby smiling baby. I push it away.

T.

No major injuries. Limbs all work. Nothing broken.

An overdose then?

Wouldn't be my first. Sadly, they are never my last either.

I get up on Bambi legs. My body feels better for expelling some of the poison even as I feel its gathering cries for more. The hunger that is never satiated. I still remember the first time I was ever sick after drinking, which seems like nothing at all in comparison to dope sick. That had been peach schnapps, and coming back up it had tasted almost the same as when it went in.

I take deep breaths as I manoeuvre around the room. It is absolutely bare. Nothing on the walls or the floor. Just the bed with the bedside table. The pills, the water.

No IV drip, no chart, no noise. In my experience, hospitals are noisy places. Even in the deep dark of night.

I go to the other door and put my hand on it.

It doesn't give, doesn't click open. It stays steadfastly still and I understand then that it is locked.

I am locked in here.

I am trapped.

CHAPTER ONE

She's so tall now. All arms and legs. A coltish version of her former self. Her face is different too, less puppy fat, more definition, Seb thinks. He misses those chubby cheeks, misses her gappy smiles and soft curls. She is turning into a young woman.

Fifteen today.

She stands in the midst of a gaggle of her friends. They are queueing up to go into the cinema and Seb is sitting obediently in the cafe watching them file in.

There was a time where she wouldn't have wanted to go in unaccompanied. He'd have sat in there too, internally grumbling at the choice of film, gearing himself up for a plotless disaster and reminding them all to keep their voices down. Now he'd give his right arm to be invited.

Just when he feels his heart can't take any more she turns, eyes looking for him, and her hand raises just for a second. So quick, it's almost imperceptible.

He raises his hand to her, smiles, nods.

A voice says, 'Still not quite grown.' And he turns to look at his once mother-in-law, Val.

'You think so?'

She nods. 'I know so.' She pats his hand. 'You've years left yet.'

'Yes,' he says, though that sense of loss, his fear at her growing up, up and away, natural of course and right, is still there below the surface.

Maybe because she's his only one, maybe because he is her only parent.

Val says, 'What we need is caffeine, because you know we won't be getting any sleep tonight.'

He heads up to the counter and buys coffee, glad of the distraction, glad to have something to do. The barista asks his name and writes it incorrectly on a paper cup. Val and Seb talk about nothing in particular, passing the time while they wait to be a taxi service. She is an easy woman. He'd heard horror stories of other people's in-laws but Val is Seb's rock. They've lived together since he joined the force and honestly, his and Tilly's life wouldn't function without her in it. More than that she's funny, sharp and quick-witted and she has him laughing as she updates him about the latest politics of her various groups. Val is someone who likes to join in and she has a book club, a knitting circle and, unlike many her age, has embraced the online world and gets herself involved in all kinds of fiery debates.

After the movie, they head home, Seb driving a hired people carrier full of giggles and raucous sugared-up excitement. They order pizza. More, he thinks, than four girls and two adults could ever eat, but they'll likely polish off the lot. Then the youngsters make their way upstairs to Tilly's room.

The door closes and the noise starts.

'Dear me, Sebastian,' Val says, her face scrunched up in a frown. She looks tired, Seb thinks, and feels a small swell of panic. She's no spring chicken, he supposes, though she never seems old. 'I'm cool from here, Val,' Seb tells her with a grin.

'Are you sure?'

'One hundred per cent. I'll bring you pizza when it arrives.'

She nods, 'Appreciated,' and leaves to go to the annexe they'd had purpose built for her.

He walks to the bottom of the steps and listens to the cacophony from upstairs, mainly giggles, and decides that there is no need at all for him to go up, in fact he'll text Tilly when the food arrives and she can take it. He'll deal with the greasy cardboard boxes in the morning once some semblance of order is restored.

–

The station is Seb's home away from home and despite the fact that he's tired from broken sleep, he's pleased to be here and grateful that all the extra teenagers will have been collected and taken home by the time he is back again. He likes his job. He'd been working on a local paper, training to be a journalist, when Tilly became a thing, unexpectedly. His dad had got him the journalism gig after Seb had flunked his first year of A levels. A lucky break, as he was constantly reminded, and one he did not deserve. It was a cushy number, his dad had said. One that eventually would lead to a plum position and plenty of financial reward.

Neither he nor Seb's mother were impressed when Seb told them they'd be grandparents, and in some ways, he couldn't blame them. Who wants their eighteen-year-old kid announcing he'd got his girlfriend pregnant? Worse was the fact they disliked Charlie almost as much as they disliked him. He was nothing if not a disappointment to them. Seb had been adopted and had grown up with the best that money could buy and yet still somehow made a balls-up of his life.

They couldn't understand it, couldn't understand him. Muttered that perhaps nature did win over nurture, and Seb had thought about that. Did he come from bad stock? The thing he'd always feared. He didn't know then and doesn't know now.

Looking back, he can almost feel sorry for the well-to-do couple who'd opened their home to him. They thought they were doing a good thing, but he could never meet their expectations.

When Charlie finally went and Seb told them he'd be raising Tilly alone they cut all ties. Cut him off and, he suspected, they'd removed him from their will.

He could have limped on with the journalism job, and he did for a bit until Val came down south, saw the state of him, how much he was struggling, and suggested he have a think while she lent him a hand. That hand was well over a decade ago.

His thinking led to an Open University degree in criminology and psychology, and Seb joining the force. Looking at the state of modern-day journalism, Seb thinks things worked out for the best work-wise anyway. He'd never looked back and he'd never spoken to his adopted parents again.

Detective Sergeant Lucy Quinn appears at his desk, a worried expression on her face.

'You OK?' he asks, almost laughing at her unusually serious expression.

'Um...'

'Lucy, is everything all right?'

'I don't know.'

'OK…'

'It's… I don't know if I should be saying anything, but I figured you'd want to know.'

'Lucy, don't talk in code. Spit it out.'

'Your ex-wife.'

He is still sitting exactly where he was at his desk, coffee in front of him, computer on, ready to go over his tasks for the day ahead, but everything around him seems to shudder. He closes his eyes.

Years he's waited for this, a call he'd thought rather than in person, rather than one of his own officers. Years he'd wondered if he'd still be listed as her next of kin.

His first thought is dead. It springs into his mind in letters.

He doesn't speak and the silence stretches out, he's holding his breath. Because he doesn't want to know, except of course he does. He blinks and the station comes back into focus. Lucy says, 'Someone's filed a missing person's report,' and he almost laughs.

'Right,' Seb says. Lucy is still hovering by his desk, chewing her lower lip, which he knows means she's anxious. You and me both, kiddo, he thinks.

His phone pings. Faye.

> How was the sleepover? How are you?

Oh god, he was going to have to discuss this with her of course. 'Yes, all fine,' he says. The first lie of their relationship sliding from his phone to hers, because of Charlie. That thought sends a swell of anger tinged with panic right through him.

He puts his phone away and manages to stand, hoping his face looks balanced and impassive. 'Meeting room?'

Lucy nods, her face flushing as though she is taking his embarrassment for him.

The anger swells again. Not at Lucy but at Charlie, who has been a source of humiliation for many years now. Who hadn't been there yesterday when their daughter celebrated her birthday, who hadn't been there for most of her other birthdays. Who hadn't ever been there, not really. Charlie was a mother so absent Tilly never even mentioned her. A fact Seb worries about endlessly.

Once they're out of the open plan and behind a closed door, he says, 'Let's hear it.'

'A man, Sid Darnell, came into the station.'

Sid Darnell.

Boyfriend? Customer? Pimp? He doesn't ask. Unsure the words would come out in any sort of reasonable tone.

'Her uh… partner?' She says it like a question.

'Boyfriend?' he manages.

Lucy nods, looking relieved. 'They live together.'

'Right.' His heart beats hard in his chest but his voice sounds steady and even. 'When?'

'Two weeks ago.' Seb lets that sink in. Two weeks. 'I only came across it because I was covering the night shift yesterday.'

He frowns. 'Have you been home?'

'What? Oh no, not yet, but that's not the point. No one realised that uh, you were…'

'That the missing drug addict was my ex-wife?'

Lucy flinches but nods again.

Just a case. Probably not even that. Drunks and druggies go missing all the time. She'll show up like a bad penny. Wherever it is she's meant to be.

He asks Lucy, 'How come it's come to your attention now?'

'Oh, we had an anonymous call from a woman this morning about a disturbance in their flat.'

'Where?'

'Pardon me?'

'They live together – you said their flat, where?' Last he'd heard Charlie was hanging out in central London but the call had come in here, to this station.

Lucy says, 'The Hartsmead estate.'

Hartsmead. Less than half an hour's drive from where they are now.

She's here. In the same borough as him. As her daughter and her mother. He almost laughs. Charlie so imprisoned by suburbia she just couldn't bear it ends up back here.

Not in the good bit of town though. Hartsmead, despite its pretty name, is the armpit of the little burb they call home. People move here in droves when they start families. They are in theory still a London borough, so the commute won't break you, time-wise or financially. They suffer from fewer inner city problems, though with county lines spreading and not enough police officers, it's not what it used to be. Nowhere is. But, on the whole, the schools are good, the grass is literally green and plentiful, and if you have some money, you can avoid the sore spots.

Like Hartsmead.

Seb visits fairly often, mind. With two sprawling estates, a lot of his work takes him there. He wonders if he's ever passed Charlie. Not beyond the realms of possibility. He hasn't been looking out for her recently. Since Faye, he's thought about her less and less.

'Sir?'

He clears his throat, more for pause than because he has any need to do so.

'Is there a report?'

She nods and slides over a single page.

Sid Darnell reported her missing thirteen days ago. The officer had ignored it. He'd come in again a week later adamant that she should have shown up by now and also convinced someone was following him.

Seb nods at the page as though in agreement, but of what he is unsure. The officer did the right thing. Chances are she'll show up. They usually do. The desolate drug-addicted. They wouldn't have wasted resources looking for an adult like her with a history of going off. He himself had reported her missing more than once. He'd spent many a night, phoning local hospitals, walking the streets. She always turned up. Chances were she would this time.

Lucy says, 'Should I have told you?'

'Sorry?'

She shrugs. 'I mean I was going over the previous reports linked to the address and saw the name.'

'Oh right. Yes. Best to have said.' Then he adds, 'She might even be back by now.'

Lucy nods. 'Maybe.'

He stands and says, 'Shall we go and find out?' Aware that he is smiling too brightly.

She nods. 'Sure.' But it almost comes out as a question.

CHAPTER TWO

SAM

My eyes sting from lack of sleep, but also from the overripe hideously chemical fumes from the pipe lying next to her. Shit. She'd been doing so well too.

'Laura.' My voice is startlingly loud in the empty room. She sold off her furniture last year, shortly after May took the kids for good. The right decision for them and, for a while, we'd all hoped it was a wake-up call for her. 'Laura,' I say again. My hand on her shoulder. She comes to, pale eyes snapping open. Combined with her crusted lips and pockmarked skin she looks like an extra from *The Walking Dead* rather than the smart young woman she is. She'd been trying to get clean for months. The most she'd strung together was three weeks. This time she'd managed ten days and here we were.

'Sam?' Her voice is a pathetic croak but she's awake and lucid, kind of.

'I'm here,' I tell her, 'I'm here. Let's get you showered?'

I help her into the bath, turn the water on and leave, pulling the door to behind me.

I open the windows and a blast of crisp air sweeps in. Not enough to get rid of the awful tang of hell smoke but it at least dilutes it. The kitchen isn't too bad, though the stench of the bin is pungent. I wash the few dishes, wipe down sides and take the bag out. It stinks, old takeaway boxes with food dried on, the kitchen roll I'd used to wipe the grim surfaces and sides. It's only been a week since I last visited her and yet she's managed to trash the place. She'd been doing so well, I'd been so hopeful for her.

At least this time, she was the only one there, I guess.

She comes out of the bathroom, towel wrapped around her too small frame.

'I'll take the rubbish down and leave you to get dressed,' I tell her.

The sun is bright but not much can make this ragged sinkhole of an estate look good. It was a nice place once, built with good intentions, but it's dilapidated and houses the lowest of the town's residents. Problem tenants from other estates often end up here and it has an apocalyptic feel to it.

As I walk to the bins, I see a tall man and two uniformed officers getting out of an unmarked car. Not an unusual sight here, where trouble is constantly brewing.

I put the bin bag into the big plastic bins and watch the police make their way upstairs. There are kids loitering round the bin shed and they give me hard stares as I walk past. I ignore them, walk to my car where I carry a small portable Hoover. I grab it and head up the stairs. Once inside, I run it around the place, cleaning the low-slung coffee table, rearranging the scatter cushions where I suspect Laura is sleeping and sitting for most of the day. When she relapses, she tends to bring on severe agoraphobia and barricades herself in one room.

Laura comes out of her bedroom. She still looks awful but slightly better than she did when I arrived.

'Hey,' she says, her eyes scanning the room.

'I put your stuff in the drawer,' I say. As ever, the temptation to take her drugs and flush them down the loo is strong but I'd learnt years ago that there's no point. The one thing you can be certain of when it comes to addicts is that they'll find a fix no matter what you do to stop them.

'Thanks.' Her hand reaches up to her cheek, working away at the skin there. The source of the little craters in her face. She was pretty once and should be still. In the last few weeks I've seen glimmers of the real her coming back. Looking at her, I think those days are past, at least for now. She looks sick.

'What happened?' I ask.

She slumps down onto the sofa with a sigh. 'I don't know,' she says, her face blank. 'I argued with Mum.' I knew that, because her mother, May, had already told me. I had stopped short at admonishing May for it. I got both sides and although I desperately wanted May to go easy on Laura, to give her a chance to improve, I knew too how many chances May had already given her.

I pull out some paperwork, and slide it across the table to her. 'You didn't show up to court,' I say. This week there was a hearing about her two children, Donna and Riley. The hearing was to determine whether Laura should have any contact right now. The way things had been going, I'd been really hopeful about the court date, about Laura starting to rebuild. May had been less optimistic, and it turned out she was right.

'They're better off without me,' Laura says now.

'I don't know about that,' I say, though they are certainly better off not living with her until she can get herself in check. I know very well the devastation of living with an addict parent. The slow destruction this illness wreaks on everyone who comes close to it.

There's a pause and then, 'How are they?' Her voice is barely a whisper.

'They're OK,' I tell her, and she nods. We tend to leave it at that. It's what she can handle. She doesn't want or need to know that Riley wakes in the night in a wet bed calling for his mum. That Donna is stubborn and hard-faced whenever Laura's name is mentioned. A ten-year-old trying to appear tougher than she is. Tougher than any kid should have to be.

'Donna is very protective of her baby brother,' I settle on, and it's true.

Laura smiles. 'She always was.'

'Your mum's doing a good job.' Laura doesn't respond to that, but her eyes stray away from me and to the drawer in the table. She's keen, I know, for me to leave so she can smoke the rest of her stash. She and May had argued because Laura had asked to visit. The court order had left such things up to May's discretion but had also said any access had to be supervised. It is a far from ideal arrangement, putting added pressure on May, who is already struggling to care for her grandchildren – kids who have been through a lot. Add in the fact that May is furious with Laura, understandably so, and it is volatile at best.

'I do need you to sign a few forms.' I point to the paperwork and pen. She picks it up, scrawling her signature without even glancing at the words.

'It just reiterates that you give your mother permission to keep parental responsibility, for now.'

She nods. The first time the kids were taken, she'd howled, screamed, shouted abuse and refused to sign anything. Now, just a year later, she doesn't bat an eyelid.

Last week she'd been different. Last week she'd been quietly hopeful and determined. Last week she'd been clean.

I stand, gathering the signed forms.

'I've left some shopping in your kitchen.'

'Thanks.'

'You know, it doesn't have to be like this.' She doesn't say anything. Doesn't even raise her eyes to meet mine. 'Whenever you're ready, help is available.' Still nothing. 'Call if you need anything, and I'll see you next week.'

'Yeah, OK.'

I look back as I close the door; her back is to me, hands ferreting in the drawer. Her children forgotten. Everything forgotten for now.

I walk back down to my car and check my phone. Mark has sent over news regarding two more of my active cases. Not even ten a.m. on a Monday and I already feel battered by my job and the thought of the week ahead.

I get in my car and drive to our offices in the local guildhall, thinking that at least I'll be able to grab a coffee before our team meeting begins.

CHAPTER THREE

CHARLIE

Time passes. Days that might have turned into weeks whizz by in this weird white room. People come in but they are hazy, indefinable shapes. Dressed in white, their faces covered. They bring water and the pills that I eventually take.

I am sick. So so so sick. Reality slips in and out; I dream endless dreams, coming to frightened, my skin damp, my heart racing. I feel a hand on my forehead, cool with powdery skin. I smell bleach, disinfectant and hear the low murmur of voices.

I sleep, I think, or more accurately, I drift in and out of consciousness. Whatever the pills are, they are strong, and I have fleeting moments where I wake and wonder where I am before I slip away again. At one point, I'm sure there is someone standing over me with a cone-shaped mask on. I see blurry eyes, the outline of a face, and I hear them speak. To me? They look away off to the side. I try to move my head but I can't, it's too heavy. All of me is heavy. My limbs are like concrete and I go to raise my hand but it doesn't move. I try to speak but no sound comes out. The masked person moves away. I feel them pass me by, a whoosh of moving air and nothing else. Then my heavy eyelids close and...

Oh god.

My skin itches, more than itches, because I know from experience that I can scratch all I want and there will be no relief. It is literally crawling. I look down and for a horrifying second, my skin seems to writhe and wriggle as if insects are under there doing their best to burrow out. I wrap my arms around my legs, pulling them to me, scrunching in on myself. I lean my head into my arms and try and think. How long since the pills? How long since the masked person… people? Time is a funny beast when you live like I do. I never have a real grasp on days, hours or minutes. I come to at some point at varying times. Usually woken because I'm starving, my whole body crying out for a fix. My nerves jangled if I've left it too long. Like now.

I pull myself to standing. As my feet hit the linoleum floor, I realise they are damp. In fact all of me is. They stick to the floor, making the itching worse and sending a sharp flash of new pain through the length of me. I force myself to breathe slowly even as panic rises like a flock of birds from my gut to throat. I press a hand to my mouth but there's no bile at least. I wait for everything to stop feeling so wobbly and when I think I can, I move, I shuffle towards the door. My hand reaching out for the metal handle. I grip it and my slick palm slips. I wipe it on the side of the thin blue gown, fleetingly wonder where my clothes are and decide quickly I don't care. I try the handle again and this time my hand is dry, or dry enough. The handle wiggles, but the door doesn't budge.

I'm locked in. Did I know that? Why would I be locked in? What had I done? I try to think.

All of me hurts, my head is pounding, and my body shudders violently. Vomit and bile spew from me. I sweat,

I cry, I hurt. The door opens, closes, seconds could be minutes, could be hours could be days… a sharp stab in my arm and then blessed nothing nothing nothing…

CHAPTER FOUR

Seb actually met Charlie in a bar near here.

It's derelict now, the bar, soon to be knocked down and smashed out of existence.

Back then, it was a live music venue. Well live music out the front, strippers out the back. And not the good kind. Those women looked OK enough under very dim red lighting, but occasionally you'd get a close-up and see that they weren't at their best – not living their best lives, as Tilly would say. They went about their routines with hard faces and a quiet desperation that Seb had struggled to find a turn-on.

It was a good pub other than that though, one that had launched a few great bands in its time, and he'd had some fun nights there. He'd gone in a few times with some of the boys from his school, in a last desperate bid to fit in where he never could. He lost contact with them after he met Charlie and had no regrets about it. They'd lived out life the way they were meant to, finished sixth form, gone to university, started out in lucrative careers with high status. They'd eventually married the right woman, had some kids.

Seb married Charlie just after his eighteenth birthday. She was pregnant and even he could see why his parents didn't approve.

The night they met, she'd been dancing on a table in that bar at the back of a crowded mosh pit. Plenty of eyes were on her, his included. She was beautiful, but it wasn't just that; she looked so free, so wild. So unlike the girls he knew.

And she was those things. They were what led to her eventual downfall and almost his, because free eventually just becomes shorthand for unreliable. And wild gets old when people need you to show up.

He drives through this shit little bit of town and it's like doing thirty miles per hour through memories that make his heart sore. Lucy says, 'Always seems to rain here.' Which actually makes him laugh.

'Isn't that just ten months of the English year?'

She smiles. 'You know what I mean though?'

He nods, because he does know. It's drizzling now but even when the sun is shining, this place looks grey. He's not sure if it's the tower blocks, the grim houses with the wire fences and the front yards full of sofas and overused but unloved electrical appliances, or the people who look knackered and hard, but certainly this place feels dull. As if the rest of the world operates in glorious Technicolor but here, all you have is grainy black and white.

There's a shortage of trees and green spaces, there's a shortage of care, love and attention and – most glaringly and worse now than ever – a shortage of funds. The community centre in the middle of the estate no longer runs Sure Start; instead it has a food bank. One that is attended by people with jobs as well as those without because cost of living means anyone in the south is struggling. The playgrounds that are nestled between the high rises are more like pockmarks on acne-ridden skin than inviting places you'd want to take your kid. You can find all sorts under the swings there, but what you rarely find is children playing. And across the other side, at the back of Hartsmead, is an encampment made up of homeless people. A slum if ever he'd seen one.

He doesn't know why the thought of Charlie being here makes him sadder than when she was in, he assumes, similar shitholes more centrally, but it does.

Probably because he, Tilly, Val and most recently Faye were literally minutes away living a life she had opted out of. Ten minutes in the car and yet it could be a whole other world.

It crosses his mind in indignation that she hadn't even visited. But then he was the one who'd eventually told her not to. And meant it.

Sometimes no mum was better than a shit mum.

—

The address is a third-floor flat in a block with various youths loitering around looking shifty. Seb gives them a hard police stare, and Lucy, still in uniform, is enough to send them scurrying on their way. They try to style it out, try to look cool and chill. It is a walk Seb recognises, one that denotes an attempt at forced casualness. It never worked. No one bought it. Kids playing at being grown with no understanding of what that meant. They aren't scared of the police anymore, but they are wary.

They aren't there for them today and he wouldn't have been anyway, which most of them know. Police budgets meant they didn't patrol just for the sake of it, though that would certainly make all the difference on a day-to-day basis. Staff shortages also meant that they often turned up too late.

A voice in Seb's head nags at him for wasting police time on this. But a man had called. He'd been in almost two weeks ago and had come in again just yesterday to say that Charlie was still missing, and then an anonymous caller, a woman, had phoned about a disturbance at their flat. Someone was going to have to follow it up. He tells himself that's why he's here, but there's a voice in his head that says, 'She clicks her fingers and you go running.'

She hadn't though, had she? Charlie. Clicked her fingers. So this wasn't the same at all.

He knows just from looking at the front door that even in this desolate block this flat is a particularly bad one. When he knocks, the door swings open, the lock seemingly busted. Sometimes policing is just a shit day full of laughable stereotypes.

Lucy presses a hand to her mouth as they step inside and he doesn't blame her. It smells bloody awful in here.

Drug dens never smell good of course; there's a certain familiarity to them, a grotty minging sameness. Blood, sweat, vomit, body odour, often sex, though a less romantic setting would be hard to think of.

In the living room there are two people curled up on a mattress on the floor. He sees fair hair hanging off the side of the mattress and that shudder goes through him again.

So what if it's her? He tells himself. Good if it's her, even. Alive, if you could call this living.

It's dark in the room. There are towels hanging at the window. Lucy takes the torch off her belt, shines it at the sleeping couple. A man with many-day stubble looks up with a 'what the fuck?' and the woman next to him shifts, exposing her face, but doesn't wake.

Not Charlie. Younger maybe, though it's hard to tell; addicts, drunks, homeless people, whichever category this woman falls into, probably all three, often look old before their time.

But it's not Charlie and his first feeling is relief, because he hadn't allowed himself to consider bumping into her, how that would feel, how he would react. Then the relief slides away because whatever her flaws, she's Charlie, and he wants her to be alive and accounted for.

Seb says, 'Sid Darnell?' to the man they just woke, flashing his badge. That makes him sit up quick. He moves his hands out in surrender and says in a nasally whiny voice, 'Nah man, nah. Upstairs.' Adding, 'This is his place though. None of it has anything to do with me.'

The next room along – a kitchen – gives a strong suggestion as to what 'it' the man was talking about refers to.

No fruit bowls, blenders, coffee machines or fresh veg here. The side is instead stacked with packages of bagged-up goodies. Heroin by the look of it, and enough to make a fair bit of cash. Seb wonders if the flat's been cuckooed. A technique gangs are employing where they take over places and use them for dealing. He relays this suspicion to Lucy in a quiet voice, adding that she ought to be careful. Often the gang members are armed. Sometimes they are children. Seb is not sure which one scares him more.

Upstairs. Another room, this one with what seems to be a child's bunk bed and old forgotten toys. They are covered in a thick layer of dust. He is thankful that whatever little ones lived here are no longer present but he also feels a gut punch at the horrific tableau. It's marred further by a puddle of dried vomit, various bottles and discarded drug paraphernalia littering the carpet. In the bathroom there is a smashed mirror, a broken sink, cracked down the middle, one side fallen, the other hanging precariously from the wall. A bathtub full of what he honestly hopes is cat or dog shit.

Seb presses a hand over his face. For all the good it does. Lucy looks suitably nauseated.

He says, 'This may be the source of our smell, eh.'

Seb rethinks that as they enter the next room. The overhead light is on in here, a bare bulb hanging from the ceiling, in sharp contrast to the rest of the flat, which is steeped in semi-darkness. Boxes, newspapers and towels cover most of the windows, as though this place aims to keep the thick horror trapped in and the daylight out lest it illuminate activities that should never be lit.

This is a bad place, a horrible place, and Charlie's last known address. Sadly, they may not be able to confirm that though, because the man Seb suspects might be Sid Darnell is sitting awkwardly, his back pressed to the wall, legs splayed out at too wide angles either side of him. His throat is a red slash; his chest, in what must have been an off-white T-shirt once, is a crimson sodden mess. The blood, which Seb imagines fell in a gush, is pooled and congealing in his blue jeaned lap. His face holds a shocked but dim expression; his tongue is out and lolling to the side. It is the surprised face of death.

Seb tells Lucy, 'Better call for scene of crime,' gesturing in needless explanation to the red gash running across Sid's throat.

CHAPTER FIVE

He calls Val, who assures him Tilly hasn't even noticed his absence. Val tells him she's asleep on the sofa. 'I suspect she's worn out after a night of incessant giggling with her friends.'

'Yes, I imagine so. They've all been collected?'

'They have, and not a moment too soon.'

He smiles at that. 'Sorry to leave you there alone with them.'

'It was fine.'

His eyes flick to the windows at the station; the day is bright but chilly. It's the Monday of the February half term. He supposes that at fifteen Tilly is now old enough to be left alone in the daytimes. That hadn't always been the case and his gratitude to Val for being there to cover school holidays, late nights and overtime was immense.

'All OK there?' Val asks. He feels a spike in his heart at that, and a rare moment of uncertainty. Should he tell her? Maybe it isn't so clear-cut; does she have a right to know? Charlie is her daughter after all. But what's to tell, she's been missing from their lives for years. No, he'll wait until he knows more. Besides, this is the sort of conversation you ought to have face to face.

'Yes, all OK, but I might be here a while yet.'

'That's fine. Fingers crossed by the time you get in, she'll have recovered and be less of a grump.'

'Yeah,' he says.

He ends the call feeling like an arse and is about to respond to Faye's text asking how it's going when Lucy pokes her head around the door to the small interrogation room. 'Harry's found her social worker.'

Seb stares blankly at Lucy for a moment and then snaps into action. 'Oh, OK, cool,' he says, though it is anything but. Harry, Finn and Lucy are the core members of the little team that he now heads. They are his colleagues and they all work well together. He respects them all and thinks they respect him too. He wonders if that respect will be slightly eroded by this. His junkie ex-wife. He imagines they all knew anyway. It's one of those open things that, thank god, no one has ever talked to him directly about. But a DI with an ex like his was bound to be a source of gossip. The gossip would be worse now of course. His junkie ex-wife who has been living round the corner. Who is currently missing, who had been reported missing by her murdered boyfriend.

He falls into step beside Lucy. 'Remember the last murder we worked?' Lucy asks.

'Cowley's exes?' he asks her. A mad case where a man's ex-girlfriends and wife had been killed, Cowley himself had been the prime suspect along with his damaged ex Stevie Gordon though it turned out both had been innocent. 'I do, yeah.' As if he could forget; it made front pages everywhere and during the investigation, the perpetrator became known as 'the Sweetheart Killer' in the press.

'Remember when we went across to Leigh Valley, to look at the murdered dancer.'

'Yes.'

'The policeman we spoke to mentioned my dad.'

'I remember,' Seb says. The policeman had alluded to some trouble Lucy's father had been in but had not expanded and Lucy had left the meeting tight lipped. Seb hadn't pushed her.

'He was a gambler, a petty criminal and a wife beater.'

'I'm sorry,' Seb murmurs.

'He was arrested for attempted murder on a cold day when I was thirteen.'

'Jesus, sorry Lucy, I had no idea. Who did he try and kill?'

'My mum.' They are outside the door to the open plan office where Finn and Harry are waiting. She pauses, her hand on the doorknob.

'That's...'

'Shit, I know. Two of my brothers aren't much better, in and out of prison, but three of us are great and my mum, she's fine.'

'Your dad's dead?'

'Yes, good riddance.'

Seb nods. Some people lived only to blight the lives of others, he understood that.

'Anyway, do you blame me?'

He frowns. 'What?'

'For my dad and my plastic gangster brothers?'

'No, of course not.' He frowns. 'What they do or don't do isn't on you.'

She nods, 'Right,' and meets his eyes with hers.

'Charlie's not all bad,' he says, annoyed at how small his voice sounds. Annoyed at how much the truth of that and the pain that accompanies it still gets him.

'No one said she was, but her actions aren't on you either, and we all get that.'

'Thanks.'

She nods and opens the door.

–

'All right, guv,' Harry says, looking up from his computer screen as Lucy and Seb walk in to the section of the large open plan that they have made their own.

'Harry, Finn.' Finn nods, tapping away at the keyboard in front of him.

'We found Charlotte Locke's social worker, which may be of use?'

The name Charlotte Locke still punches him. He knows that keeping his surname won't have been a choice. They were divorced, and he understands really that she just won't have got round to it. Life admin ranked low on Charlie's list even in the good old, or less bad, days.

'Yes, it's useful, thanks Harry.'

'Of course.' Harry frowns. 'Whatever we can do to help.'

Seb waits, anticipating Harry doing his usual and saying something awkward or horribly inappropriate. Nothing else comes. He murmurs, 'Thanks,' and sits down to look over Charlie's most recent notes.

Sid had an even longer record than Charlie. He must have been worried about her, Seb thinks, to have even stepped foot inside a police station. Seb feels his pulse pick up pace and allows himself to feel the full pelt of it – panic. Charlie was missing. Her ne'er-do-well boyfriend, no friend of the law, had been frightened enough to walk into a police station not once but twice and report her missing. That man was now dead. Murdered.

He swallows thickly, a cacophony of awful thoughts all clamouring for attention like a swarm of flies on shit. He lets it flood him, feels a sense of horror, and then he slowly, slowly, pushes them aside, forcing his eyes to look at her file as he would any other missing person.

CHAPTER SIX

SAM

'Sam, there's a DI Locke in reception for you.'

I frown at Anna, the team's office administrator. 'Who?'

Anna shrugs in a 'beyond my job description' fashion. Something she does a lot and something that generally infuriates me. Her mantra around here is 'I could never do what you guys do.' And she's right, in part because she's lazy, and laziness in our job can lead to disaster. 'Tell them to send him up then, I guess.'

A few seconds later, I find myself greeting a tall man with a serious face and a female uniformed officer. I think I've seen her about and she introduces herself as a Detective Sergeant Quinn. I'm well acquainted with the police force, all social workers are, but when DI Locke flashes his badge and explains he's from the major crimes squad that gives me pause.

'Major crimes?' I ask him. That must mean murder or serious assault.

Dead bodies are, sadly a large part of my job, but the deaths I deal with are usually accidental, unnecessary and often painfully stupid. I work with lots of homeless people in the area, many of them drug users. None of them having a good time, or why would they need me?

'Yes,' he says, sliding the badge back into his inside jacket pocket. 'Sid Darnell.'

I frown. Sid. 'Charlie's boyfriend?'

I see something on the officer's face, a twitch round his lips, which he presses together, and he nods. 'That's right. I believe she's one of your... uh...'

'Clients.' I smile. 'Which sounds odd, I grant you.'

That gets a half-smile, and it turns out he's quite good looking when he's not scowling.

'She is, yes, though the last time I was supposed to see her, which was over two weeks ago, she didn't turn up.'

'What were you supposed to see her about?'

'She's on my list, which means she needs to check in with me. We've mutually agreed every fortnight.'

'What's she checking in for?'

I shrug. 'Various things. I usually sign paperwork, you know for various benefits, a methadone prescription.'

'She's on methadone?'

'She is, or was – as I said, she hasn't been to see me to refer her for a refill. She may have gone straight to her doctor, though it's unlikely he wouldn't have called me if she had.'

'Is she uh, getting clean then?'

'She was trying.'

'Was?'

I sigh. 'I only met Charlie recently. She's new to the area.'

'She's from here,' he says.

'Yes, originally, but had been absent for several years. She was in central London. She moved back and actually has been really trying to get clean since she arrived.'

'Trying?'

'A serial relapser.'

'Did she manage to get any time at all?'

'A week at one point.' I frown. 'It would have been almost that again if she'd made her last appointment. I was looking forward to seeing her, I had some hope.'

'Is that unusual?'

'The intent isn't unusual; most of the people I work with know they are not living, they're not doing well.'

'You have a lot of clients on methadone?'

'I do,' I say, and give him a wry smile. 'They all take the prescription but often to sell or swap for heroin.'

He frowns again, making a deep dent pop up between his eyebrows, which will one day be carved there forever. 'Why give them it then?'

I shrug. 'We remain hopeful.'

'Or stupid,' he murmurs. I cover my surprise at this slip in professionalism with a quick smile.

'Sorry,' he says, 'I imagine it's meant well.'

'Everything we do, or try and do, is meant well.' I shrug. 'Doesn't mean it's effective, sadly.'

'No,' he says. 'But you had hope for Charlie?'

'Cautious hope,' I agree.

'Did you know Sid Darnell?' the small woman asks. She has a soft, kind face but sharp eyes.

'I did, yes, he and Charlie came as a pair.'

'So if Charlie came in to see you, he'd be with her?'

I nod. 'A lot of the time, yeah.'

'Was he also getting clean?'

'He was making the right noises, but I felt like that was more for Charlie's sake. I also suspect he was dealing.'

'Judging by the amount of dope we found in his flat I'd say you were right,' the detective tells me.

'Making it all the harder for Charlie.'

'She could have moved out.'

'She could,' I agree, not pointing out that that's easier said than done. A single woman is easier to house than a family, of course, but housing remains the biggest issue faced by Britain's burgeoning underclass.

'He didn't have a social worker?' Sergeant Quinn asks, though she must know this already.

'No, he had a probation officer when he and Charlie were living in central London.'

'Recently?'

'No, three months back. I believe he was supposed to connect with probation here.'

'He hasn't,' DI Locke says.

'No, that's often the case.'

'Would that get chased up?'

'Maybe,' I sigh, 'and he hadn't responded to the last few messages. I believe he was close to having a warrant issued.' I shrug. 'You know as well as I do it's not a perfect system.'

'Yes,' he agrees, and some of the tightness seems to leave his face. We are, mostly, on the same side. Social services, probation, the police. We are all under-resourced, reeling from austerity, Brexit and Covid. The truth is many people slip through the cracks, a lot of them criminals. I myself send kids back to unsafe homes, fail to place people in desperate need in hospitals or rehab and often struggle to manage my ever-growing caseload in a timely fashion.

'What was Sid like?' the detective asks.

'Lost, rough around the edges, an untrustworthy addict but not bad, I wouldn't have said. Lost and messed up. If you'd have told me he was dead I'd have assumed an OD or misadventure, but since you're here…'

'Murder,' the detective says. 'His throat was slashed.'

'Jesus, where?'

'The flat you have as Charlie's registered address.'

'On the Hartsmead?'

'Right. Two people were there at the time: Amanda Sales, who we believe may have made the anonymous call, though she's denying it, and her boyfriend Louis Ernesto.'

'Oh yes, I know them both.' I shake my head. 'Trouble follows them like a bad smell. Not surprised they ended up at that flat. We think he was dealing out of there, Sid,' I tell him. 'We've signed it off as a no-go zone, which is why Charlie was coming in to us, or supposed to be coming in to us, with no home visits, which are normally my preference.'

'The flat was down as what? Dangerous to visit?'

'Yes.'

'And, as you say, hardly the place for an addict wanting to get better.'

'A real shame considering how well she'd been doing.'

'You like her?'

'Oh, yes. A bright young woman. She sought us out, preregistered, complied with meetings at a local rehabilitation centre. You might know it, Hope Springs?'

'No,' the detective says; his sergeant makes a note. 'So, she meant well but never got much clean time?'

'No, but I believed her when she said she wanted to, and I normally don't. She had one medical detox, I referred her myself.'

'Who to?'

'Dr Alex Martin — and yes, we're related.'

'Oh?'

'My brother.'

'And your work crosses over?'

'It does, yes, he's a GP and he volunteers at the local drop-in centre I just mentioned, hence seeing so many of our clients.' I ferret around in my desk, pull out his card. 'Here.'

The detective takes it, handing me a card of his own. I take it, noting the detective's full name. I look at him. He meets my gaze evenly, but do I see a faint blush? I'm about to open my mouth but he says, 'Thank you,' and then, 'Charlie is missing,' closing down the question I'd been about to ask.

I frown. 'Missing?'

'Sid reported her to the station as missing almost two weeks ago,' the sergeant says. 'Were you aware of his concerns?'

'No, actually.'

I open up my emails and find one from Anna dated two weeks ago. It says, 'Sid Darnell called, Charlie's missing.' This will teach me not to stay on top of my inbox, though Anna probably ought to have relayed this to me in person. 'Here, he did call,' I say, feeling my temper rise while keeping my voice even.

The detective moves to stand behind me, reading the message over his shoulder. 'Did you respond to it?'

My heart is starting to beat a little faster. 'No, god... I missed the message, but even if I'd have got it I'd have just assumed she'd wandered off or found somewhere else to hang out...'

'A perfectly reasonable assumption,' the detective says, though I hadn't finished my sentence. 'They could have argued, she could have got waylaid with a new group of people, she could even have gone back to London.'

'Has she, do you think?' I ask him.

'We don't know. Like you I didn't think it seemed important.' He pauses. 'But now, in light of Sid...'

'Yes. God. I should have checked.'

'I imagine it wasn't the first appointment she'd missed?'

'No, though as I said she's new to me.'

'Three months, the records say.'

'Yes, and she's not particularly high risk.'

'If you do hear from her,' he says, standing and again cutting out the question I'm dying to ask, 'or hear anything.'

'I'll be in touch.'

'Thank you.'

—

After they leave, I go through Charlie's file, looking from the card the detective had given me to the notes about Charlotte Locke, and yes, there it is. Ex-husband Sebastian Locke, currently a detective inspector at Thamespark. DI Locke. They have one child together, Matilda Locke. I knew this already of course. Charlie has mentioned both her husband and her daughter. She was the reason Charlie had come back to Thamespark originally. 'I'm going to get cleaned up and then I'm going to go and see her,' she'd said. I'd nodded and wished she would like I wished it for all of my clients. So many of them similar to Charlie. Lost in a fug of drink, drugs, failed relationships shattered lives and lost children.

'What was that about?' Mark comes over, perching on the edge of my desk, his long legs stretching uncomfortably into my space.

I slide my chair back slightly. 'Sid Darnell.'

He frowns.

'Charlotte Locke's boyfriend,' I tell him.

'Oh right, in the cuckooed flat?'

I nod. 'That's the one, though we don't know that for sure.'

Mark snorts. 'It's likely though. Also, he's not our client.'

'Yeah, no, I know, but he reported Charlie missing.'

'When?'

'A few weeks ago.'

Mark shrugs. 'She'll show up.'

'Maybe,' I say. 'Mark, Sid was murdered.'

'Murdered?'

I nod. 'Throat slashed, left to bleed out in the flat. Someone called it in, a woman who they think may have been Amanda Sales but who wished to remain anonymous.'

'God,' Mark says, though his heart isn't in it. He is more immune to this shit than me, the daily treadmill of destruction and waste. He's a good person but he's been in the job too long, and staying in this job too long is a problem. I can imagine him young and enthusiastic, but now he's old, jaded and I don't blame him. Though it can make him a challenging boss. He needs to retire but like many people his age in this profession in this insanely expensive part of the country, he can't really afford to.

'That was her ex-husband.'

'What?'

'The detective, tall guy. DI Locke.'

'Oh. He's investigating her disappearance?'

'Looks like it.'

'Poor sod.'

'Yeah,' I agree.

He frowns. 'Is he allowed to?'

'I don't know. He's a major crimes detective, so actually it'll be Sid's death. I suppose Charlie being missing is secondary.'

'Still,' he says, 'it's an obvious conflict of interest.'

'Yes,' I say, though the detective is definitely investigating both cases – he'd just said as much. 'She missed her last appointment,' I tell Mark. 'She was due here.'

'Happens.'

'Yeah, no, I know.'

'Horrid about Sid, do they have any idea who did it?'

'Not that they told me,' I say and realise I also hadn't asked. It was the name, the connection and, as sorry as I was about Sid, my concern now was Charlie. I understand what the detective said about the low recovery rates for addicts and of course, he's suffered it first hand, I get that too. But I'd liked Charlie. I'd had hope for her, and now I'm kicking myself. I should probably have followed up when she didn't show. I hadn't even phoned. Just thought well, there's an extra hour to attack some paperwork. I can judge Mark all I want but maybe I'm just as jaded, or at least on my way to it despite all my noble self-talk about never stopping caring. Shit.

'Anyway.' Mark pushes himself up and off my desk, heading off to do whatever it is he's going to do today, firmly shutting the door of his office. Anna is on one of her endless breaks and I'm the only one in the office. I call Alex; he picks up on the third ring.

'Hey.'

'Hey yourself.'

'Not at work?'

'No, I am, you?'

'Between patients,' he says with a sigh.

'Well. I was just calling to say, we've had a couple of detectives in, about Charlotte Locke.'

'Charlotte Locke...' he says, and I can picture his face, so like mine, scrunched up in concentration.

'Charlie, thin, blonde, heroin addict,' I prompt.

'Oh, yes, with the awful boyfriend.'

'Sid.'

'Right.'

'She's missing.'

'Well...' He'll be thinking exactly what I had – addict missing, no big deal, hardly a newsflash.

'Yeah, no, I know, but the awful boyfriend, Sid, was killed. Murdered,' I add for emphasis.

'Shit. Really?'

'Really. So anyway, they'll be coming to see you.'

'What, why?'

'Well, they asked who might have seen her.'

'I haven't seen her. She missed her last appointment.' And that will have been all the thought Alex will have given it. He's not cold, my big brother, but he is forever the clinician. Steady, calm, not easily ruffled.

'No, I said I thought that was the case. But she didn't call or anything?'

'Not even for her scrip,' he says. In his position I think I would have worried about that. Or would I? I hadn't worried when she hadn't shown up here, had I? Easy to imagine my response in retrospect. The thing is, I'm worried now, though there will be no point saying this specifically to Alex, who will remind me to detach with compassion.

'Well, maybe Debbie and Barry have seen her?' I say. The couple who run Hope Springs.

'Why didn't you send the police there then?'

'I probably should have.'

He sighs. 'It's fine, I'll direct them.'

'Sorry,' I say, meaning it, ever the little sister.

'It's fine. Still on for dinner later?'

'Yes, please,' I say, grateful that I've been forgiven.

'Great, we'll see you about seven. Caroline's making carbonara.'

CHAPTER SEVEN

CHARLIE

That first day I had refused the pills I realised I was in a locked room and ran through possibilities. A section? Had I come in voluntarily? I had no memory of doing so but I didn't remember a lot of things, such is the nature of my life. I had banged on the door demanding someone come but no one had. I'd closed my eyes, laid down on the bed. The paper knickers made a soft flumping kind of sound. My skin had starting to itch and I'd wondered how long my body would last before it started to rebel. I'd been there before in withdrawal. I had even had an attempt at a home detox, years ago now, that had almost killed me.

I knew that before my body got to the stage it shut down there would be a fair few horrors inflicted on it. The sweats, nausea and vomiting were just a warm-up and pain has torn through me, making every nerve jangled, raw and alive. After that initial memory all there is is the sickness. Agonising hours of it. Days? Weeks? My head fuzzed, my body crying out, coming to, blacking out.

Today, though, I have opened my eyes and realised I have slept. Really slept, a deep and dreamless state.

I roll onto my side and assess my body. The aches have subsided, my head doesn't hurt and I no longer feel nauseous, though my mouth tastes bitter and vile. I wonder if there's a toothbrush in the bathroom and go to investigate. When I stand up, I feel... OK. My head is clear, my thoughts no longer jangled and unreachable. I'm in a room, is it a hospital room? I have been medically detoxed, I think. I have no idea how long that process has taken. Someone, or some people, have been in. I remember sobbing, desperate awful cries, and a hand patting my shoulder, holding out the paper cup with the pills, helping me sit, bringing water to my lips.

My mouth feels dreadful. I step into the small bathroom, and yes, there is a toothbrush, a blue and white one, and next to it a tube of toothpaste. I open the shower curtain and see soap, shampoo and conditioner. Outside the cubicle are two fluffy white towels.

I run water on the brush, add paste. I can handle being dirty, but I do like to have clean teeth. As a result, unlike many of the people I spend time with, I still have all of mine.

I brush them now and then I step into the shower.

I stand under the warm water for I don't know how long. Marvelling at the relief of it, shampooing and conditioning the tangled knotted mess of my hair. I step out feeling, if not brand new, definitely better than I have for years. I wrap myself in the towels and when I step back into my room the first thing I notice is that the bed has been made. On it are clothes. I go over, picking up underwear, a T-shirt and a grey tracksuit. I go to the door, jiggle the handle, try and push it open.

It's still locked, but someone has been in, and I think they knew that I wasn't in here when they came. They timed their entrance carefully. A chill races through the length of me.

I dress beneath the cover of the towel, carefully avoiding looking down at myself. I hang the towels in the bathroom, looking at the ceiling of the room as I go. I see the red blinking lights of cameras in each corner.

CHAPTER EIGHT

'I've only got about,' Dr Alex Martin pauses, hitching up his sleeve, hand gripped around a reusable rubber coffee cup, he glances at his watch, 'crap, nine minutes.'

'We appreciate it,' Seb says.

'And you'll need to walk with me,' he leans his head towards a building in the distance, 'to the other clinic, sorry.'

'That's fine,' Seb says, he and Lucy falling into step beside the man who looks an awful lot like his sister. It's not just the striking red hair, though that is the obvious similarity. They both have intense very dark brown eyes. So dark, Seb thinks, they look black.

'I have an afternoon of diagnosis and prescription calls to make and there's literally no space in the main building.'

'Right.'

'Ridiculous that we have to do our admin from a porta cabin but...' He shrugs, and Seb knows what he means. Everything is held together by plasters, especially in the NHS.

'Anyway, you're here about Sid Darnell?'

'Um...'

'My sister called.'

'Right,' Seb says.

'She means well, but she's a control freak.' Alex flashes them a smile. 'She also told me about Sid's untimely demise, which on reflection perhaps she ought not to have?'

'It's fine,' Seb says, not meaning it. He hadn't told Sam not to contact her brother, of course and it seems he should have. But still.

'Sorry to hear about it,' Alex says. 'An awful way to go, at someone else's hand.'

'Yes.'

They are at the porta cabin, and Alex pushes the door open with his back. They step inside and follow him to a room not much bigger than a cupboard. It has a wheeled chair and a desk with a phone on it.

'God, I can't even offer you a seat.'

'It's fine, really.'

Seb checks the clock above Alex's head. They probably have about four minutes left.

'You knew Sid and Charlie?'

'I prescribed for Charlotte, who was referred via Hope Springs. Sid was often with her.'

'You were prescribing Charlie methadone?'

'I was, yes, and honestly when I first met Charlotte, I had high hopes for her.'

'Really?' Seb asks, his surprise evident in the word. His face heats up and he looks at Lucy, but Alex doesn't seem to have noticed his discomfort.

'Yes, she seemed dead set when she arrived.'

'Dead set?'

'On staying clean.'

'But she was on methadone?'

'As a detox, yes. I always said to her it would be hard if she stayed with Sid.'

'Who was still using?'

'Exactly.'

'Sam said she didn't last long.'

'A week and a half is a lifetime for someone in long-term addiction.'

Seb doesn't respond, can't think what to say next. His head is filled with Charlie, young Charlie sobbing and telling him she's sorry, she doesn't know why she does it, doesn't know why she can't stop. The memory made worse because he knew that she meant it. That she was as baffled by her own behaviour as he was. Behaviour that almost ruined them both. That would have ruined him too if he hadn't had Tilly to save him.

The computer beeps. 'That means my calls are due to start.'

'Anything else you think might help us locate Charlotte Locke?' Lucy asks, quickly adding, 'We need to speak to her in relation to Sid's death as a matter of urgency.' Seb is glad to be covered by Lucy in this instance. He is going to struggle getting his involvement in this past his superior, Jackie. He'll need to frame it as investigating Sid's murder rather than Charlie's disappearance, and he needs to remember that during questioning. But find out who killed Sid and he should find Charlie. He hopes that when he does she's alive and innocent. In relation to murder at least.

Alex slides open a drawer in the too-small desk and pulls out a flyer. 'Here, it's the drop-in centre I mentioned at Hope Springs. She was there frequently. Even did a bit of work for them I think.'

The phone starts ringing and he puts his hand on the receiver. 'Anything else you need come back, but...'

'That's great, thanks.' Lucy gives him smile and ushers Seb outside.

The silence in the car feels awkward. Seb wants to break it but he can't think of anything to say. His head is a mess, his heart hurts.

'Are you OK?' Lucy asks and he's about to bite back when she adds, 'Sorry.'

All the irritation, which has nothing to do with Lucy anyway, slides away. 'I've been better, and I'm not looking forward to talking to Jackie.'

'Understandable.'

'Do you think she'll kick me off the case?'

Lucy shrugs. 'I don't know. If she does will you leave it alone?'

'No.'

'That's what I thought. Have you told Tilly?'

He shakes his head. 'No, or Val.'

'God, of course, Charlie's her daughter.'

'Right.' He keeps his eyes ahead on the road, horrified to feel the prickle of tears. If he'd felt uncomfortable in the silence, him sobbing would be much worse for them both.

'I might not tell them, yet.' He says the words as quickly as he thinks them. 'Because this is awful for me, and she's just my ex-wife. Not my daughter or my mum.'

'Yes,' Lucy says, 'that's true.'

He nods, grateful to her for not pointing out that they probably have a right to know and he can't put it off forever.

'It was her birthday party yesterday too, Tilly's.'

'Oh yes, the cinema trip?'

'Right, and four girls sleeping over at ours.'

'Bloody hell, poor you and Val.'

Seb smiles. 'Yes. I mean, I stayed up just in case, but Val had to deal with them all tired and grouchy this morning, plus parent pickups.'

'That's a lot, she's probably tired.'

'Right. I'll give her and Tilly the day to recover, you know.'

'Sounds like a plan.'

'Yes,' he agrees. Tomorrow, once they'd all had a good night's sleep and the calendar was clear at home, what excuse would he have then? His heart beats a little faster at the thought of it.

He fiddles with the CD player in his ancient Golf and feels soothed as Metallica fills the car and they drive to the morgue.

CHAPTER NINE

Seb's phone vibrates in his pocket as they pull up outside the morgue. He gets it out, stares blankly at the message.
Faye.

> Still good for dinner later?

He wasn't good and eating was the last thing on his mind. He'd have to tell Val and Tilly of course. Would he have to tell Faye? The amazing woman who'd come into his life, unexpected and totally welcome. She had slotted into their unusual little family with no hassle. Val liked her, Tilly considered her the coolest adult she knew. They all loved her, himself included. He loved her intelligence and her straightforward nature. He loved that he could trust her, that she didn't make him feel anxious, and now here he was hiding something from her.

'So sorry,' he types, 'work is mad – rain check?'

> Of course x

He feels a stab of guilt as he slides the phone into his pocket and follows Lucy into the morgue.

Sid Darnell is laid out on the table, covered to his throat, his face still stuck in the same slightly surprised expression he'd had when Lucy and Seb had walked into the flat's too warm upstairs room. The smell in the room is as vile as ever. Rotting meat smothered by bleach and formaldehyde.

'Hello Seb, Lucy.' Martina Mathewson appears from her small office at the back of the large sterile place.

'Martina, thanks for getting to him so quickly.'

'No problem,' Martina says, which is unlike her. He'd been prepared for sarcasm or a barbed comment about having other corpses to attend to or something. He sees her eyes flick to Lucy and realises she's been told who Sid is and his connection to Seb. Of course she has. He can imagine what Lucy had said; something like, 'Seb might sound stressed' – though he'd tried especially hard not to – 'this one, well it's personal.'

'Thanks anyway,' he says, avoiding meeting her eye and feeling a flash of anger that is familiar. Charlie can still humiliate him, even now, even in her absence. Charlie can make him act in ways that aren't what he considers true to himself. He thinks again of the new territory of withholding information from Val, Tilly and Faye. This had always been the struggle with Charlie. She brought out the worst in him.

He looks at the dead man. His face is so thin, it's almost skeletal, his mouth is slightly ajar and Seb can see a few dark spots where teeth are missing. His cheeks are covered in high raised spots. Not a rash, more like some kind of adult acne. He smells of organs, open flesh and the sterility of the morgue now. Seb imagines that when he was alive he smelt of damp clothes, stale beer, fags and BO. This man who Charlie had been living with – if you could call it living – for at least the last two years. A man she'd preferred over him, he thinks before he has a chance to smother it. To reason with himself as he always tried to do. She didn't leave because she didn't love him, or Tilly, she left because she loved the drugs more. Like all addicts. Sid was a symptom of a mental health condition. But... still... the thought and the feelings are there.

'Cause of death fairly obvious,' he says, pulling his gaze away from the man whose eyes are horribly open and blank.

'Yes, throat slashed. He'd have bled out.'

'Quick?'

'Yes, relatively. He might have survived it had he been in better shape and had someone called an ambulance. Was he alone in the house?'

'There were people downstairs, but out of it,' Lucy says.

'Not sure the person holding the knife would have allowed that outcome either,' Seb murmurs, wondering if the killer had gone in, stepped over the comatose bodies downstairs, nipped up, committed murder, and waited for Sid to die before leaving. He reckons Amanda was the one who'd made the call, and therefore had seen something. Unfortunately, she'd been deemed unfit to be questioned properly so he'd have to come back to her. Or maybe Sid had been dead when the others showed up and they just hadn't realised. Either scenario was possible. Both were equally horrifying.

'No, you're likely correct. He'd also taken an insane amount of heroin and would probably have died from that anyway.'

'An overdose?'

'Exactly.'

Seb swallows. He imagines Charlie and this guy using together, which he supposes they would have every day. Their tiny lives revolving round the next fix, scoring it, taking it, and repeat. Maybe she'd overdosed too, but if that was the case where was her body?

'Do you think the person who stabbed him took Charlotte?' Martina asks.

'She'd been missing for almost two weeks,' Seb says. 'It's not impossible, but the two things may be completely unrelated.' Is that what he was hoping? Probably that was the best case. Charlie had fucked off somewhere else. Sid had got in trouble, likely with a supplier or a customer, or just a petty fight over nothing, as was often the case when people like him clumped together.

Martina says, 'He died less than twenty-four hours before you found him I'd say. Rigor hadn't set in well but I'm told it was hot in there.'

'Like an oven,' Lucy tells her. 'The world's grimmest oven.'

'I hope you find her safe and sound. Charlotte,' Martina says to Seb, and he tells her thanks even though no one in the room expects her to be safe or sound. Right now, he'd take alive.

—

As they get in the car, Seb's phone rings. 'Can you grab that?' he says to Lucy, who is endlessly hassling him to consider a new car, one with a hands-free kit so she wouldn't have to act as his secretary while he was driving.

'Yes of course,' she says politely, instead of reminding him he is a dinosaur. Pity, Seb thinks, is one of the worst things, even when it's well intended.

'DS Quinn.' A pause. 'Oh yes, hello Ms Martin.'
'Speaker,' Seb murmurs.
'I'm just putting you on speaker. DI Locke is with me and can hear you.'
'Yeah, OK,' the social worker's soft voice breaks in.
'Hello Ms Martin,' Seb says.
'Sam please.'
'Sam then. How can we help?' Seb swerves to avoid a maniac pulling out of a side road without looking, resisting the urge to blast his horn.
'Well, no, I... I'm not sure if it's important at all.'
'Anything you have could help,' Seb assures her.
'Well, OK. I'm at Surrey Mead.' The local hospital. 'With a client.'
'OK.'
'She's in a pretty bad way, being put on a drip and mostly incoherent.'
'OK.'
'But she, uh, mentioned Sid.'
'I'm sure many of the j... your clients know each other.'
'Yeah, no, of course, but I know she's friendly with Sid and Charlie and I asked if she'd heard from her, Charlie. She said no, Anita, that's my client, but that Sid had been frantic.'
'Frantic?'
'Yes, looking everywhere for her. Apparently initially he thought maybe she'd gone off with someone else.'
'Charlie had?'
'Yes, Sid said she'd been sneaking around.'
'Right,' Seb says, remembering too many times when he too had thought, no, had known, that Charlie was sneaking around. 'Do you know when this was?'

'No. Like I said, she's out of it. But they're keeping her in overnight, she'll be sedated until the morning, so I'm just giving you a heads-up because if you did want to talk to her, she'll be in some semblance of order first thing.'

'OK, thanks. Can you text her full name?'

'Will do. Have a good evening, detective.'

'Yeah, you too.'

CHAPTER TEN

SAM

I hang up the call and by the time I do, I'm parked outside my brother's place. Unlike me in my generally messy shoebox flat that is actually a studio, Alex lives well. He married Caroline, one of the best women in the world and who, I like to remind him, is far too good for him.

I step out of the car, grabbing the bottle of wine, which is the first one I saw in the Co-op, and head towards their front door. They've recently had the drive redone and it's picture perfect. An Instagrammable front of house, as Caroline tells me with an eye roll. Her daughter Jessie, who is almost fourteen, will have found that important, and I know she's been consulted regarding colour. Grey for the drive itself, so dark that when it rains it looks black, and a long concrete step to match. The door is olive green and on either side of it are two beautifully potted pink flowering plants which Caroline had told me the name of and which I'd promptly forgotten. The revamp is a definite success. It is welcoming and stylish, and the smell of the flowers wafts up to me.

'Hey,' Jess answers the door, leaning forward and pulling me to her. Both she and Caroline are huggers. Very different to Alex and me, who are not tactile people. But perhaps growing up in a house built for survival rather than affection had made us that way. Not only is Caroline awesome, she comes from a large family who are all equally brilliant and who have welcomed not just Alex but me as well with open arms.

Alex and Caroline married when Jess was only five, and being her step-aunt has truly been one of life's blessings.

'Hi Jess,' I say, handing her the wine.

'Come through, dinner's almost done.'

I wriggle out of my coat and hang it on the freestanding pegs, having to reach up and get on my tiptoes. Jess at her young age is already a whole head taller.

'Sam.' Caroline grins from the cooker, standing in front of a large pan that is kicking out pleasing odours. My stomach groans in response to them. Alex heads over, handing me a large glass of red wine that I suspect will be far nicer than the cheap rosé I've bought and which they'll probably never drink. I take it and have a sip. Yeah, it's the good stuff. I imagine all the bottles I've brought round over the years festering in a box in the basement.

'Sit.' Alex points to the table, where Jess is slicing fluffy bread. I plonk down next to her and she slides me a slice. 'Try this.'

Alex goes to help Caroline serve up and I listen to the soft murmur of their voices in the background. I bite into the bread, which is thick with salt, and baked-in flecks of green rosemary. 'Oh, that's delicious,' I say, and it is. It beats the absolute crap out of my occasional sad sandwich from Sainsbury's at lunchtime. By the time I take my break, if I do, all the good ones are normally gone.

'I made that,' Jess says, grinning triumphantly.

'You're kidding!'

Alex and Caroline come over carrying plates. 'She outdoes us in all things kitchen related already, Sam.' Alex gives me a wink. The us he is referring to here is him and me. In fairness, Alex had learnt to reheat food well enough to keep me fed. I remember a childhood though where we were often hungry and almost always frightened. I love this life for him, I love the feel of his home and the warm affections that hit you as soon as you walk in.

'Lucky for you you live with two excellent cooks,' I say.

'I am blessed indeed,' he tells me, grinning, and he looks so much like our dad it makes my heart sore.

–

Dinner's nice, pudding is even better. Jess goes to her room and Caroline heads up to bed. This is the normal routine when I'm here on a weekday evening. When Alex had told me he was getting married, I'd felt slightly panicked if I'm honest. I'd met Caroline, I liked her, and I liked Jess too. But for years, it had just been Alex and me. My dad died when we were young – a cruel cancer that shrunk him to nothing and left my mother angry and resentful. Both our parents were doctors just like Alex, but our mother became hooked on prescription drugs and followed our dad by her own hand just after Alex turned twenty. He'd been in medical school, I was sitting my GCSEs. He transferred courses to our local university and moved home to raise me. He's never complained about it and overall we've both done well. He is more than my brother, he's the closest thing I have to a parent too. I guess I'd been afraid Caroline might jeopardise that. What wife wants a younger sibling loitering around after all? But she'd accepted me exactly as I am, and we did things together, just her and I – something she insisted on. I took Jess for days out and they became my family too. Caroline also understood that Alex and I shared things she never would and never could, including our work. It is no coincidence that we both help local people in the throes of addiction. No coincidence that both of us work with people suffering from the same disease as our mother.

We move to the cream corner sofa now, taking our glasses of wine with us. Alex hardly ever drinks and I don't tend to drink much around him but I've had enough to feel mellow. Enough for the hard edges of the day to start softening slightly. I drink a lot more when I'm at home, alone. I push that thought away and sink into the cushions, leaning back with a groan.

'Tough day?'

'Aren't they all?' I smile. 'You?'

'At the surgery today, so busy but not awful.' Alex works in a private clinic two days a week, having cut down his role as an NHS GP. We'd clashed when he took the role. Me bleating on about commitment to helping others, Alex sighing and saying the NHS was killing him. I got it, of course I did. I worked in another ravaged service. When the voluntary position came up via Debbie and Barry, Alex had taken it and put an end to our often circular discussions. I could see his point of view really – he saw patients quickly, and as a result, their outcomes were vastly improved. I envied him some days, especially when I was sitting beside hospital beds in dilapidated wards seeing patients often with acute trauma being fobbed off and kicked out as soon as possible. It is what it is.

'Did you see Laura?'

'Yes.' I frown.

'She's picked up again?'

'Yes.'

He sighs. 'Not good, but not unexpected.' He'd messaged me when she hadn't shown up to see him last week and I'd known what it meant, though of course I still hoped it might be otherwise.

'No, but it doesn't make it any less sad.'

'It doesn't,' he says. I lean forward, sliding my glass onto the table. My eyes are heavy. It's only Monday but I work most weekends too in some capacity and I've never slept that well. 'I saw May and the kids yesterday.'

'Sunday?'

'Yes,' I say, and it sounds snippy. Alex is often lecturing me about boundaries. 'I've got a packed week and I wanted to check she was OK.'

'And is she?'

I shrug. 'All things considered. The kids are difficult.'

'Well, yes,' Alex says. 'It's good of her to have them.'

'It is.'

'So, Sid Darnell?' I interject quickly before he asks how Laura is about them. As frustrated as I get with my clients, I feel defensive of them too. Laura is a terrible mother, of that there is no doubt, but I learnt long ago to hate the illness and not the addict. And to not give up, because sometimes people change. Not often, but it happens.

'Yes, goodness.'

'The detective is Charlie's ex-husband, I told you that?'

'You did. It must be awful for him.'

'I can't imagine,' I murmur, though I can of course. There had been plenty of occasions with Mum where she'd go missing, be brought home by the police, or Alex and I would get calls from various hospitals. In the last eighteen months of her life she no longer worked. She'd been struck off and was lucky not to have faced criminal charges. Alex was of the mind that she should have and that perhaps the right consequences were often a good thing. Either way, being struck off had meant she could no longer prescribe herself anything and she took to drinking instead. It was heart-breaking and terrifying. It would be the same for the policeman.

'I'd had high hopes for her.' My brother gave the appearance of being detached and he was certainly more able than me to set aside personal feelings, especially when it came to the realities of his work, but I knew too that he cared.

'Me too,' I say. 'I feel terrible for not checking in on her when she missed our appointment.'

He laughs. 'If you checked in on every one of them that missed appointments, Sam, you'd be chasing them all day and have no room for anything else.'

'Yeah, no, I know, it's just like you say, she had been doing well.' I shrug.

He sighs. 'I'm sure she'll show up.'

'Do you think it was her?' I ask him the obvious question I'm sure we're both considering.

'Who killed Sid?'

I nod.

'Maybe, though she has no history of violence, and in his defence neither did he.'

'No, but both high?'

'Well, yes, it can't be ruled out.'

'He must know that,' I say.

'The detective?'

'Yes.'

'I suppose he must, yes.'

We sit in silence and I feel peaceful in it. My eyelids start to feel heavier and at some point, Alex shakes my shoulder and ushers me to the downstairs spare room that may as well just be called my room because I'm in it at least once a week. I even have toiletries and a change of clothes here. I sleep deeply. More deeply than I ever do at my flat, and all thoughts of the poor detective, Laura, Charlie and Sid fade for a blissful eight hours.

CHAPTER ELEVEN

CHARLIE

The room is sterile. It smells of bleach. Like a hospital or some other institution, but a reasonably nice one. The tablets, whatever they are, have taken the edge off.

I've detoxed, I know that because it's not my first rodeo. I've been through it before, or at least I've managed to kick heroin before, a few times, normally switching it for methadone, tranquilisers or booze. I could do with a drink, I think now, and maybe a few more of those pills, whatever they are. I could do with knowing what the hell is going on. I try hard to think, to remember exactly where I'd been and what I'd been doing before I got here.

Sid and I had argued. He had a delivery, a big one from Gordon. Gordon normally only gave Sid just enough to sell to a few personal contacts but this was a different league. This was stepping into major territory. I'd been clean for a few weeks. Well, I'd been off heroin. On methadone, I'd been drinking and smoking a lot of cannabis but I had been determined that once I had the withdrawals under control I could look at everything else. I'd spoken to Hope Springs about it, had had advice from their doctor who had talked me through my options and I'd thought, really thought and felt that this time it was different. This time, I might just make it. Then the delivery and… I used. That's my last memory. Using and the relief, oh god the relief of it.

I realise now that what I'd called a detox wasn't really. This was different. Right now, the only mind-altering substance in me is whatever the pills are, and I think the dose has been lowered. They still soften things but that's all. They haven't eradicated the hunger, they haven't alleviated it and all of my worries in the blissful way that heroin does. Which means that my main problem right now isn't the physical agony, which seems to have passed, it's all the memories clamouring into my mind screaming at me for attention. It's the horrible replay of every bad thing I ever did.

It's the constant loop of my daughter's little-girl face smiling and saying *see you soon Mummy*. Over a decade ago now.

Why do you do it? I'd been asked a hundred times, and it was hard to explain to people who never have. Once you've had one fix, the real question is how the hell do you not do it?

I rest my head against the wall, closing my eyes, as if that is any kind of protection from the past. Gordon had come for his money, I can see it now. I'd been on a mattress downstairs, unable to get up but I remember seeing him giving Sid a ticking off. Sid and I had argued, for days it felt like, and maybe it had been. 'You're different,' he kept telling me, and then, 'Who are you messaging?' and the thing was I was different, or I was trying to be. I wanted to get better and Sid said the right things but his heart wasn't in it.

I don't know how long he'd had the drugs by the time Gordon showed up but there had been a steady stream of people in and out. I'd stayed half-comatose.

I can't quite remember what had been said or who exactly had been there. Some of the people who'd come to pick up had stayed. I know that. Louis was sparko, Amanda had been flitting about, she'd also been sympathising with Sid.

Someone had picked me up, I remember that, maybe two people? Paramedics? Had I OD'd? It wouldn't be the first time.

When? When was it? Night-time I think, though it's hard to tell in there. Most of the windows in the flat were covered.

The next thing I remember is being here. But where is here? It's not prison; that smells of piss, shit, vomit and desperation. It smells, I think fleetingly, like the flat. I push the thought away, add it to the ever-growing pile of things I don't want to think about. Things that are way too hard to consider. It seems like a hospital; I've been locked up in hospital rooms before, but normally I'm handcuffed to a bed. Not in a locked room. There were the people, or a person? With masks, man? Woman? I couldn't say. Did I have some infectious illness?

I stand and go to the door. I bang on it. Nothing. I shout. Nothing. I sink down, curling into myself, and I start to cry, because my own thoughts are trying to kill me.

CHAPTER TWELVE

'We're gonna go,' Lucy says, pulling Seb's attention from the stack of files he's going through. He's looking at the paper trail of Charlie's history that comes complete with a breakdown of all of her criminal activity. Petty and stupid mostly. A prison stint that he'd known about. Tilly had been seven at the time. Seb was still a beat copper then and he'd spent much of that year lying awake trying to imagine her in that place and wondering if this might be the thing that made her change. He'd considered visiting but hadn't in the end. He'd heard that she was still using inside and had had a month added to her sentence for possession.

'Yeah, of course,' Seb says. 'Thanks guys.'

Finn and Harry leave first, Harry throwing him a pitying glance he could do without. Lucy pauses, about to speak. 'I'm OK,' he says, because fine might be too far a stretch.

'I can stay,' she tells him.

'No, really, go. I need to be busy, but you get on. We'll be back to it in the morning.'

'Yeah, all right.' Her voice is reluctant.

Finally, it's just him and a few officers starting the night shift. Night shift, he thinks. Lucy had finished a night shift as he'd been coming in this morning. She was due in again tomorrow. She must be exhausted. Normally he'd have sent her home hours ago. Normally almost always seemed to go out the window when Charlie was involved. He'd make sure she took time in lieu.

He glances at the clock and sees it's almost eight, so she'd stayed late too. He should have been out to dinner with Faye, eating greasy slices of pizza. He'd texted Val, telling himself he was too busy to call, which was a lie of course. He just couldn't face hearing her voice and lying to her so directly. He'd have to have a difficult conversation, and with Tilly too. The thought of how to open that conversation makes him feel nauseous. He stands, stretching, and heads to the drinks machine, making himself a tea that comes out scalding despite the splodge of milk, which means leaving the bag in until it's almost stewed. The tea in this place makes Val's mouth pinch with rage every time she's here. The thought makes him smile briefly, until he thinks again about that conversation.

If he could find Charlie, he could avoid that and save Tilly and Val the pain he himself is experiencing.

He goes back to the stack of paperwork, and pulls out the most recent photos of Charlie. Mug shots are never anyone's best, of course, but hers are harrowing.

Tilly takes after her mother, high cheekbones and fair hair. Stunning. He blinks away tears as he looks at what Charlie has become. Ravaged, skeletal. Her once blonde hair is matted and pulled back into a high twisted knot. A far cry from the girl he'd met who'd fizzed with so much energy it had jumped from her to him. She'd made him feel alive, Charlie. He remembered that and had never felt anything like it since. But that aliveness came with a helping of agonising anxiety. Wherever Charlie went, he'd thought, fun followed. Seb wasn't fun. He knew that, he had always known that. The boys he was at school with were Britain's best and brightest. They had a firm policy of work hard play hard and when they played, they did it in the way only people with no money worries utterly secure in their futures could. Seb didn't know exactly why he felt so different to them, but he knew he did. Knew he was.

He forces himself to go back to the images, trying to look at this like he would any other case.

He charts a rough year for her and Sid in London. There are photos from a hospital stay showing various bruises, cuts and scrapes, three fractured ribs apparently. She'd been beaten up and, he pauses, reading the accompanying notes, badly sexually assaulted during a pickup. She and Sid had been going to get their usual drugs from their usual dealer and it turned out Sid hadn't paid the last bill. While Sid had taken a kicking, it seemed Charlie had got the worst of it. Neither one of them wanted to press charges and Seb can read the frustrations not recorded in the police report. It was why Britain's underclass remained mostly left to its own devices. It was hard to help those who wouldn't help themselves.

This sort of stuff crops up daily in Seb's job and while he isn't immune to the horrors, he doesn't feel endless distress about them either. If he did, he'd be ineffective. But this... her... the nauseous feeling gets worse. This is why police shouldn't work on cases where they have a personal involvement. He knows that, though he also knows there's no way he'll be handing this over. He'll need to discuss it with Jackie, but even if she pulls him off the case, he'll still pursue it.

He slams the file shut, putting away the images, as if it can erase what has happened to her. This woman he had once loved with all his heart. He picks up the tea, sips and scalds his mouth.

This is no good. He empties the paper cup in the narrow kitchen's scummy sink, binning the bag and putting the cup into recycling. He leaves the station, grabbing his car keys, gets into the Golf and heads back to Hartsmead.

—

He drives around the familiar streets, eventually parking at the bottom of the block where Charlie and Sid had lived. Not far from where, once upon a time, he and Charlie had lived in the flat Charlie had grown up in, him leaving his comfortable suburban home to be with her. Teenage parents to-be with their whole, admittedly complicated, lives ahead of them. But, Seb had assured himself. All you need is love.

His phone vibrates. Faye.

> Hope you're not working too hard x.

He stares at it, slides it back into his pocket and gets out of the car.

Spring is on its way. The February half term always holds that promise. Normally he's fairly cheerful, having recovered from the winter gloom. The awful point where Seb feels as if the dark might engulf you. Faye had said next year they should go and spend Christmas or at least half of January in Mexico and right now, he'd love to do just that. Head home, grab Tilly and Val get on a plane.

He stands, his back pressed against the car door. He could call her. He could get in his car and go and see her. This woman who represented all the good things in life, like festive periods in the sun with no drama. A kid whizzes past him on a BMX and Seb murmurs, 'Watch it.' The kid turns and gives him the finger. Seb watches him go, fading to a small blur in the distance. It's early evening but would be pitch black without the lights that pepper the estate. They cast the entire place in a murky glow, making everything look slightly unreal. If only that were true, he thinks as he heads to the stairwell.

He'd learnt when he lived here, moving from the wealthy suburb he'd been raised in to Charlie's flat on the estate, never to take the lift. The buggers rarely worked and on the odd occasion they did, they couldn't be relied upon not to get stuck.

He steps into the grey stairwell and the stench of piss hits him, grim; it will be almost unbearable in the summer.

He heads up, passing various youths smoking spliffs and loitering. He gets lair from one of them, a young man, a boy really, who snarls when Seb flashes his badge but does stop antagonising him. He hears the kids scatter as he gets higher. No one dumps their drugs anymore. They understand that the police are stretched and have little time left over for petty crime. It's better in other bits of town but here on Hartsmead they couldn't keep up with the calls or the endless shoplifting. It wasn't totally lawless but it came close, which is how flats like the one Sid and Charlie lived in came into existence, how slum-like encampments were set up and left to fester. He stands at the door, which is cordoned off with yellow police tape. The lock didn't work but the SOC officers had padlocked it earlier. No one was getting in, including him, which begged the question he'd asked himself the whole way over: what was he doing here? Why had he come?

He doesn't want to go home is why.

A door opens, making him jump, and a small old man steps out, squinting at him. He's dressed in fleece pyjamas that make him look even smaller, his feet are in slippers.

'You don't look like one of them,' he says, and Seb hears decades of cigarette smoke in his voice.

'Oh, no,' he says, pulling out his badge, stepping forward and holding it out to the man. Most people don't even give it a second glance. The small elderly man reaches out, taking it from Seb and studying it intently.

'Heard that dimwit was killed.'

'Sid Darnell?'

'Yes, Sid Darnell. You want to come in?'

Seb hesitates; this is on tomorrow's to-do list. Harry and Finn would be knocking on the doors of people they hadn't managed to speak to. 'Did any officers come to see you yesterday?'

'Might have done, I was at my daughter's.' The man turns, heading back in, and Seb follows him, deciding he may as well get something from this visit. The man pauses at the door once they are inside, double locking it and pulling the chain across.

Inside it smells musty, but old people musty rather than the decay of next door. They settle in a small living room where a freestanding heater is giving off almost unbearable warmth despite the mild weather outside.

'Tea or anything?' Seb's eyes flick to the table, which is full of dark ring marked mugs and old newspapers, yellowing at the edges.

'I'm OK, thanks.' The older man settles back into his chair with a gasp that suggests bits of him ache. Things Val assures Seb he has to look forward to. 'So you knew Sid Darnell?' he asks the man.

'Couldn't help but know him and his rag-tag crew.'

'Crew?'

'Yes, endless people in and out, none of them good. Aside from the pretty girl, who was mostly all right.'

'Charlotte Locke?' Seb says, amazed when his voice comes out even. Amazed that even though saying her name is like vomiting razorblades it also brings a stab of fear. For her suffering, her safety.

'Yes, Charlie she said.'

'Right. She's missing.'

'Sid mentioned it, was quite upset actually, came banging on my door accusing me of all sorts.' The old man chuckles and it turns into a wheeze. 'As if I'd be capable of harming anyone, and if I was it would have been him, not her. Always felt she'd fare better on her own.'

'I think she was in trouble before she met Sid Darnell actually.'

'Maybe so, but that girl had a bit of get up and go. Something about her that might have won out if she'd kept better company.'

'Perhaps,' Seb relents, though inside he is indignant. *He* was better company. *Val* was better company. Tilly was the best company you could get. But this guy doesn't know that of course. This guy knows skinny, feral junkie Charlie who Seb is certain could still turn on the charm at times. But he understands what he means, of course. There is something about Charlie.

He'd grown up in far cushier circumstances than she had, nice house, two wealthy parents and a private education. Val was solid now but as she was raising Charlie, she'd had a violent husband and had been unable to leave before the damage was done. She said herself she might never have left. He died and no one mourned, least of all Charlie, but Seb knew that she bore the pain of it deep inside. Carried it around like a hot toxic little gift. The poison slipped out and infected her, drove her to become what she was now. His upbringing was affluent and lucky in many ways but there was no love in it, and to this day, Seb still can't quite fathom why they'd adopted him, a kid who never quite measured up. He'd seen in Charlie something he recognised in himself. Hurt, and the ability to navigate it. He'd thought she was tough, strong. The strongest person he knew. Addiction, it turned out, was tougher and stronger than she was by far.

He gets his pad out now, flipping it open, and asks, 'Can I take your name?'

'Huh, oh yeah. Guy. Guy Hockey.'

'Thanks for speaking to me, Mr Hockey, OK if I take notes?' He holds the pad up.

'Yeah, course, and call me Guy. Mr Hockey is my father,' he says with a fleeting smile, and Seb wonders, not for the first time, if we ever actually feel grown up.

'Guy then. I'm sure you know by now that Sid Darnell is dead. He was killed, we suspect the night before last.'

'Inevitable.' The man sighs. 'Though I'm surprised it wasn't just an overdose to be honest.'

Seb doesn't tell him that in fact, Sid had enough low-grade heroin in his system to have killed him. He is still trying to work that through in his own head. He is assuming that the killer couldn't have known, or why stab him?

'He had a risky lifestyle.'

'They live like animals. This is the first peace I've had since they arrived almost, what, three months ago now?'

'Do you know if Sid and Charlie had known each other for a long time?'

'Oh yes, since they were kids she said, though the "romantic" thing was fairly new.'

'Why put it in air marks?'

'Well,' he sniffs, 'a girl like that, only with a loser like Sid because of her own problems, you know.'

Seb does know, but either way that is the fact of the matter.

'So they arrived about three months ago?'

'Well, his sister was here first.'

'Oh?' There was no mention of that in the paperwork, nor was Sid's sister listed as next of kin as far as Seb knew.

'Yes, not for long, stopped off for a bit with her two kiddies. Nice girl, told me she'd been leaving her partner. Odd term that isn't it? Used to just be said when partner was the same sex.'

'Was her partner female?'

'No, the kids' dad. She stopped at the flat while she was waiting to be re-housed. Would have been in a hostel otherwise. Maybe she was claiming a hostel room, actually, would make sense then that she wouldn't have wanted anyone to know she was there.'

Seb thinks of the children's room in that awful place. Guy says, 'She was gone the day before Sid arrived and I suppose at least he did that for her.'

'Yes, is she still in the area?'

'A few towns across I believe, Guildford way perhaps.'

'Thanks.'

'Her name is Maria I think. Not Rita Simmonds's girl – that's Sid's mum – but same dad.'

'So she left.'

'She did, and Sid arrived the next day, with Charlie in tow. Both of them sick, drug sick, you know.'

Seb nods, because he does, but asks Guy, 'How could you tell?'

Guy sighs. 'See it all the time, don't you, around this estate. Junkies everywhere in their various states, scratching about, looking, high or craving. These two were craving, twitchy. I met Charlie first, properly came out onto the balcony a nice sunny morning, she was standing there smoking.'

'Still sick?'

'Yes, but managed to smile. I introduced myself, said I'd been here years, which I have. That I didn't want any trouble. She told me they wouldn't be bringing any, had come here to get away from it.' He sighs, shaking his head. 'I said to her that she didn't look well, she said she didn't feel it but was planning to get to a doctor later that day. I must have looked dubious because she told me she'd been clean for three days, and that she was aiming to keep it that way.' His voice trails off into silence.

'She didn't though?'

'No, though I think she did better than him. She went out later that same day. The second she was gone almost someone showed up at the flat.'

'Someone?'

'Yes, a dealer, didn't know that then but he's been a regular fixture ever since along with any old waifs and strays they pick up.'

'So Sid used on day one?'

Guy nods. 'I doubt he had any intention of getting clean, but she did, I could see that. I'm an early riser and Charlie would often be up and out on the balcony smoking. We got to talking. Some days she looked better than others. She seemed to have a quiet determination and I really felt if she just got rid of him she'd fare better.'

Seb waits a moment, forcing himself not to scoff at that, the amount of times he'd heard her say it, it'll be different this time, I'll do it, and believed her. Each relapse more heartbreaking than the last, until he came to the conclusion that she was incapable. That she would poison not just his life but Tilly's too.

'If you go now,' he'd told her, 'don't come back.' And for years, she'd kept to that. Until now.

'Sid reported Charlie missing two weeks before he was killed,' Seb says, 'and you say he contacted you?'

'Oh yes, battering on my door at five in the morning in a right old state. I was very annoyed, and then I figured she'd finally seen the light, packed her bags and gone. That thought cheered me up.'

'Did Sid say she'd packed?'

'He said she'd taken an envelope of photos that she carried around, of her kid he said. I didn't know she had a child until then.' The man sighs. 'She'd have made a good mother in different circumstances.'

That's about all Seb can take. He stands, telling Guy, 'Don't get up,' as the old man struggles to get to his feet.

CHAPTER THIRTEEN

Seb had spent the rest of the evening driving round the area, eyes peeled, heart sore. By the time he got home everyone else was asleep and this morning he was up and out at six, leaving a note for Tilly and Val to say don't wait up.

He's a coward, he thinks, a terrible gutless coward, but he'd lain awake most of the night running through the conversation he knew he had to have in his mind. He'd exhausted every possible reaction he might get from Val and from Tilly and come to the conclusion that none of them were good.

By the time Lucy, Finn and Harry arrive at the station, Seb is on his second pot of coffee and he has found Maria Darnell.

'Hey.' He looks up as the others file in.

'How long have you been here?' Lucy asks.

'Not so long. I, uh, spoke to one of their neighbours yesterday.'

'Did you?'

'Yes, Guy, older man to the left.'

'He was on the list, not in when Finn and I popped by,' Harry says.

'Yeah, he said he was at his daughter's.'

They all settle around a table, steaming mugs in front of them. Seb puts his own down, already full of caffeine.

'His sister Maria Darnell stayed there apparently, before Sid and Charlie arrived.'

Harry says, 'Didn't see her name anywhere.'

'No,' Seb agrees, 'I think it was an informal arrangement. She and her kids had been placed in a hostel just outside of Guildford and were waiting to be housed.'

'Ah, so she wasn't meant to be there.'

'No, and officially she was at the hostel. I've left a message for the housing association who own it; hopefully they'll get back to me, but my guess is that she was nipping in every once in a while but actually living in the flat.'

'The tenancy of which went straight to Sid?' Harry asks.

'Right, she and Sid were half-siblings, and it was Sid's mum's flat, not her mother's.'

'His mum was still listed as his next of kin,' Lucy adds.

'I saw that.'

'I didn't realise you were going back yesterday,' Lucy says, and Seb waves a hand, avoiding her gaze.

'I was driving past, thought I'd look.' He sees Finn and Harry swap a glance and tenses his jaw.

The door to the open plan office opens and DSI Jackie Ferris swoops in. 'It's raining,' she announces with a frown, taking off a long raincoat, which swamps her. 'Seb,' she says, indicating for him to follow her.

Shit. He stands, trailing behind her and into her office. Lucy mouths 'good luck' as he goes and Harry gives him a thumbs up which he supposes means the same thing.

He has no intention of backing off the case, and so he'd likely need all the luck he can get.

—

'Sit,' Jackie says as she takes the chair behind her desk.

He does, and finds he's holding his breath. He lets it out slowly, irritated with himself. He's not scared of Jackie, he is one of the few people who isn't, but he knows that he should have spoken to her, yesterday probably. Just as he'd put off talking to Val and Tilly he'd done the same with his boss. They've worked together for almost three years now and one of Seb's first cases as DI had involved investigating historical corruption in the force Jackie had taken over. He'd handled a difficult situation well and also found her to be firm but overall fair. However, she didn't suffer fools gladly and, perhaps because of the corruption, she tended to be a stickler for rules. Understandably so, and he really shouldn't be on this case, but he also wasn't prepared to step down.

'Are you all right?' she asks. It's a surprise opening. He stares at her for a moment, weighing up the best approach. Honesty probably. Dishonesty makes him feel nauseous, makes him feel like the broken man Charlie had walked out on, a man who used to lie all the time to cover her tracks. That aside Jackie herself is straightforward and expects the same from other people.

'I've been better,' he tells Jackie now.

She nods. 'Understandable. How's Tilly doing?'

'I haven't had a chance to speak to her yet.' Jackie raises an eyebrow. 'I will, I just…'

'You were hoping to find her mother so you don't have to.'

'I'm hoping to find her, and sooner rather than later, yes.'

'The dead man, Sid Darnell, he was her boyfriend?'

'Apparently so.'

'Reported her missing, what, a week before his death?'

'Two.'

'Two,' Jackie says, and he wonders if she's thinking what he is. Most people turn up within twenty-four hours. When they don't, nine times out of ten, it's bad news.

'She's a junkie,' Seb says, managing somehow to keep his face impassive, 'they have a habit of wandering off.'

'Did she do this when you knew her?'

'All the time,' he tells her, his jaw tightening at the bombardment of familiar feelings the memories conjure. A bird fluttering in his chest, unsettled, agitated, stressed. The Charlie effect.

'Do you think she killed him?'

'No,' he says quickly. 'I mean, we can't rule it out.'

'No, we can't.'

'She was missing before he was killed, if she'd done it she'd have been more likely to go missing then.'

'She could have come back and done it.'

'Yeah,' he relents, 'it's possible.'

'And awful for you to even have to consider, I'm sure.'

'That my daughter's mother is a killer?'

'People in her situation are volatile, Seb, you know that. All kinds of fuckery happens.'

'I know.'

'I'm not trying to be extra unpleasant, I just want to make sure you can handle this, because you know as well as I do that you shouldn't be working on this case at all.'

'I need to.'

'Will that need cloud your judgement?'

'I hope not.'

'Your ex-wife –' he nods, he'd managed to get Charlie to sign divorce papers by paying her to do so – 'is a suspect?'

'I know… I…'

She holds up a hand. 'You shouldn't be working this but, you are my best detective. We'll go from the angle of Sid's murder and we'll call it temporary during preliminary enquiries, I'll do some paperwork that makes it look like we're considering other options. If need be we'll put Ken in charge for official purposes.'

'I... thank you.'

'Don't thank me. It's not a final call, it's a pursue it for now, and check in with me. Ken's coming in to help out from today if he has any concerns, no matter how minor, he'll also let me know.'

'I'm glad to have him. Is he happy with that?' Ken had been threatening to retire for the past year but had instead moved to part-time hours. He hadn't worked a full investigation for a while though.

'He is, yes, and he'll be here by ten. Use him, use your team, and if it gets too much, just say.'

'Yeah, I will.' There's silence. The bollocking he'd been expecting for swooping in and taking this on without consultation doesn't seem to be coming.

'Good. And just so you know, the others will be checking in on you too, and if they have any concerns, I'll hear about it.'

'I understand.'

She nods. 'OK, find Sid's killer, and let's hope we find her safe and well too.'

CHAPTER FOURTEEN

SAM

'Laura.' I bang on the door again, the file of paperwork slipping out of my arms and onto the floor.

'Shit,' I mutter, leaning down to pick it up. My fingers are numb with the cold. I fumble, my anxiety making it even worse. She had missed signing one of the forms yesterday, which meant May's next benefit payment might be held up as a result, which isn't good. May is on a pension, struggling to make it work with two kids to feed and clothe and it's my fault, as I should have checked the paperwork over before I left. I'd been so unsettled seeing Laura and knowing she'd relapsed that I hadn't done so.

I hear a door slam and jump half out of my skin.

'She's not there,' one of the students who have lived next door since September says.

'Oh?'

'I don't think she is, anyway, had a fight with someone then the door slammed so hard our place shook. I came out onto the balcony, saw her getting into a car.'

I frown. 'Who was she fighting with?'

'I don't know.'

'What time was it?'

'Um, just before Kelvin and me went out, for student night.' Mondays in the centre of town are now overrun by university students with NUS cards and a hunger for large quantities of cheap beer.

'Which would make it?'

'Nineish.'

'Right, and she's not been back?'

She shrugs, this pretty girl with plump skin and shiny hair who looks out of place on this estate, though student lets were becoming far more common here and social tenants would soon be the minority. This is definitely one of the better blocks too. Facing out towards town, on the sprawling estate's outskirts rather than right in the fray. 'I mean, I don't think so.'

'OK. Thanks.'

I leave and start to make my way back to the office. Putting my phone on dial I call Barry and Debbie's place. Barry picks up. 'Hello, Hope Springs, recovery is possible.'

'Barry, hi.'

'Sam.' His voice is warm and I feel that background spark that I always get for Barry. I have an inappropriate crush on him. Inappropriate because I know him in a work capacity and he is a happily married man with a wife who is equally as lovely as he is. 'How are you?'

'OK.' I swerve to miss a tiny Fiat pulling out too sharply; the young woman behind the wheel grimaces and holds a hand up to me. I give her a strained smile. No harm done, but still. 'Actually I'm a bit concerned.'

'Oh?'

'Yes, have you seen Laura?'

'Laura Doyle?'

'Right.'

'Not for a few days no. How is she?'

'She picked up again.'

'Sorry to hear that,' he says, and the sincerity in his voice lets me know he is. Barry isn't the kind of man who just offers empty platitudes. He's the kind of man who says what he means and means exactly what he says. Hence the crush.

'Yeah. Now I can't find her.'

'Can't find her?'

'I mean, she's not at her flat.'

'Hmm, not unusual?'

'No. But I messaged her yesterday when I realised she'd missed signing a piece of paperwork, she said she'd be in.'

'Well…'

'She's not exactly reliable. I get it.'

Barry sighs. 'Is it to do with the kids?'

'Yes, and not having it done will hold up May's benefit payments.'

'That's not good.'

'No. Her neighbour said she heard her arguing with someone.'

'Oh, do you know who?'

'Nope, then she left, got into a car.'

'I mean…'

'I know she could be anywhere with anyone. Maybe Tiny?' I ask. A close friend of Laura's, the pair had known each other when they were both children in the care system, and Tiny was one of the few permanent residents at Hope Springs.

'He doesn't drive,' Barry tells me, and I think maybe I knew that. 'Plus he was here all day yesterday, we're painting several of the outbuildings.'

I sigh. 'Hopefully she'll show up.'

'I'm sure she will. In the meantime, if May needs assistance to tide her over, we might be able to help in the short term.'

'Thanks Barry,' I say. 'I'm just going to May's now, so I'll get back to you on that.'

'OK, and Sam?'

'Yep.'

'Look after yourself too, won't you?'

'I will. Thanks.'

I hang up the call. I know I'm extra on edge because of Charlie. I hadn't given her a second thought, and now look.

—

May has the door to her small but neat house open before I'm even out the car.

'Samantha,' she says with a wide smile. She has pale skin and pale hair, was once a redhead like Laura, but it's faded now. The new lines around her eyes belie her tiredness and I can only imagine how exhausted she is. Years of raising her own two single-handedly – she has a son who lives in warmer climates and Laura, who has been nothing but a cause for concern – and now two grandchildren in what ought to have been her golden years.

'Come on in, I have coffee on.'

'Music to my ears.'

We sit at the kitchen table. It's after nine; both children will be at school by now. I look round the homely space, kids' artwork pinned to the refrigerator, images on the walls of May younger with two babies of her own. Laura gap-toothed and grinning. Almost unrecognisable when compared to the woman she has become.

'It's peaceful in here,' I tell May.

'Oh yes, until three fifteen, when it all kicks off again.' She's smiling when she says this but I can hear the strain in her voice. She had no choice really. I understand that, know she's not the kind of woman who could have slept at night knowing her grandchildren were languishing in care. But it's a hard path nonetheless.

'Did you find Laura?'

I shake my head, and May makes a clicking noise with her tongue.

'I'll be able to get around it though, the signature, she's signed everything else and is uncontactable.'

'How long will that take?'

'I don't know,' I admit. 'Sorry.'

She sighs. 'The day-to-day stuff is fine, under control mostly, but Donna needs new shoes, Riley has a trip coming up and whilst the cost of it is covered, I need to get him kit.'

I ferret around in my bag, pulling out an envelope which I've stuffed two twenties in. I slide it across to her.

'Sam,' she says as it sits between us.

'You can pay me back when the money comes in.'

'You shouldn't have to lend to me.'

I shrug. 'This sorts out the shoes. When do you need to get the rest of the kit?'

'Next week.'

'That should be fine, this ought to all go through by then and Barry at Hope Springs has said they may be able to help, so call him, OK?'

She nods. 'Thanks.'

'Don't mention it.' My phone beeps and I groan.

'Need to go?'

'Team meeting, which I'm liable to be late for.' I pick up the coffee and drain it. 'I'll let you know once everything is sorted, OK?'

'Thanks, Sam.'

She sees me to the door and I head into the office. I call Laura on my way. Straight to voicemail. I have lots of clients who are runners, it's par for the course. But Laura is fairly predictable unless there's a man involved. Just the thought of it makes my heart sink. The last man beat her so badly she wound up in intensive care.

CHAPTER FIFTEEN

CHARLIE

The masked person comes back in at some point and I'm so glad to see him, her? Glad and this time much more aware. I push myself up to sitting.

'I've been sick,' I say.

The masked figure nods. 'I know, but you're doing very well.' Voice muffled and not much more than a whisper.

'Am I in a hospital?'

'You're in a safe place.' The person leaves a wheeled tray and is gone as soon as they arrived. I'd seen outside the door that there was at least one other person too.

I stand and bring the wheeled table across so it's alongside the bed. On top of it is a covered plate, a bottled juice and another small paper cup with a new handful of pills in.

I lift the lid. A sandwich. Am I hungry? I realise I probably am.

I eat, taking slow small bites, amazed that I can taste everything, the slightly stale brown bread, thick butter, ham. It's like a child's sandwich and reminds me of ones I'd made once in what feels like another life. Always with the crusts cut off.

I finish eating, drink the juice and swallow the pills. 'You're in a safe place,' the person had said. Man, woman?

Tall, thin, hair covered in a scrub cap, wearing those rubber shoes they wear in hospitals.

I think I can hear something. I stand up, manoeuvring to the door and pressing my ear against it.

No. Now all I get is a thick eerie silence. I try the handle, locked. I call out, my voice is weak and hoarse my throat hurts. I haven't spoken in what… days I suppose. I've slept a lot or blacked out when it all got too much. I look at my arm where the needle had been and see other pinprick marks, new fresh ones; my veins are notoriously hard to find, sunken as they are. They've kept me drugged then? A medical detox? Someone who knows what they are doing well enough to turn me into a human pin cushion. Well enough to prescribe. I feel… clear, and I realise as I make my way back to the bed that although I'm freaked out, physically I'm starting to feel a bit better.

CHAPTER SIXTEEN

'Hope Springs,' Lucy reads aloud, her voice thick with sarcasm.

Seb grins at her. 'You don't like it?'

'I mean it's...'

'Twee?'

'Yeah. Ha. But Sam Martin said they do great work here.'

'Yeah,' Seb says, not adding that when he'd thought about it, realised the name was familiar, it occurred to him that this had been one of the places he'd suggested to Charlie right before she left forever. That there had been a period of hope, which was worse, he'd decided retrospectively, than just accepting her the way she was.

Inside there is a reception area. They flash their badges and the young woman behind the counter smiles. 'Barry said you'd be in, follow me.'

They fall behind her and Seb steals glances at a large common room type area, with two long dormitories, one either side of the corridor, and several smaller rooms.

They finally end up outside in a large garden where small groups of people are tending to both the outside space and some outbuildings. It's a much bigger enterprise than Seb had realised, much bigger than it looks from the street. The place had been running for just over a decade. Debbie Marlon, Barry's partner, Seb understands, had inherited the building and a lump sum, so rumour had it. An ex-addict herself, she'd decided to do this with the legacy. An admirable choice.

'Barry.' The woman taps a tall man on the arm. He spins round, throwing Seb a grin that shows a glint of gold tooth and holding out his hand.

'DI Locke?'

'Yes, and this is DS Quinn.'

'Great to meet you both, gimme a sec.' He walks over to a young-looking man. Not much older Seb supposes than Tilly, though his face is made up of harder lines. He's standing next to a thin shed with a paint-dipped roller in his hand. Seb watches Barry take the roller and demonstrate cutting into the shed's corners. Then he hands it back to the kid and the kid has a go, and Barry slaps him on the back. More big smiles are exchanged and then Barry is gesturing for them to follow him into the main building.

'Teaching Jimmy the finer tricks of painting.'

'The kid?'

Barry nods. 'Eighteen actually, but yeah, a kid really. His mum spent some time with us, though she never did get Jimmy back.'

'Sorry to hear that.'

Barry nods. 'That's the reality. Worse for Jimmy having to suck up the care system. They pretty much washed their hands of him when he hit sixteen. You know they do that now?'

Seb nods. 'I'd heard it's getting worse.'

'That it is.'

'Jimmy works here?'

'Yep, and has a studio upstairs.' Barry points and Seb sees a staircase to a second floor.

'What's up there?'

'That's where Debbie and I live and there are three studios. Right now, we've got Jimmy in one, Tiny in a different block and two other tenants.'

'Like him?'

'Not exactly like him, but they are all people who just needed a little time to get back on their feet, you know.'

They are in an office now. Barry ushers them in, pulling out chairs and settling them down. 'Did you get offered coffee?' He frowns.

'Oh, no, but that's fine, really.'

'Yeah, guess it's the least of your worries when you have murder on your mind.'

Seb gives him a polite smile; he could do with a coffee really, but it is probably a bad idea as he'd woken up this morning with a gut full of acid and a head full of worry that had certainly ruined his first cup of the day.

'Sam Martin said you knew Sid Darnell?'

'Oh yeah. I mean, I knew Charlie more, but Sid has been in with her a few times and they both drop into Alex's clinic for their methadone. I guess you knew that?'

'Yes, we know. So both were trying to what, get clean?'

Barry laughs a kind of warm bellow. 'Charlie had designs to, Sid was just tagging along for the scrip I'd say.'

Seb smiles politely, already sick of hearing about Charlie's grand plans which hadn't included looking up her daughter despite being around the corner.

'When did you last see either of them?' he asks.

'I saw Sid three days ago, came in here looking for Charlie.'

'And you didn't know where she was?'

'No.'

'Would you have told him if you did?' Seb asks. Barry shrugs.

'Would have depended on what Charlie wanted. We deal with lots of domestic violence situations here if that's what you're getting at?'

Seb swallows memories of Charlie small and enraged pounding his chest with her fists. Images of her years later in a hospital. She'd been beaten up… assaulted. 'Yeah, I guess I am.'

'Hmmm,' Barry says. 'Not in their case. Sid was a loser, no doubt on that one, but violent? I don't think so.'

'Don't think so?'

He shrugs. 'Could be wrong.'

Seb nods. 'We think Charlie had been missing for over a week by then, almost two. He came into the station a day later and the day before he died.'

'If he came to you guys he was really worried.'

'What makes you say that?'

'Sid was scared of the police, was scared of his own shadow really, which takes me back to your question on his violent tendencies. Let's say Sid was more likely to be the recipient than the culprit.' Barry shakes his head. 'Sid wasn't tough enough for any of it.'

'Oh?'

'Yeah, mad for someone with that lifestyle, but he just didn't suit it.'

'How do you mean?'

'He was paranoid, which they all are, but he was also frightened outwardly and unable to manage ninety per cent of the time. That got him into some real trouble.'

'They were dealing from that flat?'

'Oh yes, and their supplier is a genuinely terrifying man.'

'Gordon Anselm,' Seb reads from old notes.

'Right, I imagine you know him?'

'We certainly know of him.' Seb had looked at the man's file in horror. He'd overseen some awful things, was suspected of a litany of murders, deals gone bad and severe beatings but he'd got away with most of it.

'He is every bit as awful as you'd think and I still don't really understand how he and Sid came into a deal together. Like I said Sid wasn't tough, not the kind of man you'd necessarily want fronting a house like that.'

'Do you know what the deal was?'

'He could use the flat as his base to deal more widely across the estate.'

'And why were you surprised?'

Barry pauses, and Seb imagines he can see the cogs turning. This is a man who likes to think through what he has to say. A man not dissimilar to himself.

'I know who you are,' Barry says, meeting Seb's gaze. Seb is certain he can feel Lucy's eyes boring into him. He doesn't look to check but keeps his face impassive, meeting Barry's gaze.

'Right.'

'I know Charlie had come back here hoping to get her act together.'

'So I heard,' Seb says, glad that his voice sounds calm rather than bitter. 'Instead she did a deal with a terrifying dealer.'

'Which is why I was surprised.'

'Addiction is a funny thing, as I'm sure you know.'

'Oh I do, and a powerful thing, but Charlie meant it.'

'Meant what?'

'That she wanted to get clean.'

'And Sid?'

'Sid wanted Charlie,' Barry shrugs.

'Love's young dream,' Seb murmurs before he can help himself. He instantly regrets it as Barry gives him a look that can only be described as pity.

'A toxic relationship of course. Co-dependent, as addicts tend to be, but Charlie at least had some level of self-awareness.'

'And Sid?'

Barry shakes his head. 'Sid was unlikely to improve, but Charlie called the shots and I tell you she was determined, so when I found out about the Gordon arrangement, yeah I was surprised. I figure he did that deal without her knowing and once you do a deal with a man like that,' he shakes his head, 'no going back.'

'Well I guess we'll never find out from Sid.'

'No, we won't.' He waits a beat. Seb tries to feel some basic human decency towards Sid and finds if he has any, it is certainly scant. This would be a good example of his personal life clouding his work. A good example of why he should probably be avoiding this case. But he wouldn't, he couldn't. Right or wrong, it still feels to him like Charlie is at least partly his responsibility. 'Drug deal gone bad?' Barry asks Seb.

'That seems most likely,' Seb agrees, but he doesn't think that, not exactly. It's not that black and white, because Charlie missing really does lead one to conclude that she was involved in some murky indefinable way, but Seb doesn't know if he is quite ready to believe that.

'Which begs the question, where is Charlie, and why did she run?' Barry prompts.

'You think she ran?'

Barry shrugs. 'Most obvious explanation.'

'Maybe she knew something was brewing, something dangerous.'

'My thoughts exactly.'

'And you'd suspect Gordon?'

'Or associates, yes.'

Seb nods agreement. 'Normally the most obvious conclusion holds the answer.'

'Normally so. Look man, this must be awful for you, I'm sure all kinds of things are running through your mind, but I don't think she'd have killed him,' Barry says.

Seb feels his jaw tighten even as the words are a relief of sorts. 'Maybe she felt she had to?'

Barry shrugs. 'Maybe, but she'd been gone almost two weeks, and he obviously didn't know shit about where. Seems silly for her to come back.'

'Yes,' Seb says, though he can think of plenty of motivators, money being the likely culprit. Maybe she came back for the stash, maybe she took it in the first place and left Sid in the lurch and that's what got Sid killed. Actually, that feels almost... right?

'For what it's worth,' Barry says, 'I liked her.'

'People usually do at first.'

Barry laughs, his big booming sound. Seb can see why the people around here like him. 'Maybe so, and look, sorry I couldn't be more help. If I think of anything or hear anything... I'll be in touch.'

'Appreciated.'

'You take care, detective,' Barry says as Seb leaves, and he can't work out if he's touched or patronised by this statement of care.

-

'He seemed nice,' Lucy says as they step into the car. 'Like genuinely.'

'As opposed to pretend nice?'

'You know what I mean, like he cares about them.'

'Them?'

'The addicts he deals with.'

'Yeah,' Seb relents; his bad mood is not on Lucy. His bad mood is stress and a severe lack of sleep. He'd only really been home for about four hours. Sneaking in late, sneaking out early. Telling himself he was just trying to get on, that was all. Really, he knew he was avoiding a difficult conversation that he'd have to have at some point.

They stop at a drive-through Starbucks and arrive back at the station with coffees for everyone wedged in a cardboard tray.

'Hello son.' Ken catches Seb as he heads to the kitchen. Son instead of sir lets Seb know that Ken has been fully briefed.

'Jackie find you?' Seb asks.

'She did yes, said you could use a hand.'

'Yes, thanks. Uh, Sid Darnell…'

'I'm up to date on the notes and figured perhaps we could have a chat later this morning,' Ken says.

'Yeah, that's fine.'

'Team's waiting,' Ken tells him.

'Right,' Seb says, standing at the door to the kitchen.

'And we've all got your back.'

'Thanks,' Seb murmurs. He steps back into the main bit of the room, Ken behind him, and calls for everyone to come over.

The small team gather around and wait for Seb to speak. He uses a second to take a sip of his coffee, which is much better than the station brew that is often left on so long it becomes unbearably bitter, and clears his throat.

'Lucy and I have just been to see Barry Matthews, who is one of the co-founders of Hope Springs. He seems to genuinely care about the people he works with, as does Sam Martin.'

'The social worker?' Harry asks.

'Right, and thanks for those details, Harry.' He clears his throat. 'Sam Martin is Charlie... Charlotte Locke's social worker. Charlotte Locke is, or was, Sid Darnell's partner and has been missing for...' He looks to Lucy, who says, 'Sixteen days.'

'Sixteen days,' Seb repeats. 'You all know I have a personal connection to Charlotte,' he says, finding using her full name, which he has never done, somehow easier. 'I promise I won't let it interfere with my approach.' He pauses. 'And to be clear, this is a murder investigation. We are looking for the person who killed Sid, and Charlotte Locke is a key person. We need to speak to her ASAP. Sid Darnell reported her as missing and he called again the night he was killed, which is when Lucy took the call and connected the name to me. We went to the flat to speak to Sid and found his body.'

'Well now it's a murder case at least,' says Harry with his knack of saying the wrong thing at the wrong time. Lucy softly punches his arm and Harry mutters, 'Sorry.'

'You all know who Charlie was, who she is to me and my daughter Tilly, and I appreciate you trusting me to oversee this case nonetheless.'

'Course we trust you, if anything you'll likely be more diligent. If it was my baby mother...'

'For god's sake Harry,' Finn murmurs. Which immediately takes the sting out of the clumsy words and almost, almost makes Seb smile.

'It's fine, Finn,' Seb tells him. 'And Harry, yes, you're right. I have a vested interest, but like any other missing prison I want her back, safe and sound. The main thing is that we have a murder on our hands and that's what we need to work. Finding her may help solve that, so that is one strand of our investigation.' He looks at their faces receives nods and murmurs of agreement.

'So, this morning, we need to go and get statements from anyone in Sid and Charlie's block who haven't already been questioned. Finn, are you and Lucy OK to do that?'

Both nod. 'I spoke to their direct neighbour, he happened to step out onto the balcony by chance. His name is Guy. He repeated something Lucy and I were told a few times yesterday and again today by Barry at Hope Springs, which is that Charlie had seemed to have some desire to stop using.'

'She got clean?' Harry asks.

'I don't think it was a fully successful attempt, no, but Sam Martin and her brother Alex, a doctor who works closely with many of these people at the drop-in at Hope Springs, said the same thing as Barry. Both felt she was genuine in her intentions at least and she had had periods where she was detoxing using methadone.'

Harry snorts. 'Swapping one thing for another,' he says. Seb ignores that, though he doesn't wholly disagree. 'Sid would have OD'd if he hadn't been slashed right?' Harry says now.

'Yes, and there is no evidence that either he or Charlie actually got clean. Just that she wanted to.'

'What do you think, guv?' Finn asks.

Seb sighs, running a hand across his eyes. 'I honestly don't know. I haven't seen her for years, but I do know she can be convincing and that like all addicts she may even mean the things she says. I also know that Charlie herself is the obvious suspect here, and whilst I'm not ruling it out, I do think the fact she went missing and hasn't been seen since at least buys her the benefit of the doubt.'

'Have you said that to Jackie?' Ken asks.

'I have,' Seb says, 'and she agrees, so let's work on the assumption that it was someone else but keep an open mind as regards her involvement. Harry and I will go and speak to Gordon, whose name has cropped up and who many of you may already be acquainted with.'

'I am,' says Harry. 'Came across the slippery fucker a few times when I was on the drug squad.'

'Right,' Seb says, 'we'll go and see him now. Ken, you said he's expected to be in his office all day?'

'Yes, and his office is attached to a car dealership A legitimate business at first glance but also a place fairly blatantly used for money laundering, among other things.' Ken stands, handing Seb a thin file. 'Some of the info in here might be useful if you need to threaten him, though I will warn you none of it will stick.'

'Got it,' Seb says, 'and thanks.'

'Of course.'

'OK, everyone good to go where they need to go?'

They all nod.

'Lucy, Finn, you head off now. Harry, carry on trawling social media while I have a quick chat with Ken.'

'All right, guv.'

CHAPTER SEVENTEEN

'How is he actually?' Finn asks Lucy as they step out of the station and into her small Fiat.

She sighs. 'I mean, he's visibly stressed.'

'Shit, really?'

Lucy nods, half smiling. Finn rarely swears but she too is unsettled to see Seb like this. He has a reputation as having a stoic disposition. When she'd first met him, she'd thought he was a bit cold even, but as she'd gotten to know Seb, and she did know him well by now, she thought, she'd realised that he was just a man of few words. He considered what he was going to say and often times said nothing at all.

'I mean, I guess of course he is?' Finn says it like a question. Lucy glances at him as she starts the car; he's chewing his lower lip and looks visibly worried. Like her, Finn had got his chance on major crimes because of Seb. Their boss had an eye for spotting talent and an uncanny ability to bring out the best in them all.

'It must be hard,' Lucy says, 'and then having to go and talk to all of these people who know her, like better than he does now, I imagine.'

'Yes. Has he told Tilly?'

'I'm not sure.' She has a niggling feeling that he hasn't. He'd spoken to Sid and Charlie's neighbour who happened to step out onto the balcony. Quite late, looking at his written notes, and he'd been in by the time she arrived this morning. If she had to hazard a guess, she'd say he'd purposefully got in late and left early. 'I don't think he's had a chance though,' she says, feeling disloyal even as she says it, which is stupid. If anything, she's trying to stick up for him.

'Maybe he wants to try and find her first, like not to worry her or Val?'

'Yes, that makes sense,' she agrees, but in the back of her mind, a voice says he ought not to even be on this case. Not that that was her call, thank goodness. She'd been surprised Jackie was allowing it to be honest. It could backfire badly. She didn't think it would, but still.

They drive out and park up on the Hartsmead. It's a bright day but while the sun is lovely, the estate itself is awful. It smells bad, the cause some overflowing bins at the bottom of several blocks of flats. Finn frowns at them as they pass. 'Should they be like that?'

'I'd say no,' Lucy tells him, though she'd been aware the last few times they'd been here that it had fallen into an even worse state of disrepair. The big social housing dream that had come to this. The other side of the estate that backs on to a park is mostly privately owned and is notably better kept than this side. She knows many of the buildings have creeping damp. They had been called out to enough suspicious deaths that turned out to be people taken early due to respiratory failure. Animals were kept in better conditions than some of the people here, she thinks.

There is a large piece of wasteland right at the edge of the estate, backing on to woods, where some of its inhabitants aren't even lucky enough to be tenants in crappy flats. They head there now. Three or four tents litter the place, and a barrel where a fire had burned out sits squat and blackened. It looks apocalyptic and the few people shuffling round the scene fit right in.

'Jesus,' Finn says.

'Yeah, pretty rough.'

'Sid and Charlie hung out here?'

'Two of the people in the flat with his body listed this space as their address.' She makes quotation marks around the word address.

'And that's who we're looking for now?'

'We're looking for anyone who might know anything, but yes, Amanda Sales and Louis Ernesto.' She pulls out her phone and shows him images of both. The pictures are mug shots.

'You go left, I'll go right?'

Finn nods. 'And call if there's trouble, yeah?'

'Yep, will do.'

—

It's a horrible scene but Lucy trudges through, stopping to speak to a few people as she goes. One man sitting outside a tent with no shoes twitches while he talks to her. She shows him the picture of Amanda and Louis and he pauses, frowning at it. 'Oh yeah, know them.'

'OK, do you know if they are here now?'

He shakes his head, making clotted clumps of black accidental dreadlocks sway around him. 'No, no.'

'OK, thanks.' She had been crouching down to talk to him and heaves herself upright, feeling her knees protest as she does so.

'Amanda left town, I think. Maybe,' he adds like an afterthought.

'Where to?' She frowns.

The man shrugs. 'Don't know where to, saw Louis recently and he said she'd gone and good riddance. Guess they had a bust up, you know?'

'Guess so.' She's now awkwardly standing looking down at the top of his head where she's almost certain she sees something moving among the matted hair. 'Do you know where Louis was going?'

'He was heading over to see his mate Colin.'

'Who's Colin?'

'Colin, Colin, you know Colin,' he says as if she's extremely stupid and should definitely know whom he means.

'OK, Colin, got a surname?'

'Nope, nope.' That twitchy head shake again.

'Do you know where I can find him?'

'Yeah, yeah. Squat on the other side of town.'

'Do you have an address?'

'Ummm, big old house on Stowater Street.' She knows exactly where he means; Finn and Harry, who both still work normal beat shifts, had been called out there a few times.

'OK, thanks. What's your name?'

'My name?'

'Yes, in case we need to contact you again?'

'Mickey, Mickey Bolton.'

'Thanks Mickey.'

'Yep yep. Looking for who got Sid?'

'We are, yes, any ideas?'

'Nope nope. Nice guy. Wouldn't hurt a fly.'

'You knew him?'

'Yep yep, knew him, we all know each other.' A network of people hiding away beneath the lovely suburban sheen of this commuter town.

'So no enemies then?'

'Oh well, Gordon. Don't say I said.' He looks madly over one shoulder then the other.

'Sid was dealing for Gordon?'

The man shrugs, scrunching in on himself and clamming up. 'Don't know, can't say, know nothing.'

'That's OK, Mickey. I won't mention it, all right?' She can see the real fear on him. A man in this state, living no kind of life, but still not wanting to be Gordon's next victim. The will to live, she thinks, is so strong even when you're already dead.

She takes down his details; he has no address, of course, and no phone either, but she gets his name and age, adding a description for her own notes. She's walking away when her phone rings.

'Finn.'

'Lucy, you'd better get over here.'

CHAPTER EIGHTEEN

SAM

I scowl at Mark. 'She's my client, and I have a duty to look out for her.'

'You have a duty of care, but there are limits on what you can provide.'

'She's been gone. Overnight now.'

Mark shrugs. 'She's a grown woman and can stay anywhere she wants.'

'I know, but...'

'But she normally picks up the phone to you. You're worried. I get it.'

'Do you?'

He sighs. 'Of course I do, Sam. I do the same job, remember.'

'Well, you're mainly here these days.' I sound like a petulant child and I know it, yet I can't seem to stop myself from being that way. It's guilt of course. This job always makes me feel like I'm not enough, but Charlie is missing, she hadn't come to our appointment and honestly, I hadn't given it a second thought, and now she's gone and Sid is dead. I should have followed up. I should have at least called her. So Laura being gone even just one night is putting me on edge. The second of my clients to go missing – coincidence? I'm not so sure, but realise if I attempt to explain the link between the two to Mark he'll be exasperated.

'I am yes, because there are only so many years we can be out there before it takes its toll.' His words are sharp but the meaning I suppose is kind.

'So you're saying I'm overreacting?' Definitely no point coming up with unwieldy theories right now.

'I'm not policing your feelings here.'

I make a scoffing sound before I can stop myself and he frowns at me, a reminder that he is my boss and his patience probably has a cut-off point. I look at my feet.

'I'm not, but you have other clients. Too many, I know. The paperwork you needed signed has been sorted, so right now there's no pressing problem?'

'Other than she's missing.'

'Or out, and hasn't told you, which she probably does all the time.'

'Not really. She's gets bouts where she's scared to leave the flat, remember.'

'But gets out when she needs to score.'

'Well, yes, but out and back again quickly.'

'Look, I know you're stressed.'

I let out a puff of air. 'Worried, Mark.'

'Right, and that concern is what makes you good at the job, but you need to rein it in. These people are unwell and you know as well as I do that most of them won't get much better.'

'Ever the optimist,' I say, thinking that this is similar to talking to Alex. It's the same circular discussion, where they seem intent on reminding me that most people fail to get better. Most, but not all — and that means some people improve. I know in my heart of hearts that a lot of my problem is the failure to save my own mother. I'm not stupid. But knowing the reasoning doesn't stop me hoping, or believing.

'Look.' His tone softens. 'I get it, I do, and I hope Laura gets home safe and sound as much as you do.'

'But I can't do much about it?'

'Not today.'

'I have to head over to Hartsmead later, so I'll give her a knock if she's not called back?'

'Yeah, OK, but that's it. No need to survey the entire block again.'

'Got it,' I say through gritted teeth.

'Look...' He pauses, looking awkward, takes his glasses off and rubs the lenses with the bottom of his flannel shirt. 'The thing with Charlie and Sid is making us all anxious.'

I look down, avoiding his gaze. I don't feel anxious – well I do, but mostly I feel responsible. I should have called, should have visited. If I had, maybe things would be different.

'She was doing so well.'

'She was, in large part thanks to you,' he says, which is too generous. Too simplistic. Addicts never did well due to someone else. Not really. They only ever threw the towel in when they wanted to.

'Thanks,' I say then add, 'I'm okay,' which is a lie.

'Great, team briefing in ten.'

–

I take my time making coffee and give myself a few minutes to calm down while I do it. I have a bad feeling about Laura but I also understand what Mark is saying. My nerves are jangled. The shock of not only a missing client but also her partner being murdered is sharp and brutal. It's a unique anxiety and one that takes me straight back to childhood where each day was like walking a tightrope. Each day pregnant with worry for my mother who lurched from one devastating situation to the next. The fact I've grown up and willingly chosen to work amongst these people is an irony not lost on me. I wear my issues openly. I am textbook. Which some days makes it even more depressing. My phone buzzes in my pocket and I make a grab for it, glad to be distracted from my own thoughts. 'Hello, Sam Martin.'

'Sam, it's DI Locke.'

'Hello detective, any news on Charlie or Sid's killer?'

'Nothing as of yet, but the woman who was in the flat when we found Sid…'

'Amanda?' I stir two sugars into my coffee cup, rinse the spoon and put it on the drying rack.

'Yes, Amanda Sales.' I know her but she's no longer registered with us. She aged out of the care system at just eighteen, that was two years ago. She'd been adamant she didn't need our help though I was aware she'd done poorly since then.

'Look,' he says, 'it would be best if we could come and talk to you, in person.'

I glance at the clock. 'I've got a team briefing then I need to head to the hospital. I've got a client there, the same one I mentioned who said Sid had been worried about Charlie.'

'Oh yes, could we meet you there and deal with that too?'

'Yes, that's…' I resist the urge to push him for information now; he'd said face to face. 'Of course.'

111

CHAPTER NINETEEN

CHARLIE

When I wake up, there are clean clothes and two folded towels on the chair along with a small wash bag of toiletries and a hairbrush.

I feel... different. I feel like I'm on my way to getting well. I take the toiletries and head into the shower room. I hate hospital gowns, like everyone I suppose. But I've been in one so regularly I'd forgotten that I disliked them. Or maybe I just haven't cared. Dignity is something I let go of years ago. What dignity is there ever for a mother who has abandoned her child?

I'm being watched. I've gathered that much. Cameras blink in each corner of the room. I'm not in prison, there are procedures that have to be followed there. I'd assumed some kind of rehab but again, there surely would be some sort of system. I've waved at the cameras, shouted hello and banged on the door to no response, and despite feeling a lot better physically, I feel a flutter of panic in my chest. Captive, I'm being held captive. But why?

I turn on the shower, reaching my arm out to test the temperature. The first initial of her name greets me. Once black, now the ink is faded blue green. I see the tattoo every day. Remember having it done, sat in a prison cell, a big woman with short hair, a mean face and a stubby little needle. 'Who's Tilly?' she'd asked.

'My kid,' I'd told her.

'Must miss her, huh?' She'd meant because I was locked up, and I'd nodded agreement, though by then, I hadn't lain eyes on her for almost four years. Now a decade has passed. In the blink of an eye.

I thought about her every day. The horrible slithers of time between opening my eyes and finding something, anything that will take it away. Nothing I've discovered is more effective than heroin for that. It's like lying beneath a warm, weighted blanket. It is oblivion, and that's all I've ever wanted. Too chicken to die, too weak to live.

I ranted about my kid to anyone who would listen when I was out of it. I woke up in cold sweats screaming her name. Sid held me on more than one occasion while I waited for the sobs to subside, for the horror to pass. Mostly, though, I'd shut it down, kept it hidden inside. The loss of her. The unforgivable horror of leaving. Choosing a needle over my kid. I'd judged my mum for choosing my father with his ready fists but I was no better; I was worse, in fact, because my mother had never abandoned me, not willingly.

Now I find I am assaulted by memories. Of Tilly and of Seb. A young man smiling at me as if I was the most important thing in the world. For just a minute, I'd almost believed it too. Not just in me. I'd believed in him, I'd believed in us. We were babies when she came along, not grown enough to take care of ourselves, and yet he'd risen to the task. While I collapsed under the weight of it. I'd really thought having her would sort me out. At that stage I was just a party girl, or so I thought. Liked a drink, a joint, a few lines and the odd pill at the weekends. I'd been horrified to discover how hard it was to stop when I was pregnant. Had spent the entire time gagging for something, anything to change the way I felt, which was awful. It wasn't the drink and drugs that were the problem, I decided, it was sobriety. She wasn't even one the first time I smoked heroin. I'd been out, drinking, clubbing, phone switched off to avoid Seb. Someone offered me a hit and I was coming down, back to reality with a bump and thought – why the hell not?

I shampoo my hair, add conditioner and start to untangle some of the knots. When I get out, I comb it through. There's a sliver of mirror in here attached to the wall; when I touch it, I realise it's not glass but a soft plastic of some kind. Everything in here, I realise, has safety in mind. I can see my face, my body wrapped in the white towel. I methodically comb my hair and think about the last time I'd done that for her, for my daughter. I blink away tears. I will go to her. Please god, let me get out of wherever here is and I'll go and find her. I'll say sorry and mean it and know the words can't make up for it but need to be said anyway and maybe, just maybe that could be a start?

When Sid had told me about his flat, the tenancy that had become his, I'd made a decision, taken it as a sign. It was time to go home, to face the music. The terrible tune my footsteps left as I walked away. From her, from him, from the few things that made me anything more than rotten to the core.

We did OK, Sid and me, for the first few weeks. I'd even found their house, Seb and Tilly's. I'd stood outside it, seen her through the window talking to my mum, who has aged but looked well. I knew she lived with them. Initially I'd still call her from time to time, demanding money that more often than not she'd send. Another woman burdened by maternal guilt. Maybe it ran in the family. Or maybe what ran between us was shit parenting. It was weird seeing the two of them. Tilly a young woman now, my mother older but not elderly. They looked easy together.

I'd seen Seb step out the door with a tall beautiful woman with glossy red hair and a magazine smile. The pair of them looked shiny, effortless. I saw my daughter leave the room with Mum in and hug the woman at the door and I felt a pain so overwhelming it almost felled me where I stood.

It took two days before I gave in. Before Gordon knocked on our door to 'have a word' with Sid who had 'worked' for him way back when, and while I didn't agree to the devil's deal, I did nothing to stop it either. I'd stay off the gear, I'd told myself. Even though I was on a mixed bag of methadone, illegally sourced Valium and the occasional warm tinned beer. Not quite sober but cleaner than I'd been for as long as I could remember. On my way, surely, to something better? I had a social worker, Sam, who seemed to believe it was possible, and her belief gave me some hope. But it only took two days.

Sid had dallied, siphoning enough for personal use off the large delivery from one of Gordon's rag-tag crew, and I'd thought, no – this is my sign. Reinforcement of all that I am. All I'll ever be. A strung-out junkie who damaged everyone I touched.

I put the clothes on that have been left on the bed, a soft white tracksuit, and find underneath there are several books, all about addiction and healing. Some I'd been handed before, sitting in creaky hospital beds while well-meaning doctors crowded me. Once at a meeting I managed to get to, a place where people talked about all the bad feelings I had but also laughed among themselves, when I couldn't imagine even smiling again, someone had pressed some of these into my hand as I left. I'd walked out, put them in the nearest bin and gone on my way.

I'm holding one of the books when I hear something, no, someone? A voice, faint, but there.

I stand, go to the door, pressing my ear against it and, yes, a voice. A woman's voice, yelling 'Help me.'

CHAPTER TWENTY

Seb gets to the hospital and makes his way inside, Harry following closely behind him. Harry is smaller than Seb but always seems to take up more space and make more noise. He's a big gesture kind of person and even his footsteps on the soft linoleum hospital floor are heavy and reverberate down the hallway. Finn and Lucy are still at the camp at the back of the estate waiting for scene of crime officers and Martina to appear.

Lucy had called Seb, voice shaky. 'It's Amanda Sales,' she'd said.

'You found her?'

'Oh yes.'

'And?' he'd snapped, impatient to get on, to get this done, for it to be over.

'She's dead, Seb.' A pause while she'd spoken to someone, and Seb already knew somehow what she was going to say. 'Same as Sid.'

Same as Sid. Amanda had been in a tent for one, throat slashed. Lucy had told him she'd spoken to someone else who was staying there. He'd mentioned that Amanda was planning to leave, that Louis had said as much and thought she'd already skipped town. Which reinforced what Seb already believed. Amanda had seen something, or more likely someone, the night Sid was killed.

Two murders. Charlie missing, a link to both dead people? Or just coincidence?

The hospital is like a maze but Seb knows his way around quite well and finds the acute ward quickly. He and Harry flash their badges and ask for Sam. 'By bed four, end of the ward.'

They pass other people in beds, curtains open, their indignity out on display for all to see. Better than A&E, where the same beds litter the hallways; the hospital, one of the largest in the area and surrounds, is often bursting at the seams.

'Hello, Ms Martin,' Seb says when they reach her. She's sitting next to a bed where a young woman with lank hair and dead eyes lies. It's by the window, which is slightly ajar, but it's still so hot in here that Seb feels sweat break out on his upper lip.

'This is my colleague, Detective Sergeant Fritz.'

She nods. 'This is Anita.' The woman in the bed doesn't respond. Sam leans forward. 'Anita, I'm going to go and talk to the police now, but I'll be back shortly.'

The woman turns, frowning. 'Am I in trouble?'

'No, it's not about you, they want to talk to me about a woman called Amanda Sales.'

Anita frowns. 'Louis's girlfriend?' Sam looks up at Seb, eyebrows raised.

'Yes,' Seb says stepping forward. The woman's eyes move to meet his. 'Do you know her?'

She shrugs. 'I mean, kind of. I'm friends with her friend, Charlie? Sam said you might want to talk to me about her?'

'Charlie Locke?'

That frown again. 'Don't know her surname. Lives on Hartsmead with Sid.'

'Yes, that's her,' Seb says. 'She's missing.'

'Missing?'

'Yes. We're trying to find her.'

'Ask Sid, he's been looking for her.'

Seb pauses, looks from Sam to Anita and addresses both when he says, 'As well as Charlie being missing, I'm sorry to say Sid was killed.'

'And Amanda Sales?' Sam Martin asks. Seb had said on the phone that's who he wanted to discuss.

'I'm afraid she is also dead, that's what I wanted to tell you.'

Sam nods, lips drawn in a thin line. Anita's face scrunches up and her expression makes it look like she's concentrating really hard, as if she's scared not to keep iron control on her thoughts lest they slip away. Sam had warned them Anita was out of it, and was clearly in a bad way to have landed here. 'Killed?' she says. 'Like how?'

'Murdered,' Harry pipes up and Seb scowls at him; he says sorry, eyes to the floor. Seb is reminded, not for the first time, why he usually gives Harry work based at the station. He likes him and he's good at what he does, especially research and assisting Finn with all things technical, but his people skills really do leave a lot to be desired.

'Oh shit,' Anita says, glassy eyes wide.

'You knew them both, yeah?'

'Well, like I said, we all knew each other.'

'Any idea who might want either of them dead?'

She shrugs, the hospital gown jumping up around her slim shoulders, bruised, stick-like arms poking out from it. 'Dunno. Maybe they owed money to... I don't know.'

'Gordon?' Seb asks.

'No idea who you mean.' She looks away, out of the window that isn't letting in enough air.

Seb and Sam exchange a look.

Seb says, 'Sam mentioned to me that Sid had told you he was a bit upset. Had Charlie and Sid been arguing?' and feels his pulse pick up pace at the question; the images of her last 'domestic dispute' haunt him still.

'They always argued,' the woman says. Her eyelids are drooping and heavy. Her breath smells foul. Sam had told him she'd been in here for two days with some kind of infection and it's coming off her in waves, the decay. Seb dreads to think of her outside an institution wandering the streets from one mishap to the next. Like Charlie, his brain offers, and the thought makes his heart ache.

'What about?'

She waves a hand and the tube it is attached to yanks a machine around, wobbling it. She doesn't seem to notice. Seb assumes that along with the antibiotics she'll be on a medley of opiates. Detoxing when people are this far gone is a tricky business. Even alcoholics might struggle to go cold turkey, but intravenous drug users are at real risk.

'Loads of things,' Anita says. 'Most lately, Sid thought she might be sneaking round on him, you know.'

'Sneaking around,' Seb frowns, 'like cheating?' He knew from various police reports that Charlie had been picked up more than once for soliciting while she was with Sid. Did that not count? he wonders.

'Yeah, said she deleted some messages from her phone.'

'Her phone?' Seb says. Charlie's number, which Sid had given in his first missing person's report, was currently switched off. Going straight to a standard inbox message. Not, Seb had been pleased to discover, a message she'd recorded herself. He had been selfishly glad not to hear her voice. Not yet anyway.

'Mmm,' Anita says, her voice thick, dropping eyelids heavy.

'Do you think she was?' Seb asks. 'Cheating?'

Anita shrugs. 'Wouldn't have thought so, but Sid was really paranoid about it, thought maybe she'd run off with him.'

'Did he have any idea who the person was?'

'Nah, but they'd been having some issues, you know.'

'Issues like?'

'I think Charlie wanted to sort herself out.' The woman yawns, reminding Seb of his cat Mimi when she's about to stretch out and hog the whole sofa. He can see dark grey fillings and black spaces where teeth once were.

'Sort herself out?' This is the third time he's heard this now. She'd come home to get well. She hadn't come to find him or her daughter though. *Yet*, a little voice adds. The voice that always gives her the benefit of the doubt. The voice that had cost him far too much wasted time and energy already. He does his best to push it away now.

'Yeah, you know she was on methadone and whatever?'

'Sid was collecting a prescription too.'

'Yeah, but he was selling it on, don't think Charlie knew, plus she didn't manage it, I don't think, stopping. Hard when she was living with him, I'd say that's why she went clean break.'

'Do you think she did then, sort herself out?'

The woman shrugs, her eyelids starting to press together. 'I think if any of us could have managed it she'd have been on the list.' Her head slips to the side and her breathing becomes long and drawn out.

Sam looks from Lucy to Seb. 'Shall we go grab a coffee in the cafeteria? I don't know about you, but I could use the caffeine.'

—

The tables are full of NHS workers in scrubs and crocs, masks slipped around their necks, eating plates of too dry, fatty fried breakfasts. There are other people not in uniforms with stricken faces. Family members, Seb thinks, relatives and friends, waiting to find out if loved ones will live, die or be irrevocably changed. He hates hospitals, is always reminded of the endless trips to A&E with Charlie, then to too warm wards where she was offered help she almost always refused. He'd argued, cried and begged alongside her sick bed on more than one occasion. And now, here he was again. His phone vibrates and he pulls it from his pocket glancing at it. Faye. God.

Seb puts it into his pocket and queues for coffee, bringing them over to Harry and Sam who are now in conversation about the logistic of Sam's job. He catches 'here, there and everywhere' from Sam and assumes she means the many places she needs to be in a day, which like him could mean a hospital, an office or a courtroom.

'What's Anita's story?' he asks when Sam has finished her sentence.

'They don't know exactly, but an infection of some kind which has put pressure on her heart and caused a heart attack.'

'Heart attack?' Harry frowns. 'She can't be more than thirty?'

'Twenty-four, actually, but she's battered herself and has been doing so for years.'

'Gosh,' Harry says, 'that's so sad.'

'Yeah, I know.'

'Do you get tired of it?' Harry asks, and Seb finds himself leaning forward slightly, waiting for her answer.

Sam sips her coffee and sighs. 'Yeah, of course, it can be frustrating, but,' she shrugs, 'they're mostly ill, not bad. You know that, surely. Prisons and police cells are full of people who need assistance with their mental health. Often their crimes,' she puts the word in speech marks with her fingers, 'are a perfectly reasonable response to horrific trauma, and instead of receiving help, they get locked up, locked away and come out worse than ever with a record.'

'Crime is crime, though, and can't go unchecked. Besides, addiction has a solution,' Seb says, his voice harder than he'd meant it. 'I mean people do recover, right?'

Sam smiles and it transforms her face, which seems to sit in a perpetual perplexed frown. 'Yes, they do, or I wouldn't bother.'

'You've seen it?'

She nods. 'A few times. Debbie and Barry who run Hope Springs, for example.'

'They were addicts?'

'Yup, met in a rehab.' She laughs. 'Imagine that story on your wedding day.'

'That's such a nice outcome,' Harry says.

Seb adds, 'It seems like a cool place?'

'Oh yes, it really is, and a labour of love.'

'I met Barry,' Seb says. 'He said Debbie was away.'

'Yeah, she travels a lot, attends conferences and stuff I think. She was a nurse for a while when she first got clean and sober, but she doesn't do much of that now,

Hope Springs is a full-time job, but I know she keeps her training up to date.'

'They are a registered charity?'

'That's right, they've had to fight for funding but they've also had a few generous donations.'

'Who from?'

'Can't give specific names, though you could ask them. From what I gather some of it has come from family members of some of their previous residents.'

'Residents?'

'Yeah, they have studios on the second floor and dorms out back. If people get to ninety days they'll often get offered a place there. Usually temporary, but long enough to get back on their feet. They also have links to local housing services and give them some work experience.'

'Any other names of success stories?' Seb wants to speak to one of these people, he decides.

'Um, Owen Sanchez comes to mind, he works there full time, and Tim, can't remember his surname. Tiny, who Barry practically adopted, he's young, has his nickname as he's huge but utterly harmless. A few others – ask them.'

'Yeah, we will,' Seb says.

'They all seem to know each other, your clients?' Harry says.

'It's a small community.'

'Of addicts?' Seb's voice sounds scathing even to him, his personal anger pushing to the forefront.

Sam pauses, meets his eye and he feels his face flush. 'My mother died of a morphine and barbiturates overdose.'

He frowns. 'God, I'm sorry… I…'

She puts a hand up. 'No need to apologise, I just wanted you to know, I get it. She looked respectable. She was a doctor just like Alex, but living with her, loving her, trying to care for her when she didn't care for us or herself.' She shakes her head. 'It's hard. I think it is an illness, but it's hard on them and harder perhaps on the people around them.'

'Is that why you do this job?' Seb asks her.

She nods. 'I think it probably is, yes.'

'And your brother Alex volunteers at Hope Springs?'

'He does, yes, though I think it's fair to say I tend to have a more optimistic outlook than him.'

'Oh really?' Seb asks.

'Definitely. Whilst I believe most people want to get well, he thinks most of our clients prefer it this way and that trying to change them is a waste of time.'

'The numbers would agree with him.'

'You're right.' She shrugs. 'But people aren't numbers.'

'Why does he come to the clinic then?'

'My brother is also a good man, detective. My father died of cancer when I was very small, just seven, Alex was thirteen. That's when our mum spiralled. She died three weeks after Alex's twentieth birthday. Instead of going off to university as had been his plan he changed his place for the local uni here and took full custody of me. I was fourteen.'

'Wow,' Seb says, 'that's a lot of responsibility.'

'Well, you should know, detective.'

'I guess I do a bit.'

'So Alex may have a more cynical view, but he also believes everyone deserves medical treatment and sometimes someone may improve. He's close to Owen, as I'm sure you'll discover if and when you speak to him.'

'What does he do at the clinic exactly?'

'Holds a full drop-in surgery for the day, appointments nine to four, drop-in from five to seven, but he overruns all the time.'

'And this is voluntary?'

'It is, though Barry and Debbie have funding and have offered to pay him. He may act the cynic but I know he's always pleased when he sees people doing well.'

They all pause, taking sips of their coffees, and Sam says, 'I don't think Charlie was cheating, by the way.'

'Oh?'

'She helped out at Hope Springs a few times, attended some meetings, maybe she was talking to people she met there. She did mention to me that Sid was a bit scathing.'

'Not very supportive,' Harry blurts out.

Sam smiles. 'Well, partners in crime I guess. She gets well, the logical conclusion would be Sid was on his own.'

'Maybe that's what she's done,' Seb ventures.

'Maybe, but I don't think she'd leave him without a conversation – we discussed it in fact. She was fond of Sid and I don't think would have hurt him intentionally.' She shrugs. 'I might be wrong.'

'But you don't think you are?'

'No.' Which leaves them with – where the hell is she?

'Amanda and Louis?' Seb moves on from these excruciatingly personal topics. He'd wasted years daydreaming of the day Charlie would wake up, see the light and stop, and he had to admit his views were probably more aligned with Alex Martin's than Sam's. He was, he felt, happy enough to have given up. It hurt a lot less than the hope had.

'Turbulent, often violent.'

'Which one?'

'Both, a truly toxic relationship. She was in and out of here after he'd battered her but I've seen him come in covered in burns and marks from stiletto shoes too.'

'And they knew Sid and Charlie?'

'Yep, I suspect Louis ran drugs for them and Gordon on occasion. Certainly he and Amanda were at that flat as often as they were at certain points.'

'Do you know Gordon?'

Sam shakes her head. 'I know of him, of course, like everyone. He runs all the skulduggery around here.'

'A bad name?'

'The worst, but as long as drugs are criminalised men like him are endless.'

'Even in your job you think they should be decriminalised?' Harry asks her, surprised.

'Yes. There will always be addicts, but regulation would make fewer criminals.'

'In your opinion.' Harry sort of scrunches his nose at her, as ever blunt and to the point. He never, Seb thinks, has a thought or feeling that doesn't register on his face.

'In my opinion, yes.' Sam smiles that smile again. 'You'll want to start with him, Gordon. Sid and Amanda both had links, I'd say they both sold for him one way or another.'

'Yes,' Seb agrees, 'I think you're right.'

CHAPTER TWENTY-ONE

SAM

I had forgotten to tell the detective about Laura. Which may be a good thing? Chances are I'm overreacting. I call her phone again. It doesn't ring, it just clicks to voicemail. I wonder if she's sold it. In her last relapse she sold her bed and has been sleeping on a thin rolled-out futon mattress ever since.

I remain sat at the table where they left me. I pull out my phone and am thinking of texting the detective, considering how I might phrase it, when my phone rings in my hand, startling me.

'Hello.'

'You sound harassed.'

'The phone made me jump, is all, when it rang.'

'That's what they do Sammy,' my brother says, cheerfully. I resist the urge to stick my tongue out at my device. Instead, I say, 'What's up?' because it's unusual for him to call me in the middle of the morning.

'Can't just ring to say hi?'

'I saw you mere hours ago, you don't miss me that much.'

He laughs and I find myself grinning. 'Yeah, no, you got me. I heard a rumour.'

'You shouldn't listen to gossip.' I feed him back one of his favourite pearls of wisdom.

'Yes, all right,' he chuckles, and then says, 'Amanda Sales?' His tone serious.

The smile drops. 'Bad news travels fast.'

'It's true then?'

'How did you hear?'

'Mickey called me.'

'Asking for an extra scrip?'

'Of course.'

'Huh.'

'He said the police had been out to that encampment.'

'Never quite shuts down, does it?' I say. It's been on the 'hot list' of things to do for years and occasionally the police would show up and attempt to move people on, but the same people would arrive back again. One time a few of them moved closer into town, set up camp on the edge of a children's play park. Locals there had kicked off in a way residents of Hartsmead never did and as such, it pretty much got left alone now. Another hot spot left to fester, but I suppose from the law's point of view at least the hot spots were all in the same place. A cluster of ripe pussy zits that no one quite had the courage or desire to pop.

'Nope. Anyway, he said the policewoman was called away, and he followed her. Saw them cordoning off. Everyone knows.'

'Guess they do.'

'Such a shame.'

'It always is.'

'Do you think Louis did it?' he asks, and I frown at the receiver.

'Why would he?'

'Well, you know what they're like.'

'I mean, maybe. If it was just her that was dead that would be logical I suppose. But there's Sid too?'

'Right,' he says.

'It's more likely to be Gordon related, isn't it?'

Alex sighs. 'You might be right.'

'That's what the police are leaning towards,' I tell him, thinking of the poor detective and his pinched face. The toll this must be taking, hunting down his ex-wife, the mother of his kid.

'Is it?'

'Yeah, I'd say so. I mean maybe initially they thought it was a row between Sid and Charlie gone bad.'

'He'd reported her missing by then though, Sid?'

'Yes, but she could have come back.'

'I guess. But now?'

'Now it seems if it's not a matter of the heart it's likely it'll be money related. Money for them will lead back to Gordon one way or another.'

'I hate him,' Alex says, the heat of the anger in his words so intense it hits me in a blast. I close my eyes.

'Yeah, me too.'

I decide to walk back to the office, and even though I know it's fruitless, I call Laura again on the way. No ring tone, no voicemail. I try May, who picks up on the second ring.

'Hello dear.'

'Hi May, any news?'

'Ah, you have none then?'

'No, I'm afraid not,' I say, adding, 'sorry.'

'No need to be.' She sighs. 'Look, I suppose in some ways, much as it pains me mentally, I've written her off, at least for now.'

'I understand that,' I say, wishing I could do the same, knowing that despite her bravado, somewhere inside, May will be in agony. I'd seen her in the pits of despair about Laura, driven wild with worry. Taking in the kids had moved her focus though and somehow allowed her to compartmentalise – at least for now. In light of Charlie's disappearance and two gruesome deaths, though, I'm concerned. OK, I'm more than concerned, I'm stressing. I like Laura, had been hopeful for her chances of success, and I've known her for years too. Seen her lose everything. Liking clients is always a mistake in my job. I have a bleeding heart, is what Alex would say. And maybe he's right. Maybe I'm still just a scared little girl trying to save a mother who doesn't want salvation.

'OK,' I say to May now, 'I'll let you know if I hear anything.'

'Please, I'll do the same.'

I hang up and pull the detective's card out of my pocket and put his number into my phone. I can almost hear Mark tutting in my mind.

'Hello Ms Martin.' He picks up on the second ring.

'Detective, hi. I, uh, one of my clients is… well she might be… missing.'

'Missing?'

'Yes, well she hasn't been home for at least two days.'

'Is that unusual for her?'

'It is these days,' I say, trying to choose my words carefully and avoid sounding as if I'm being hysterical. 'She has long periods of being quite agoraphobic. Normally I take her out to appointments and she has things delivered in.'

'Has she gone missing before?'

'I mean...' I shouldn't have rung, he's going to dismiss it just like Mark and Alex both have, and who knows, maybe they're right to.

'It's OK, I'll take it seriously if you're concerned, and in light of the fact that we have another missing woman and two murders nearby. Would she have known any of the people involved?'

'Oh, she'd have known Louis and Amanda for sure. I'm not sure about Sid or Charlie; as I said she has struggled to leave the house of late.'

'OK, her name and possible contacts?'

'Laura Doyle. Last time she went missing, or last time I didn't hear from her, she was pretty much being held captive by her ex-boyfriend.'

'What's his name?'

'Alan Humphreys.'

I can hear the murmur of voices, muffled momentarily.

'He works for Gordon?'

'He does, yeah.'

'Are they still involved?'

'I'd hope not.'

'But you can't be sure?'

'No, I can't be sure.' I pause, then add, 'She lost her children.'

'Oh?'

'After the thing with Alan. They were left alone in the flat.' I swallow thickly, remembering the call from her neighbour, finding the kids tearful, dirty and hungry.

'I'm sorry to hear that,' Seb murmurs. 'Are they OK now?'

'Yes, they are with May Doyle, Laura's mum, doing much better.'

'That's good.'

'It is.'

'When did you last see her?'

'Monday.'

'Certain she's not still involved with Alan?'

'No, not for ages.' My voice is firm but – am I certain? I like to think she was done with him, the man who'd taken so much from her: dignity, sanity, her children.

'Anyone else that she may be involved with romantically?'

'No,' I say without having to think about it.

'Are you sure?'

'Yes, I'm over there every few days, I'd know if someone had been in.' I don't add that she is petrified of most men; after Alan it's understandable.

'You've tried calling?'

'Her phone's off.'

'Right, silly question. Leave it with me.'

'You'll look into it?'

'Yes. I mean we probably wouldn't normally, but two young women, both addicts, both missing, and two murders. We'll dig.'

'I appreciate it.'

CHAPTER TWENTY-TWO

'So you can't track either phone down.' Seb stands over Finn, frowning at the computer screen as if that might make it give up information they don't have and really need.

'Both phones are off, so yes, right now, that means they are untraceable.'

Seb looks from Harry to Lucy. 'Coincidence?'

Lucy shrugs. 'People like them sell phones, lose them. Could be anything.'

'It could,' Seb agrees.

Ken comes over. 'Here you go.' He hands Seb two images. One of Charlie, he's seen it a few times over the last few days and yet still it's like a sucker punch to the gut. So thin, so ragged. The next one is of a woman he knows is younger, though like Charlie she could be anywhere from twenty to fifty. Her face is too thin, her forehead lined, her skin dank and grey. The two of them are also fairly similar in looks generally and Seb thinks Laura, like Charlie, could probably clean up well if ever she had the inclination. She has faded blonde hair, blue eyes, good bone structure. 'They could be sisters,' Ken says.

'Yeah,' agrees Harry. 'Weird.'

Seb's heart picks up, because actually, it's not weird. Two murders, his mind offers. Two linked murders. Three makes it a serial, but alongside that, two missing women, if indeed they are missing. 'It's a pattern of sorts.' He looks to Ken, who says, 'Not yet.'

'Two murders, both people who have been in Sid and Charlie's flat. Both of whom were there at the time of his death in fact.'

'Yes, and it needs looking into obviously, but right now whilst the murders are linked by demographic and method the rest is unknown, isn't it. Most likely link is the dealer,' Ken says, which is true, but still. Seb looks at the photos, feels that quiver in his brain that he gets. Gut feeling some detectives call it, but Seb doesn't feel things there. For him it's almost always cerebral to some degree.

'What do we have on Gordon?'

'Enough paperwork to write a novel,' Ken tells him.

Seb frowns. 'Give me the highlights.'

Ken sits down in front of his own screen. 'Born locally, his dad was a known wide boy back in the Eighties, hired muscle for another big wig, Ian Foxton. Gordon himself was in and out of cells and prisons. His mum raised him and six other kids on Hartsmead. Gordon was the oldest. He has a sealed juvenile record. It was rumoured, though never proven, that he killed Roger Kendall when he was just fifteen.'

'Who took the charge for it?'

'No one, and Roger was stabbed in broad daylight too, but it was the Nineties, not so many cameras around, and I can tell you because I was there, none of the locals wanted to talk to us.'

Lucy snorts. 'Some things never change.'

'Ha, yeah.' Ken nods agreement. 'Anyway. He never went down for it, but he stole Roger's stash, and gained a reputation. He started running drugs all over the estate, linked in with some of the biggest firms in London. Both of his younger brothers and two of his younger sisters work for him, as it is rumoured does his mum. He's made plenty of money, took over Ian's businesses,' Ken puts that in speech marks, 'and launders it through various outlets. The one he spends most of his time at is a car dealership across town.'

'That's where we'll find him?' Seb asks and Ken nods.

'There or at home.'

'And home is?'

'His mum's place.' Ken grins. 'The hard man who's yet to fly the nest.'

'And she's still on the Hartsmead?'

'Yep, ground floor maisonette, three blocks from where Sid and Charlie were.'

'OK.' He looks at Lucy. 'Shall we go find him?'

'Yep.' She stands.

'Finn, keep looking into Laura and Charlie. Make a list of any immediate crossovers and people they were close to. Same with Amanda, Sid and Louis. In fact, Harry, why don't you and Ken see if you can go and talk to Louis today?'

'I've got an address,' Lucy says, leaning forward and scrawling it on a piece of paper, which she hands to Harry.

Harry takes it. 'Right you are.'

'We'll meet back here this afternoon – let's say three.'

—

'Do you think it's all connected?' Lucy asks as they get into his car.

'I don't like coincidence, as you know.' He smiles across at her. 'But they may not be connected and it could be just that.'

'You think the killings are connected to each other though?'

'I'd say so,' Seb says not adding, not wanting to admit, that the missing person or persons in this case were of more interest to him. He was on major crimes, but murder made up the bulk of his cases. The murders were the only reason really he was even still on this case. Jackie probably shouldn't have allowed him to be. Though, in his defence, he was the best detective they had, and the case was local. 'I've asked Martina to try and work out if Sid and Amanda were killed with the same knife. She said it won't be definitive but she can give us a close approximation. She's hurrying through the autopsy. We'll see her later, on our way back to the station.'

'Yeah, OK. Where are we going now – the car dealership or his mum's?'

Seb glances at the clock display. 'Just after one, let's try his work first.' He puts work in quotation marks, lifting his hands briefly from the steering wheel.

They pull up at the dealership, which looks entirely innocuous from the outside. On its forecourt are several BMWs and Minis alongside a sign saying they are 'specialists'.

'Tilly wants one of these,' Seb murmurs as they pass a pastel blue Mini with a grey, white and black union jack for a roof.

'They are pretty cool.'

'But very fast, like little go-karts.'

'You're a few years off of that though, surely,' Lucy says.

'Two,' he tells her, 'which will fly by.'

'I've heard that happens as you get old.'

Seb actually laughs, surprised he has it in him. 'Better than the alternative,' he tells her.

'It is,' she says, grinning. Lucy is in her mid-twenties. Dedicated and sharp as a tack but still at the age where you think you have forever. Seb had missed it really. He'd gone from being a confused teenager to being a dad and working out fast that in order to do it properly he had to be a grown-up. He'd studied, with Val's help, joined the force, good salary, good benefits, decent pension, and sworn he'd put Tilly first no matter what. Mostly he had. He'd been unsure whether working major crimes was a good move. The rock stars of the police force, but more than that for him, a big case meant puzzle solving, it used his immense intellect and he liked giving people closure if nothing more. He also liked seeing justice served. But the job came with downsides. The hours on call, the danger. Without Val's support, it wouldn't have been possible, and while he couldn't imagine himself in a nine to five, he was quite sure if he'd needed to, he would have done it. He'd do anything for his daughter.

Except be honest with her, a niggling voice says at the back of his mind.

Later. He wasn't lying, he was just withholding information, and he'd rectify that. As soon as seemed right.

They step inside a large, air-conditioned showroom and Seb pushes thoughts of his personal life away, determined to treat this professionally like any other case. A woman with impossibly long nails smiles at them from behind a desk.

'Hello, can I help you?' She stands, getting up and walking around. Her eyes flick to Lucy, who is in uniform, and the smile slips. Seb flashes his badge and the woman sighs. 'What do you lot want?' He notices that the softened voice is gone, all pretence at smooth civility fading fast.

'Gordon if possible.'

'He's not here.'

'Are you sure?'

She scowls but doesn't respond. 'Do you know where we might find him then?'

A shrug. Seb feels his frustration rise.

'He's your boss, right?'

The scowl deepens. 'Actually he's mostly a silent partner; I oversee the day-to-day running of things here.'

'And your name is?'

'Marissa Anderson.'

'Any relation?'

'His sister, if you must know, not that it's any of your business. Everything here is above board, as I suspect you already know.'

'Do we?'

'You're in here often enough.'

Seb smiles, but he's read the reports. He knows there are beat officers who'd been trying to bag Gordon and associates for years without much joy. Occasionally they'd get a low-level lackey but the man himself, for all intents and purposes, looked like a legitimate businessman. On paper, he'd gone into the system a juvenile and come out not just rehabilitated but ready to thrive. A real success story. Seb wondered, as he'd read over old files from Jackie's predecessor's reign, whether some of the old boys had gained from Gordon's meteoric rise. Seb's first big case had delved into the local force's corruption under the care of Mac – a man praised for his greatness who turned out to be utterly corrupt. With Jackie in charge, someone like Gordon would have been watched far more closely, Seb thinks, and maybe none of them would be here now.

'Wonder why that is when it's all above board.'

'Prejudice is what it is.'

Seb doesn't respond; instead he asks, 'Where might we find your brother?'

'No idea, I'm not his keeper.' A customer comes in and she heads off, plastering a smile on her face and turning her back on Seb and Lucy, letting them know the conversation is over.

CHAPTER TWENTY-THREE

CHARLIE

I feel better for having clothes on, even if they wouldn't be what I would choose for myself. In fairness, I've not worried much about what I was wearing for years, or even if I was clean and tidy. There was a time in what feels like another life when I cared about my appearance. There was I suppose a time when I cared about lots of things. The only personal hygiene I've kept up is cleaning my teeth. My father had several missing and his grinning holey maw is one of my overriding memories of him. That and his fists, pounding me, pounding my mum. I wince just at the memory.

I'd taken the pills from their small cardboard semi cup, slipped them into my mouth then headed to the bathroom where I spat them out whilst pretending to cough up phlegm, into the toilet and flushed. While I was fairly happy to take them when I thought this might be a hospital, I'm now pretty certain it's not. The pills come in what looks like a single segment from a box made for eggs. I've seen them before, always in medical establishments. Hospitals, psych wards, prison. But this isn't any of those things. This place may have procedures of its own, but I'm not familiar with them.

I'm pretty sure the tablets are some kind of downer, opioid based, but they are not a patch on heroin, they don't wipe everything away, and I suspect that by not taking them my clear head will get even clearer – which will bring its own problems, of course. Without eradication, the sharp edges, mainly bad memories, push to the forefront of my mind, threatening to slice me to death.

Back in the white windowless room with the locked door, I hear something, a banging. I go to the far wall of my room and press my ear against the wall. A voice yelling, the click of a door opening and closing. Two voices. Just murmurs, and I can't make out any words, just snatches of sound. Sobbing, I think, incoherent and distressed. I jump because the door to my own room opens. Someone is here, a slight person in a mask. I'm about to jump up, jump forward and push my way past when two large men come in, also masked, and flank me on either side.

They take an arm each and I wriggle underneath their grip, trying to escape, yes, but also trying to memorise as much about them as I can. Big men both, one thin but ropey, the other a barrel-chested bouncer type. One with brown skin, brown eyes, one white with dishwater blonde hair which may have been red once like my mum's. Faded now to the colour of a Caramac bar. 'Let me go,' I yell as hard as I can. Surprised at my own strength, surprised at the freshness of limbs not weighted down by my usual chemical concoction. I have energy, I think. Even through the pills in the small paper eggcup. I am healing.

They drop my arms, the smaller masked figure retreats and I note that their head is covered by a white cap, face by a mask and body by a white coat. A doctor? One of the people who'd been in and out while I sweated and squirmed, half-dead from withdrawals, confused and disorientated. I try to think about time, try to work out how long I've been here. Days? Weeks? Surely not months. Detox can be done in a week, more likely two. I feel... fresh. I feel like I haven't felt for as long as I can remember. Weeks, I'd say.

'Whose next door?' I ask. Silence.

'Why am I here, and where is Sid?'

The smaller figure pauses at the door. 'Worry about yourself, Charlotte.'

The door closes behind them. I am left on the floor panting from the exertion. Healing, but not healed. I remember hearing that at Hope Springs too, recovering not recovered. You can get clean, they'd said, but it will be an effort, and something you can't ever take for granted. I'd wanted it, or I'd thought I had. Wanting and getting turned out to be worlds apart.

I lie flat on my back, cold linoleum beneath me. I put my knees up, pressing the soles of my feet against the floor, a welcome cool-down of sorts. Above my head are the kind of awful fluorescent lights that are built into the ceiling, surrounded by wide panels that look flimsy. The ceiling isn't that high. As I lie still, I find myself trying to fend off a shaky wobbly feeling. I squeeze my eyes shut. I'm spinning out. That's all. It's a combination of things, the lack of proper drugs, missing a dose of the pills, whatever they are – benzos? Diazepam? And of course stress, though stress has been my constant companion for as long as I can remember.

No, that's not entirely true. There had been weeks, months even when Tilly was inside me, Seb was by my side, a brief moment in time where I felt like maybe calm was within reach. Maybe love could save me.

I'd only been home with her for a month the first time I scored. Coke on a night out. A one-off, I'd told myself, just like the guy whose bed I'd ended up in was a one-off and something I kept to myself. The first of many lies that would fester and infect my marriage. That night, I assured myself was just a reminder that I couldn't go out and I didn't. Not for a few months. I started smoking again first, when Seb went to work I'd stand outside on the balcony inhaling stick-thin roll-ups while Tilly squirmed and squawked inside. I was scared of her. The responsibility was overwhelming. Before I knew it, I was sneaking drinks in the day, nipping over to old acquaintances. Going to places and people on the estate I'd known for years. Before I knew it... I became something awful.

I open my eyes. Better now. I force myself to roll over until I am on all fours.

On the table next to my bed there is a tray, food, this time cooked. Eggs and toast, orange juice in a plastic bottle. I realise that for the first time in years, I'm hungry. Starving hungry. I eat quickly and then I lie back on the bed and start to memorise every inch of this room that looks like a hospital but it is in fact a prison of some kind.

CHAPTER TWENTY-FOUR

SAM

'Hi Tiny,' I say to the man who is anything but. Tiny is more mountain than person. Enormous at six foot five, and weighing at least two hundred pounds. He's a gentle giant though. A fixture in the homeless community and a permanent resident at Hope Springs. He's been here I don't know how long exactly. An ex-addict who has several special needs which give him a childlike quality and a big heart. He works for Hope Springs doing general maintenance and any other odd jobs that crop up.

'Hello Sam.' He gives me a huge smile; it really does make him look like a kid, with his bald head, a giant baby even, and I find myself smiling back. His backstory is genuinely awful. He was picked up living rough in his teenage years by a couple of wronguns who got him hooked on drugs and working the door at a now defunct trap house. He'd been useless on the door and didn't have a mean bone in his body. In fact, he stood demurely while his horrible recruiters beat him to almost within an inch of his life. Barry had been called to go and see him when he finally woke up at the local hospital saying drugs were bad but did anyone have any? He'd been clean ever since and Barry treated him like a family member. He's a feel-good story in a mass of everyday tragedies and I find myself genuinely smiling on a day I'd woken up feeling like utter crap.

I'm here because I run a drop-in advisory service. I'd spent the journey from our office to the drop-in centre mulling over my chat with the detective, the awfulness of two murdered people and the horrible fact that the detective not only didn't laugh in my face when I suggested Laura was missing but took it seriously. He was looking into it and considering whether it might be related to Charlie. Both gone without a trace, both linked. Both women under my care. Acid broils around in my stomach and shunts up. I press a hand to my mouth, swallowing it down and making a mental note to collect Tums on my way home and to not tell Alex, who will start going on about a stomach ulcer again.

'How are you?' I ask Tiny.

'I'm OK, still mostly here but I've also been labouring for Den's firm.' Dennis Pulaski is a local carpenter who sobered up here at Hope Springs, set up a successful company and employs people on Barry and Debbie's say so.

'That's great.'

He nods agreement. 'I enjoy it. I've been sorting out the garden here today though.'

I glance out of the tall French doors which lead from the common room where we're standing to the outside. 'Looks great,' I tell him, and it does. There are buildings out there in the distance too and, as always, I'm impressed by just how sprawling this place is.

'New plants have arrived, hoping they bed in before we get too much rain.'

'Yes.'

'Oh hey, have you seen Laura?' he asks. I know they are tight and that he finds time to check in on her, often carrying out errands and dropping off shopping. 'He's the brother I never had,' Laura had told me more than once.

'I haven't, and was kind of hoping you might have.'

'Nope, not for two days.'

'Is that unusual?'

'Yeah, she calls me at least once a day, sometimes more.'

'Have you been over there?'

'No, but I will today, I think, after I finish here.'

'Let me know if you catch up with her?'

'I will do.'

I stand pondering what he's just said, eyes on the rolling lawn, the beautiful flowerbeds that run either side of it. Hope Springs is in such a lovely setting. Barry and Debbie have done wonders here. Worked small miracles really. A restful oasis on the edge of a bustling suburban market town. The neighbours had complained initially. Not that there was anyone that close by, but near enough. Most had become supportive since. Rather than being a place where addicts loitered it kept people out of the town centre, off the residential streets. Barry and Debbie also spoke in schools and Hope Springs had even appeared on the odd news bulletin.

'Gorgeous out there, isn't it?'

I turn to smile at Debbie. 'Everything is better when the sun is shining,' I say.

'Ahhh, but without the dark winters we'd forget to appreciate this.'

'You may be right,' I say, though I don't really think that. I hate the winters and tend to struggle with October onwards as the dark seeps into the days, stealing all the light. My mother was the same: seasonal affective disorder,

Alex calls it, and prescribes me mild anti-depressants to weather (ha ha) the storm. They help a bit but not as much as winters somewhere hot would.

'Tiny's been planting.'

'I just saw him,' I tell her.

'He's doing very well.'

'He is,' I agree. 'This place has worked wonders.'

'We do what we can,' she says, but it comes out on a sigh.

'He mentioned Laura.'

Debbie frowns, and I say, 'Laura Doyle.'

'Oh yes, how is she?'

'Well, that's the thing; I've not been able to contact her for a few days.'

'Do you need to speak to her?'

'Well, I did, about some paperwork, to do with May and the children.'

'Oh that's right. I remember Laura, of course. Sorry, I feel like maybe Barry knows her better than I do.' Laura had spoken in glowing terms about Debbie but I suppose that Debbie interacts with so many people she's bound not to be able to recall them all immediately. 'She lost the children as I recall, May is her mother?'

'That's right, yes, she has full custody, just for now.'

'Yes. How are they getting on?'

'Well, all things considered.'

Debbie shakes her head. 'Such a sad situation.'

'It is.'

'I'm sure she'd be an excellent mother if only she could win out with the drugs.'

'Yeah, I think so too.'

Debbie reaches out and squeezes my hand. 'I know you do, and you're worried about her now aren't you? I can see it on your face.'

'I am,' I relent. 'Which may seem silly given she's an adult and it's only been two days.'

'Not silly. Now I know who you mean I remember she does get herself tangled up in trouble.'

'She does.'

'She was in here quite recently, you know.'

'Oh, when?'

'Tuesday morning, met with Barry I think.' I last saw her Monday. I'd not been able to contact her since Tuesday evening. I was almost 100 per cent certain that she was using when I saw her, and that was normally the only thing that made her leave the house. For a moment, I am delighted that she'd somehow made it here rather than to pick up. Then I remember she hadn't made it back home, or so it would seem.

'Is he here?'

'Right out back at the dorms across the field – hang on, I'll give you a coffee to take out to him.'

—

I walk across with two insulated keep cups. Barry is carrying bin bags from one of the low outbuildings to the outside bin cupboards when I approach and his face breaks into a smile. 'Sam. Drop-in today?'

'Yep.' I hold out the cup and he takes it with an even bigger grin. Our fingers touch briefly and he tells me, 'You superstar.'

'From Debbie, two sugars not three, she said to tell you.'

'Damn, that woman's strict.'

'Three sugars?'

He shrugs. 'I developed a sweet tooth the day I gave up the booze. Lucky I do all the physical labour around here or I'd be enormous by now.' I suppress a smile at that; Barry isn't exactly slim. He sees it and sighs. 'Let an old man have his fantasies, Sam.'

'No, I...'

But he's laughing. 'It's fine, I was so underweight fifteen years ago I could barely stand, a few extra pounds isn't so bad in the big scheme of things.'

'No, I guess not.' I don't add that he looks perfect to me.

'Drop-in quiet?'

'Deathly so,' I tell him. 'It's the sun.'

'Oh yes, lovely to see it but,' he shrugs, 'means many of our clients also start to think it's a good time to get out and about.'

'Yeah.'

'Not what you came across here to talk to me about though?'

'No. I wanted to ask you about Laura?'

'I saw her Tuesday morning.'

'That's what Debbie said, any specific reason?'

'Yes actually, she wanted to talk to me about going into a residential rehab and doing a detox.' My heart soars at that even though I understand that isn't what had happened.

'She did?'

'Yes, and she seemed genuinely interested too.'

'Did she say why?'

'Said she'd seen you, signed a load of paperwork.'

'She did, yes.'

'What was it for, if you don't mind me asking?'

'Just extending May's guardianship.'

'Ah, well,' he sips his coffee, 'said your visit made her think about things. Also said she missed the kids, so that makes sense.'

'Was she... serious?'

'I'd say so, but I called her Tuesday afternoon to say Alex and I had found her a spot and her phone was off.' He shrugs. 'Often the way, and the space is a month away so plenty of time for her to come round. At least she's thinking along those lines.'

'Yes, that is good.' I pause, taking a sip of scalding hot coffee and hissing as it burns my lips.

Barry shakes his head. 'Gotta sip it or put in loads of milk, they hold the heat these cups.'

'They do,' I say, and then, 'No one's seen her since then, Laura.'

'Have you asked Tiny?'

'Yep.'

'That's unusual, she's pretty much at home these days isn't she?'

'Unless she needs to score.'

'Huh. Well she probably went and did that then. Like I said it was a hopeful chat but I have loads of convos like that and loads of people leave here and go back to doing what they're doing.'

'Yeah, maybe.'

'You don't sound convinced?'

I give him a smile. 'I'm probably overthinking it, and you're likely right.'

'But?'

'But normally, no matter what's happening, she'll be in touch with me, you know. Especially as I'm the link between her and May.'

'Hmmm,' he says, wandering back into the dorms. I follow him.

'Help me do the sheets?' He points at a stack of them, one eyebrow raised.

'Yeah, OK.' I suppress a smile; this is what makes Barry so good at what he does here, he has a seamless way of getting people to do things. We put the molten coffees down and take the soft nice-smelling stack to the row of five beds. He separates out a sheet, handing me one end, taking the other. We shake it out, letting it float down and tucking the corners in.

'Your instincts are telling you something's up?'

'Yes,' I agree, 'though I'm prone to doom-mongering.' We move to the next bed and repeat the same manoeuvres.

'You're used to assessing situations for danger and pressure points, Sam, like all children of addicts and alcoholics.' His bluntness makes me flinch, mainly because he is of course correct.

'I mean, Alex doesn't live on high alert, does he?'

'You're not Alex.'

'He had it worse than me.'

'You both had it pretty bad, Sam.'

'But we deal with it in different ways.'

'That is true.' He grins. 'But honestly, your instincts may be right.'

'You think?'

He shrugs. 'Charlie is still missing, and there's been a murder in this small circle.'

'Two.'

He pauses, sheet gripped between his big hands. 'Two?'

'Yes, sorry, I should have started with that perhaps. Amanda Sales.'

'As in Louis and Amanda?'

'Right.'

'I'm sorry to hear that.' We put the next sheet down, tuck it in. His face is screwed up in thought. 'Amanda was there when Sid died, right, at their flat?'

'Right.'

'You think maybe she saw something?'

'It's possible,' I admit. 'The police seem to think the deaths are connected and an anonymous call was made by a woman. Amanda was so out of it at the time she couldn't be questioned.'

'Then hell, Sam, you have every reason to be worried about Laura.'

'I told Mark I'd leave it alone, but I've got a spare key.'

'To Laura's place?'

'Yes.'

'Should you have that?'

I sigh. 'Not really, it's a breach of protocol, so I'd appreciate it if you didn't mention it to Mark.'

He grins. 'My lips are sealed. I assume you want to go and check it out?'

'I do.'

'That sounds... risky.'

'I know.' And I do. I'd get in professional trouble if Mark found out, and I might also be walking into a volatile situation. There was always the chance she'd hooked back in with her ex. I didn't think it was the case, no matter how bad things got she'd managed to stay away from him, but you never knew and he'd threatened me along with May in the past. There was a restraining order preventing him from coming near either of us but if he was at Laura's and I let myself in… it would certainly muddy the waters. Plus, he might just do the things he'd threatened to before.

He sighs. 'Well let's finish up here and I'll come with you.'

'Really?'

'Really.'

CHAPTER TWENTY-FIVE

Ken looks at the man and finds the usual swell of displeasure these types of idiot always conjure up in him. Harry had just broken the news of Amanda's death, a woman Louis had been involved with for at least two years, who he had lived with, and the man's first response had been, 'It wasn't me.'

'Do you have an alibi, son?' Ken asks, knowing from experience that he'll catch more flies with honey, at least to start with.

'I was here.'

'Alone?'

'I was here with Miriam.'

'Miriam?'

'She's upstairs, in bed.'

This building is in disrepair and really ought to be knocked down, but it was currently being squatted.

'Go and wake her up then,' Ken says, his voice becoming sharper. 'Now.'

Louis stands, sighing to let them know it's an awful inconvenience. His voice is all posh Surrey vowels, his taut muscular frame full of what Ken thinks of as fridge magnet tattoos. Body art isn't for him, but he had seen plenty of full sleeves and whatnot that were obviously carefully curated works of art over the years. Even if they didn't appeal to him, he could see their worth. Louis's entire upper body, arms and neck included, are covered in doodles that seem mismatched and do not look good. Nor does the little star at the edge of his greasy skinny face. But each to their own, he supposes, and in fairness to Louis, he had managed to get a woman into bed last night, which is more than Ken could say for the last decade since his divorce.

Louis reappears three minutes later alongside a thin woman with dark hair who also has 'face art' and one of those awful middle of the nose rings, like a prize fighting bull, Ken thinks.

'Miriam?' Ken asks.

'Yeah.' She blinks and he sees her pupils are dilated.

'Were you with Louis last night?'

'Yeah.'

'From what time?'

'Um, maybe three in the afternoon?'

'Where were you?'

'Here.' She yawns.

'Were you here before Louis?'

'Yeah, I've been here a few days.'

'How many?'

'Not sure,' she says, 'sorry.'

And he believes her. Time has no meaning for these people living outside the normal confines imposed by society. It was like the endless and fascinating discussion Ken had with his grandchildren about the slavery of capitalism; while he didn't disagree entirely, he was quick to point out there didn't seem to be a better solution yet. This sort of lifestyle, he understood, had once been it. Drop out, live on the fringes, build communes and alternative spaces. But these people, junkies most of them, drunks if not, and really it was all much of a muchness, still lived in a kind of prison even if they didn't realise it.

He hoped against hope that the new generations would find a better way. On a personal level he admired his grandkids' desire to be fulfilled rather than wealthy, though it was an easier aim when you only had yourself to worry about.

'Right,' he says with a sigh, 'Harry, give the young lady a card.' Harry hands her the office details, Ken holds one out to Louis. 'Do you have a number for Amanda's parents, by the way?'

'Um, maybe.'

'Can you check then?' Ken says, struggling to keep his voice even. The number they'd found was no longer recognised and while he knew Finn would get it, it might take some time.

'Here,' Louis hands them his phone. Ken photographs the number and writes it down.

'If we can't get hold of them, Louis, would you be prepared to make an ID?'

'Of, like, her body?'

'Yes.'

'Oh.' A silence, and then, 'I'd rather not.'

'Well, you might need to,' Ken says, his irritation clear. 'For goodness' sake, it's the least you could do for her.'

Louis frowns. 'Hey, I'm sorry she's dead, of course I am, but she wasn't a saint, you know.'

'Maybe not, but she was your girlfriend, and you'd been together years.'

'It was over ages ago.'

'Yet you were still staying together most nights?'

His eyes flick to Miriam, who for her part seems to have little to no interest in any of this. 'Yeah, more convenience, you know.'

'Right. And as for who killed her?'

He shrugs. 'She pissed people off all the time. Had a fight the other day with that Laura chick.'

'Laura?' Seb had mentioned her, the social worker's missing client. 'Laura what?'

'Um, don't know her last name but you know, lives on the estate, lost her kids, always blubbing about it.' Louis rolls his eyes. 'Like, can't afford to feed 'em, don't breed 'em,' he says, looking all pleased with himself. A well-practised line, Ken suspects. He reckons that eventually Louis will tire of this lifestyle; judging by his voice he wasn't born to this kind of life and eventually he'll probably slope back to Mum and Dad, maybe get a laser on the face star and put his head down in some cushy job he didn't deserve. Or he'd die first. Ken tries to push these thoughts away and asks him, 'What was the fight about?'

'I don't know, but that weirdo mate of hers, Tiny, got in the middle of it.'

Ken pauses. He'd seen mention of Laura in Seb's notes. The social worker, Sam Martin, had definitely mentioned her. Seb felt her disappearance might be linked to Charlie's and Charlie was at least part of the key to solving Sid's, and now Amanda's, murder. He hoped for his boss's sake that his ex-wife showed up alive.

Harry says, 'Rings a bell.'

Ken nods. 'I think we're done here,' he says, indicating to Harry that it's time to go. 'We'll be in touch,' he tells Louis.

Louis has nothing to offer in parting other than a disinterested grunt.

'What a colossal dick,' Harry says, and Ken can hear the heat in his voice.

'You're not wrong, son,' he agrees. 'Let's make some enquiries around and about and while we do that, we'll ring in to the station, get Finn to check Laura's name with the notes.' He glances at his watch. 'I imagine Seb and Lucy ought to have found Gordon by now, so we'll hold off calling them for a bit and see what we can find out ourselves, eh.'

'Good idea. Where to then?' Harry asks, and Ken suppresses a sigh. He likes Harry, likes the whole team, but at times he does despair with the lad's lack of impetus. He's definitely a follower, not a leader. He reminds himself that that's fine because they have Seb to lead, and he supposes in Seb's absence he can do some hand-holding. 'Shall we go back to the estate, ask around the makeshift shantytown?'

'Oh yeah, good call.'

CHAPTER TWENTY-SIX

Gordon's mum lives on the edge of the estate in a not at all unpleasant two up two down. The front garden is much nicer than the neighbours' and, Seb notes, Gordon's ostentatious brand new Mercedes sits in front of the house. The fact it hasn't been vandalised, stolen or had any hubcaps stripped is a reminder that, around here at least, Gordon is top dog.

Seb knocks and a small woman in an old-fashioned apron answers with a scowl. 'Pigs?'

'Charming,' he murmurs, flashing his ID and urging Lucy to do the same.

The small aproned woman folds her arms and the scowl deepens as she takes more time than necessary to look over their badges. 'Here to harass my boy, no doubt.'

'We are here to ask him a few questions.'

'Humph.'

A tall man with dark hair and exceptionally blue eyes appears behind her, leaning down and giving her a quick squeeze. 'Thank you, Mother, I'll take it from here.' The woman pauses but heads back into the house.

'Do come in,' the man, Gordon, says with feigned politeness. He leads them through to a small front room. The bay windows look out onto the street outside. Gordon sits with an 'ahhh', stretching his legs out. 'Dan said you'd been nosing about.'

'We were looking for you,' Seb says. 'Figured you'd be at work daytime on a weekday.'

Gordon grins at Seb. 'I oversee things from the comfort of my own home, that's how it goes once you get some success. Only mugs work for a living.'

Seb ignores that and says, 'This is the home you grew up in?'

'It is, yes.'

'You're the only one who hasn't left?'

Gordon shrugs. 'I own this and many other properties now, but wouldn't want to leave my mum on her own and she'd find moving unsettling.' Seb realises that this man, who had most likely committed murder before he hit adulthood, is quite serious and loves his mother. Though the Krays were rumoured to have been good sons as well.

'Anyway, I imagine you're not here for a chat about housing choices.'

'No. We wanted to talk to you about Sid Darnell.'

Gordon's eyes narrow. 'Heard about that.'

'Oh yeah, who from?'

Gordon smiles. 'Can't remember.'

'We've heard Sid worked for you.'

Gordon frowns. 'Nope, not in the motor trade, Sid. Or property, as far as I know.'

Seb forces his face to remain calm and pauses before he replies.

'We're from the murder squad. I'm not particularly interested in your nefarious activities outside of that fairly specific crime.'

'You want to know if I did Sid in?'

'Did you?'

Gordon laughs and it comes out like a snort.

'Did I say something funny?'

Gordon's face drops, all pretence at amusement gone, and Seb sees now a man capable of murder and great violence. His eyes have gone from twinkling to flat in a nanosecond and the atmosphere in the room has changed too. He meets Seb's gaze levelly. The difference is immediate and chilling.

'You know, I'm sure, about my previous misdemeanour.'

'Murder?'

'Yes, luckily for me as a juvenile.'

'Right,' Seb says. 'And you saw the error of your ways?'

'I don't live life filled with regrets, but one thing I do value above all else is my freedom.'

'Didn't like it in prison?'

'No, and before you start with well who does, plenty of people, as I'm sure you know, detective, become institutionalised, and fast.'

This is true. Seb has seen lifers come out and quickly reoffend, unable to cope with life outside of those awful clanking locked gates.

'Not you though?'

'Not me, no, and nowadays, I really am a businessman first and foremost. Whatever nefarious activities you think you know about are minor things.'

'Like large-scale drug sales.'

'I'm a man who knows people who know people. I may act as a go-between from time to time.'

'Right.'

'What I don't do is act in haste or stupidity. I'm unlikely to bring my life toppling down for a lowlife like Sid Darnell, am I?'

'Even if he owed you money?'

Gordon grins, but it doesn't have the forced and pretend bonhomie of earlier, this smile is ice cold. 'If I wanted someone dead and I were smart about it, it would be an open and shut case and none of you would turn up here because no roads would lead my way.'

'You'd put someone else in the frame, you mean?'

Gordon shrugs, settling back into the chair. 'I didn't kill him, detective, or Amanda.'

'You know about that too?'

'I do, yes.'

'You're the only link.'

'I'm not a link.'

'We know Sid and Charlie were selling for you.'

'Charlie, eh,' Gordon says, the smile widening. Seb feels as if he is standing in front of this man naked and exposed. His face flushes and he finds himself being the first to look away.

'Now now, detective, no need to be embarrassed, I suspect she was a looker in her day and a smart lady too. Shame she couldn't exercise control.'

'She's missing,' Seb says, forcing the words out and hating himself for the desperate sound of them. He sees Lucy's pen pause over her pad.

'I had heard that, yes, and believe it or not, I'd like to find her as much as you would.'

'Why's that then?'

Gordon waves a hand. 'Let's just say, Sid had something of mine, and now I can't find it.'

'You think she's got it?' Seb's heart picks up pace.

'I'd say it was a strong possibility, detective.'

They leave. Walking to the car, Seb can feel the tension in his jaw.

'Are you all right?' Lucy asks.

'Yeah,' he says, and then sighs. 'I mean, I don't know, honestly. It's plausible, isn't it, what he's implying?'

'That she took the drugs and ran?'

Seb nods.

'Plausible, but if she's still using, which it seems certain she is, she'd have left some kind of trail. Even if it wasn't one we picked up, surely Gordon would?'

'Maybe,' Seb says. 'She is clever though, Gordon is right about that.'

'But is she a killer, Seb?'

'No. God, I don't know. I'd have said of course not, once. I'd have defended her until quite recently. But she came back here, she was minutes away. She didn't give us, didn't give Tilly, a second thought.'

'You don't know that.'

Seb laughs, but the sound is brittle, not amused. 'Don't I?'

'Barry at Hope Springs believed she was attempting to improve, Sam said the same. Sounds like she came back here with good intentions at least.'

'Right before she let her waster boyfriend do a drug deal with that maniac.'

'I get it's not ideal.'

'Not ideal?' Seb can feel his voice rising and forces himself to moderate it. It's not Lucy's fault. This is no one's fault but Charlie's. 'I'm sorry, I didn't mean to snap.'

'You didn't, and look, Gordon was provoking you, wasn't he, looking to get a reaction.'

'Well he did that,' Seb says, thinking for the first time that he probably shouldn't be on this case. He should probably go to Jackie and say it's too much. But he knows he won't, can't. He needs to be the one who finds her, however bad the discovery is.

'It's understandable that you're pissed off.'

'Understandable but unhelpful. As angry as I am, Lucy, I want her to show up alive, and preferably innocent of murder.'

'Look, the chances are whoever killed Sid also killed Amanda.'

'Yeah, and?'

Lucy shrugs. 'I doubt Charlie killed Sid, disappeared, came back and went for Amanda.'

'Maybe the two aren't linked.'

Lucy frowns. 'Martina is pretty certain it's the same person. Same method, same weapon.' She had pretty much confirmed this.

'None of it makes any sense. It's like it's two separate cases. Maybe it is. Maybe the deaths and her disappearance aren't linked at all. Maybe this Laura is absolutely nothing to do with anything.'

'I know it's possible, but that's unlikely, isn't it? You're always telling us coincidence is rare.'

There's a silence. They are in the car now, heading back to the station. Seb's hands are tight on the wheel; he feels so many things, but more than anything anxiety. Like a low-level thrum inside his head, electric and dangerous.

'Have you spoken to Val and Tilly?'

'No,' he says, and Lucy doesn't push it, instead turning her gaze out the window as the streets of Thamespark change from the squalid estate to tree-lined roads and quaint one-off Surrey shops.

CHAPTER TWENTY-SEVEN

SAM

I check my phone as I walk up the stairs to the police station. I'm meant to be headed over to the courthouse but I'd messaged the client and said I was delayed. I'd decided that I didn't really need to be there, it was hand-holding really. A family case that would amount to nothing much today. The paperwork would be where I was most needed. Or so I told myself as guilt snaked around my belly. I'd wasted time going to Laura's flat, where I found nothing useful. Mark would be furious, but hopefully he wouldn't find out, and even if he did… it's not that we're unsackable, far from it. If something goes wrong in our job it can be headline news of course, but there aren't exactly hordes of young hopefuls lining up to replace us either.

I get to the station's reception area. 'Can I speak to DI Locke please?'

'Is he expecting you?'

'Well, no,' I say.

'I'll see if he's here.'

'Sam?' I spin round and see him and DS Quinn walking into the station. 'Can I help?'

'Um, yes, please.'

He turns to the woman on reception. 'I'm fine from here, Cara,' he says to her. 'Lucy, do you want to head in and update everyone? I'll be up shortly.'

'Yes, of course.'

The detective says, 'Follow me,' leading me to a small room just off reception. It has a couple of armchairs, a low-slung coffee table with some bland out-of-date magazines on, and in the corner a coffee vending machine that he points at. 'Get you anything?'

'Oh, no thank you.'

'Don't blame you, it's genuinely dreadful.'

I smile at that. 'We have the same machines at the guildhall.'

'Government-issued coffee.' He screws up his nose. 'This is our family room,' he says and I nod.

'I've been here before.'

'Sorry, of course you have.'

'Not for a while though.' I lean forward. 'Maybe some of the same mags, mind.'

'Wouldn't be surprised.' He smiles again, but it's strained and he has dark circles beneath his eyes. He looks tired and I can't blame him. I'm full of worry too. I feel responsible not just for not following up with Charlie but also for the fact that not following up may have something to do with Laura. That I hadn't given it a second thought is what is bugging me. That's a new level of cynicism – self-protective, Alex would say, smart even, but if I'd thought about it, if I'd just made a phone call… 'You're not here to discuss that though?'

'No, I'm not. No sign of Charlie?'

'No.'

'Have you spoken to Gordon yet?'

'Just now.'

'And?'

'And I don't think he knows where she is either.'

'Oh,' I say, weighing that up. 'He's the most obvious suspect, isn't he?'

'I'm not at liberty to say and at this stage I wouldn't want to speculate.'

He pauses, then, 'Do you have something new?'

'No. Maybe. I don't know.' I sigh. 'That client I mentioned, Laura?'

'Looks like Charlie and is also missing?'

'Well, I think that.'

'Who doesn't?'

'My boss.'

He grins. 'Mine too, to be fair, and perhaps my team, who are too polite to tell me.'

'And you?'

He shrugs. 'It's a coincidence, and I never like them.'

'Me neither.'

'So I was at Hope Springs, and I saw her friend, Tiny.'

'You mentioned him before, is that his real name?'

'No. I, uh, don't actually know his real name, but Barry would.'

'OK.'

'Anyway, normally he'd know where she was at – they speak every day, sometimes more than once, and he's worried too.'

'Right.'

'You think I'm overreacting?' I ask him.

'No, actually.'

I pull out a copy of Laura's file and hand it to him. 'If you're willing to investigate,' I say, 'maybe this might help.'

'Thanks,' he says, 'I'll look into it.'

He's standing and I do too. 'Thank you, detective.'

'Thank you,' he says, as if I've brought him anything of real value. Anything more than a hunch. But perhaps he shares it too.

–

I check my phone as I step out, two missed calls from Mark. I ring him back.

'Sam, why aren't you with Deana at the courthouse?'

'I'm on my way there now. Sorry,' I say, adding, 'Hope Springs drop-in overran.'

'Ah,' he says, 'good to see it picking up a bit?'

I wince, my own deception reaching out to trip me up. 'Yes, in the end a few people Alex had referred actually.'

'Well that is good news.' His voice gets slightly warmer. Alex is my trump card where Mark is concerned. Alex provides us with a free and exceptionally useful service and also often helps us speed things up within hospitals and GPs where he can. 'Don't worry about Deana then, I'll go back to her now and say you've been held up and will call her later?'

'I did message,' I say, 'but yes, that would be good, thanks Mark.'

I hang up feeling like such an arsehole, though the detective's response had made me think that perhaps my fears aren't totally unfounded. I could have just called the detective, but I figure time is of the essence and if there's anything in Laura's file that might help, well, he has it now. I'm sweating and I pull off my jacket, shoving it into my backpack. I get my phone out again and dial Alex; chances are Mark won't mention it, but I'd better give him a heads up just in case. I'm relieved when I get his voicemail.

'Alex, hey. I, uh, may have been a bit late for something and name dropped you to Mark. No biggie but if he asks about referrals you made to the drop-in at Hope Springs just say oh yes. Hope all is well, thanks.'

My phone pings a few minutes later.

> I assume this is Laura related? Let's talk later

No x, no smiley. Alex is pissed off.

CHAPTER TWENTY-EIGHT

CHARLIE

There's definitely someone in the room next to mine and there seem to be various people working here. They have started talking to me via some kind of loudspeaker that feeds into my room from which a dismembered but soothing voice sends instructions. It is still as creepy as hell. I've learnt the hard way not to race for the door and not to fight the two henchmen for my freedom, because I won't get it. I won't get past them, and if I behave too badly I feel the sharp stab of a needle and then there is nothing. Whereas before I arrived here, nothing was my daily goal, now I want to avoid it at all costs. Now my head is clearer than it's been in years, I feel brand new and yet I'm a prisoner. Physically. And this is not an official institution. I had been expecting Sam Martin to show up in my early days. I'd wondered in fact if she'd been here during the mad detox where reality bled into hallucinations and mania. It seemed most obvious that I was being detained on some kind of section and while I couldn't quite get hold of what had happened to get me here, I'd had a psychotic break once before and certainly had overdosed several times and been put on suicide watch.

This place, though, isn't official. This place is a riddle wrapped in a mystery. I am in no way free to leave, nor do I know why I'm here.

The disembodied voice startles me from my strained listening – it's silent out there now – and my manic thoughts. 'Sit on the bed, Charlotte; we'll be dropping food and meds at your door.'

My stomach rumbles with my newfound hunger. I'd forgotten what it was like eating for any reason other than to stay alive, and really, my only reason for living had been to score. That awful will to live that seemed to just keep on going despite me. Every day the same, blending into the next until weeks, months, years had gone by. Since I'd come home to Thamespark I'd been trying my hardest. I'd get a day, maybe two or three, a week once, rattling, skin clammy, teeth gnashing, body shaking. Eventually it was too much and I'd buckle, give in and feel that momentary relief. Sad every time I came to and realised that dose hadn't been the one to kill me. Now I can feel the beginning of thoughts forming. Ideas pinging around my brain. The possibility perhaps of staying like this… normal. Hungry, tired, sad, agitated. Alive.

There is a clicking sound, the door to my windowless room opens, a tray is pushed in on a wheeled gurney. Later there will come a request for me to send it out. Three times a day now, and I find myself waiting for each meal. There is a person on the other side, and behind them two more people. Muscle, in case I get any ideas.

The door clicks closed and I sit at the small table to eat my food. I read one of the recovery books while I eat because I have nothing else to do, which may be the point. I'm finishing up when I hear that sound again, wailing.

I bang on the wall, certain that there is someone next door to me. I'd heard screaming, cries and the sound of another door opening and closing. I pause, wait, bang again. Nothing, but also no voice breaking into my room either. *That's interesting*, my brain says. My thoughts are like sludge but the next one comes eventually. *Why?*

Why?

Everything is information. That's what Seb used to say. Assess the situation, Charlie, everything is information. He'd been just nineteen then, both of us so bloody young. But he'd always seemed like a grown-up to me. Always seemed to know who he was even if he wasn't quite sure where he was going. Laid back, even tempered. Solid. I'd loved that solidity until I hated it. Until it felt like a personal insult. Look how he could be, calm under pressure, thoughtful, reliable while I fell to pieces. When we got Tilly home, I was terrified. The kind of gnawing fear that starts inside and settles in hot prickly sweat on the skin. I loved her, god I loved her. I wanted to care for her, wanted to protect her. But I always knew, I think, that I wasn't up to the job.

Not like Seb. 'Everything is information, Charlie. She's crying, that's telling us something.'

'That noise can drive you mad,' I'd said as her cries cut through me like a knife.

He'd smiled, our squawking daughter pressed against his shoulder. 'Either she's hungry or uncomfortable.'

'Right,' I'd said. My only thought had been that this sound would make me crazy, why wouldn't she stop?

He'd pulled me to him, Tilly sandwiched between us. 'It's OK, we're learning. It's a lot.'

I'd nodded into his warm chest but I'd also thought that it didn't seem to be a lot for him. The sleepless nights followed closely by mornings so early, you couldn't call it day. He didn't seem to feel trapped by it all, suffocated by her. He was easy and gentle. He smiled while I sobbed.

He looked at her the same way he looked at me, as if he'd do anything... anything at all to see her smile.

I never told him that's how I felt, how could I? But the shame gnawed away at me. Mingled with memories of my father, drunk and hollering for silence. No different from me after Seb left to work and I couldn't take it. Couldn't take her.

Silence. The silence here is telling me something. I'm banging on the wall. Last time I did that, the voice came over the loudspeaker. It told me to stop. It also told me meds were coming, and that was a distraction in itself.

Motherhood smothered me until I could take no more. Until I ran. Not knowing as I left in my break for freedom that I would make myself a brand new prison. It had taken me almost a decade to realise it, almost a decade to understand that I had a choice. That I *always* had a choice. Each day I made a decision, whether I realised it or not. I'd wake up and pick up – a drink, a drug, a person. I could use so many things to hurt myself; I could find so many ways to hurt others. I blink back tears, my stomach full, my eyes away from the book and focused on the plain white wall ahead of me.

Despite this place's appearance, despite the food, the meds and the care, I'm being held against my will, and I don't think anyone knows I'm here. Even if they did, who would look?

Sid. Sid would look. Silly bugger that he was. He'll be lost, I think fleetingly, without me.

I bang on the wall again and this time there is a returning bang.

It makes me jump and my eyes scour the room. The blinking red light of the ever-present camera. Still filming.

I bang once. A single bang back. Twice. Two back. Someone else is here. Someone like me who is being held against their will.

CHAPTER TWENTY-NINE

'Laura Doyle,' Finn says as Seb and the team lean over, squinting at the screen. 'Lost custody of her children a year ago.'

'Sam said that they're with her mother, May.'

'Yes.' Finn's eyes scan the files. 'She was in an abusive relationship which endangered the children. The partner also got her using and had her turning tricks when they ran out of money.'

'Charming,' Lucy murmurs.

'Yes,' Finn agrees, 'she was in a bad way.' Finn brings up photos of Laura that they have on file; in them she is beaten, battered, and barely alive.

'Did she go back to him?' Seb asks.

'Actually, no, but the heroin habit was firmly in place. There have been two hearings regarding her getting the kids back. She's been deemed unfit at both, though was granted supervised access. Says in her medical notes that she suffers from mild agoraphobia since this,' he gestures at the abhorrent images, 'but does leave the house when she needs to.'

'Sam told me that will mainly be when she needs a fix.'

Harry makes a clucking sound with his teeth. 'Persistent the addicts are, eh.'

The comment makes Seb pause. Harry as ever is blunt and unthinking. He sees Ken shoot the young man a look and it actually makes him smile. 'They are persistent, Harry, yes.'

Harry looks from Ken to Seb, relieved. He doesn't mean anything by it but his inability to engage his brain before he speaks, and the way he almost always realises a second too late, is an issue. It worries Seb in terms of his long-term career prospects. Harry would never be able to talk to the press, for example.

'Sam said she'd been in to the drop-in centre on the Tuesday to talk to Barry. Sam had seen her on the Monday and said she was using after a fairly good week the one before. Sam was, understandably disappointed. Laura missed signing a document. When Sam went back Tuesday morning, she wasn't there and hasn't been seen since.'

'Why was she at the centre?' Ken asks him.

'She was talking to Barry about her options for getting clean.'

Ken frowns. 'Charlie had the same conversation?'

'I believe she mentioned it, yes, and had got as far as being referred to Dr Alex Martin, Sam's brother, and they had begun making a rough plan,' Seb says. 'Laura had been on methadone for the three weeks preceding her disappearance, though she'd smoked crack at least once during that time.' Seb shrugs. 'Possibly more. Her picking up a prescription is no marker of clean time. They all collect whatever they can get for free, don't they?'

'Still,' Lucy says, 'it's another link, isn't it. In fact there are a few links – both involved at Hope Springs, both covered by Sam Martin and received medical care from Alex Martin.' Her eyes flick to Seb. 'Both women lost custody of their children too.'

'Yes.' Seb officially had full custody after Charlie had left.

Lucy gives him a quick smile and squeezes his arm. He swallows, thankful for his team, who must realise that whatever he might be saying outwardly, this case, this situation, is killing him.

The desk phone rings. Harry grabs it, then says to the rest of them, 'Martina. She's finished the autopsy, shall I put her on speaker?'

Seb nods.

'Martina, you're on speaker, we're all here.'

'Thanks Harry, hello all of you.'

Murmurs back.

'Exactly as I thought, Amanda died from the knife injuries, a single slash across the throat. Killer could have moved back in time to not be covered, so could have walked in and out of that encampment undetected.'

'Same weapon as Sid?'

'Yes, now confirmed, and the same method. Fast and extremely efficient. No hesitation, no pause and straight through all the veins that matter, instant death, and a fairly quiet affair, I'd imagine, too. More so if the victim knew and trusted her attacker.'

'Right,' Seb says. 'How long had she been there?'

'In the tent? Only a few hours. Lucy, you and Finn must have only just missed the killer.'

'Bloody hell,' Finn murmurs.

'Anything else, anything at all you can send off for testing?'

Martina sighs. 'I've sent her clothes off same as Sid's, but honestly Seb, no. Whoever did this left no trace of themselves.'

'Great,' Seb says.

'Sorry not to bring better news, though I'm fairly certain it's the same weapon and the same method of killing.'

'OK, thanks.'

They hang up and Seb flips the whiteboard over. He makes four columns; one side of the board has Charlie and Laura, the other Sid and Amanda.

Underneath Charlie and Laura's names, he writes, 'Mentioned getting clean. Used Hope Springs. Known to social services. Both mothers lost custody. Same social worker – Sam Martin. Different GPs but both had received prescriptions from Dr Alex Martin at Hope Springs. Don't live with their children. Friends in common. Same drug supply.'

'Am I missing anything?'

'Both been in toxic relationships?' Harry says.

'Well, perhaps, though Laura was a recent victim of domestic violence. Sid and Charlie are recorded as having argued but no physical violence as such.' Lucy stares at Seb, blinking. 'But yes, I get what you're saying,' he acquiesces. He's not even sure why he'd jumped in there. Why he felt the need to make the distinction at all. Just because this latest 'partner' didn't beat Charlie up, others had. He'd seen the evidence.

'Anyway,' he says, 'Sid and Amanda.'

'Both addicts,' from Harry. Seb scrawls it in their columns.

'Both partners of addicts.' Finn. Seb writes it down.

'Both also involved in Hope Springs.' Finn again.

'Yep, and there's another link to the others – both also involved with and known to social services. What's different?'

'No kids.'

'No kids.'

'These two were definitely murdered in the same way with the same weapon,' Harry says. 'The others are just missing so far.' Lucy shoots him a look. 'And I'm sure they're fine,' he adds.

Seb gives him a smile that comes out like a grimace. He doubts very much that Charlie is fine, though he's hopeful that she's alive.

'We saw Gordon, who mentioned a package that Sid had. He thinks Charlie may have it now.'

Harry lets out a low whistle. 'This would put Charlie in the frame of course, certainly for Sid — maybe she killed him, took the package and ran. We think that it was Amanda Sales who made the anonymous call, which means she probably saw something and would explain why she's been targeted.'

'Mad to think she knew Sid had been killed, saw the culprit, and went to sleep downstairs.'

Seb shrugs. 'She was high.'

'It looks like it's all connected, but I can't imagine a scenario where Charlie stole drugs, killed Sid, ran, then came back for Amanda, all without anyone noticing,' Lucy says, adding, 'and I suspect if Charlie and Laura were dead we'd know by now.' As if reading his mind.

'Which leaves us with two possibilities,' Seb says. 'They had something to do with the deaths, or they're also victims, and have either run away or been taken.'

—

They spend most of the afternoon at their desks, raking over every single thing that connects Amanda, Sid, Laura and Charlie.

Jackie comes in at about four demanding to know why Laura's disappearance had been added to the case file. She stands frowning at each of them individually while Seb explains Sam's suspicions.

'The social worker sounds far too involved to me.'

Seb nods. 'I think she feels bad for not following up with Charlie when she missed her appointment. Plus, she cares.'

'A health hazard in her job,' Jackie snaps.

'Maybe so,' he agrees, not adding that it is perhaps better than the alternative. Jackie has the hump over two dead bodies and no real suspect. She's also annoyed, though trying to hide it, that one of her officers' family members is missing in the midst of it all and now they've brought her another potential missing woman. Seb shouldn't be on this case, and if anything goes horribly wrong Jackie could be the one who gets the backlash. He appreciates that she's giving him a chance but knows too that they'll need to come up with something concrete, and fast. Two deaths means there will be more interest. Due to the demographic, it won't be front-page news. Not yet, at least; if and when it was he'd be pulled or moved back, he suspects. Which means he needs a break in the case and he needs it soon.

'Chances are she's just wandered off and got herself into trouble,' Jackie says.

'She may have.'

'That's not what you think though, is it?'

'No. I think it's too much of a coincidence that she and Charlie are missing, and two people are dead. All of them are connected by various threads.'

Jackie wanders to the board, where the lists of things connecting all parties is written in neat columns.

She turns back to Seb. 'You should look into the connections then,' she tells him, her lips pressed together in a thin line to let him know this displeases her. But, as most things seem to displease Jackie, he takes it with a pinch of salt. She can be abrasive and brash but she's a good person and a good boss underneath it. He knows younger officers are scared of her and while he gets it, her bark is worse than her bite.

'Thank you, ma'am.'

She sighs. 'You're OK?' she asks.

He nods. 'I'm OK.'

After she leaves, Harry lets out a low whistle. 'She must feel really sorry for you, she was almost nice.' Lucy stares at him open mouthed, Ken and Finn look embarrassed on his behalf but Seb bursts out laughing.

'I think she probably does, Harry.' His laughter diffuses some of the tension.

CHAPTER THIRTY

He's the last one left and checks his phone, a text from Val:

> Home for dinner?

He pauses, unsure how to respond but knowing full well he's not going to manage sitting through a meal with this awful secret festering inside. 'I'll be home but not for a few hours,' he types, then adds, 'sorry.' Because he is. He should be home now. He hasn't really seen Tilly since her sleepover, which meant her ensuing exhaustion, and, he suspects, fairly grumpy teen mood would have fallen in Val's lap. He's been avoiding his family for a few days now which makes him feel awful. The conversation is looming and imminent. Maybe he'll feel better when it's done. It will have to be had because he is no closer to finding Sid's killer or Charlie than he'd been three days ago. He looks around their small corner of the open plan area at the station. He'd commandeered this bit and it was cordoned off now with large boards on wheels. Not a private office, nothing so fancy, but it gave the illusion of their own space if nothing else. Kept them working as a team.

He messages Faye.

> Are you home?

Immediately...

> Yes, do you want to stop by?

> Please.

It takes him fifteen minutes to get there; the traffic is terrible. His mind whirrs with a million different thoughts, none of them good, until he's parked next to her bubble-gum pink Mini. He steps out and walks to the door.

Maybe he looks awful, because her wide smile drops and she steps forward, reaching out and hugging him, pulling him close to her. Seb's arms wrap round her, his hands getting tangled in her long ponytail. She pulls away, studies his face; his eyes are wet, his pulse racing. The last few days catching up to him, his mind full of images of Laura Doyle, beaten, battered, bruised. Two dead bodies and the sympathetic looks on his colleagues' faces.

'Come on,' she says.

He follows her inside. She ushers him onto the sofa, points to a bottle of whisky in the corner in a repurposed drinks bar that he knows she'd sanded, painted and hardly used because like him Faye isn't a big drinker. He shakes his head; the last thing he needs now is alcohol. 'Tea then?'

'Please.'

She makes it and he watches her through the small archway leading to her kitchen. Her movements as ever fluid, unhurried. Everything about her exudes solidity and calm; her flat is an extension of it too, a small place but carefully decorated and comfortable. It's what he liked about her initially, what he knows he has grown to love about her. It wasn't as it had been with Charlie. It wasn't all high passion and consuming thoughts, and he didn't know what that meant exactly but the way she, Faye, made him feel was good, and he hopes it's the same for her.

'Here.' She puts a steaming mug down in front of him. 'What's going on?'

He tells her, in faltering sentences, swallowing more tears and unable to meet her eye. Because he tells her too that despite everything she's ever done, Charlie, to him, to Tilly, to Val, probably to everyone she's ever met, despite all that, he needs to find her. Alive. He needs to know she's safe.

There is a pause when he is finished speaking. He keeps his eyes down, waiting, finding his breath is held. He feels her before he hears her; her arms reach out, wrap around him and pull him in. It is then and only then, that he lets the tears flow.

CHAPTER THIRTY-ONE

SAM

It's been a long day and when my phone rings, Barry's name flashing on the screen, I actually think about ignoring it. I won't though. For better or worse, my phone is on twenty-four hours a day, even though I'd lied to Alex and said I kept it switched off overnight. The thing is, I've had clients call me at one, two, three in the morning. Sometimes on the cusp of disaster. Once I managed to intervene in a suicide attempt. If I point these things out to my brother, he reminds me I'm not god. That annoys me, because I don't think I am. But I do always wonder what would have happened if my mum had had just one person she trusted to reach out to. If she'd still be here, if our lives would have been different. Right now, I have a new and equally painful dose of guilt heaped on top of it because I'm wondering what would have happened if I'd gone looking for Charlie? If I'd at least tried to find out about her missed appointment. If I'd have asked around I'd have found out Sid was looking, Sid was concerned. Maybe we'd have found her. Maybe Sid would still be here.

'Pick up call,' I tell Siri, and then, 'Hi Barry.'
'Sam, hey.'
'All OK?'

'I'm not sure, and I may be overreacting.'

'Ha, my speciality.' I've just pulled up outside my block of flats. It's almost eight. I haven't eaten all day but am full of caffeine from the endless cups of coffee that have seen me through. I note that my hand shakes slightly as I take my phone out of the cradle, disconnecting it. It's hunger for sure. 'What's up?' I've turned the engine off but not moved to get out. I don't think there's any food in my fridge or cupboards so I'll need to go and get something in. I wish I'd thought of this sooner.

'It's Tiny.'

'Oh?'

'Have you seen or heard from him?'

I laugh. 'What, since I saw him this morning?'

Barry sighs. 'I'll take that as a no then.'

'No, sorry,' I say, hearing the serious tone in his voice. 'What's happening? Is he not there?'

'He didn't come back after lunch.'

'Was he supposed to?'

'Yes, he literally went to grab a sandwich that was what, midday, eight hours ago.'

'That's unusual?' I ask, but I know it is. Tiny is reliable and completely trustworthy. He often does shopping runs for Laura, taking her bank card with him.

'Yes, he'd have told me if he wasn't around.'

'He's not just in his place?'

'No, and I used my keys to check. I don't think he's been back since I last saw him.'

'Yeah, that's not good. What does Debbie say?'

'She's gone to check in with a few people now, we're both worried.'

'Yes.'

'Sorry to put it on you, but I figured with Laura and everything else around here it might be pertinent.'

'No,' I say, 'I'm glad you called.'

'Look, if we hear anything I'll let you know, and maybe we could check back in in the morning with each other if he doesn't show up before then?'

'Yes, let's, and I'll do the same,' I tell him. 'I'll contact you if I hear anything.'

'Thanks.'

I hang up the call, then I start my car and drive over to my brother's.

—

Caroline is in her sweats when she answers the door. Even in casual clothes with no make-up, she somehow manages to look put together. Her set is matching and a royal blue that brings out the colour of her eyes. Her hair is scraped up but held in place with a cream band.

'Sam,' she smiles warmly, 'what a pleasant surprise.'

'Sorry to just turn up,' I say, knowing full well I do this way too often and should probably call in advance.

'Don't be silly, come in, come in.'

'Where's Jess?'

'Sleepover,' she says. 'Alex is working late.'

I glance at the clock on the microwave, it's coming up to eight thirty. 'Didn't he start early today?'

She nods. 'He did, yes. Have you eaten?'

'Um,' my stomach rumbles in response, 'not this evening.'

'Sit, I've got a chili on the go and plenty spare.'

'Are you sure?'

'Of course.'

She serves up and hands me a plate of food; I wolf it down and she brings me an orange juice. 'You were starving, Sam.'

'I uh, didn't get time for lunch.'

She shakes her head. 'Not ideal.'

'No,' I say, resisting the urge to apologise. She's always taken this maternal role with me and far from finding her worry irritating, I like it. My own mother would disappear into her room for days on end leaving Alex and I to fend for ourselves much of the time; I'm glad Alex found someone who is almost the opposite of her. And like a silly little child, I'm glad I get some looking after too, though I'd never say that aloud to anyone.

'Glass of wine?'

'Uh, maybe a small one.'

She pours two and indicates that we head into the front room. The TV is paused mid programme, some reality TV show. I realise I've interrupted her evening, probably a rare one of solitude. I gulp down the wine and stand, stretching. 'I should get home,' I tell her, half hoping she'll insist I stay.

'Of course,' she says, smile bright but eyes flicking to the TV screen. She wants to get on with her own evening, and who can blame her?

She walks me to the door, where I pause. 'Tell Alex I called by?'

'Yes, definitely. I'll leave a note if he's especially late.'

'Do you think he will be?' I ask, surprised; my brother, unlike me, is normally especially boundaried around working hours.

'I'm not sure. I know he has some research papers he's been looking over.' She yawns. 'He's been late a lot recently, honestly wondering if he's having an affair.' It's said in a jokey tone but I can hear some concern underneath it.

'He's probably just found some area of interest and has got lost in it, as you said.'

'I think you're right, and that makes me worry too. You know how he can get.'

'Yes,' I say, remembering my brother ultra focused throughout his training, then working insane hours as a junior doctor. 'He does have a tendency to push himself.'

'You're both the same in that respect,' she says; we are, I suppose. 'I'm sure he's fine.' She smiles.

I smile back. 'Me too,' I say, feeling a small spike of concern nonetheless. He has boundaries but he also has a hungry, curious mind and can go off on many tangents. He'd written several papers for various publications. I imagine he may be doing just that now. I feel a tinge of guilt that I'm unsure what projects he has on the go – he knows everything I'm working on, everything I'm thinking about and worrying about. I should know what he's doing too.

'Thanks for feeding me.'

'Any time.' She smiles.

I get in my car, feeling a hundred times better for some food, though slightly light-headed from the downed wine. By the time I get to mine, I'm completely exhausted, crawl into my bed in my underwear and despite worrying about Laura, Charlie and now Tiny, I am out like a light.

CHAPTER THIRTY-TWO

'Ah, Sebastian, I was beginning to forget what you looked like.' Val grins from the doorway of the kitchen. 'And Faye too, what a pleasant surprise.'

'Is Tilly here?'

'Tilly is at Kai's, and before you stress about it there's a whole group of them there.' Seb would probably have had something to say about this just a few days ago. Now he's relieved she's not here and especially grateful that Faye is.

He shrugs out of his coat and he and Faye head into the kitchen, where Val asks if they've eaten.

'I have,' Faye tells her, 'thanks Val.'

Seb shakes his head. 'I'm not hungry.'

'Seb, you need to eat. You're working very long days...'

'I know,' he snaps, then, 'sorry, I know, and thank you but, I... I need to talk to you.'

Val smiles and it makes the corner of her eyes crinkle. 'Sounds ominous.'

Faye says, 'You sit, Val. Why don't I pop the kettle on.'

'Tea after eight, so it must be serious.' Val's still smiling but the smile slips away as she realises neither of them are. 'Oh,' she says, 'is it Tilly?' Her eyes widen in panic.

Seb reaches across the table, takes her hand in his. 'No, well not directly.'

'Seb,' Faye says gently.

Val's hand feels so small in his. She's getting old, he supposes, which is weird; he doesn't think of her as young, obviously, but she's tough, sprightly. In her sixties, which isn't decrepit by any stretch. Not old, but too old to have to worry about her child still, although maybe you never stopped.

'Charlie came back to Thamespark.'

'Charlotte? She's here.'

'She was.'

'What do you mean was?'

'She's missing.'

'Missing?'

'Her... she was here on the Hartsmead estate with her boyfriend.'

'Boyfriend?'

'A man called Sid Darnell.'

Val frowns. 'I know that name... he was on the local news.'

'He was murdered, that's the case I'm working.'

'He was murdered, she's missing.' Val's face is chalky white.

Faye puts a cup in front of her, murmurs, 'Here, I put sugar in.' Val glances up. 'Thank you dear. That's kind.'

She takes a sip, then she stares at Seb. He hates this. Hates having to tell her, hates that he'd hidden it for two days. 'You're looking for her,' she says, but it's a statement of fact, not a question.

'I am, yes.'

'Is that the right thing for you to be doing?'

'I have to do it.'

'I see.' Another sip of tea. 'How long has she been or was she in town?'

'At least three months.'

'She didn't think to stop by?'
'Doesn't seem like it, no.'
'Wonderful.'
'I was told she had been trying for the whole time she was here to get clean.'
'Trying? But failing?'
'She'd get some days, most recently over a week.'
'But relapsed?'
'Yes.'
'Living in a flat with someone who was a reported drug dealer?'
'Yes,' Seb says. That much had been on the news reports.
'A man who is now dead.'
'Yes,' he says. 'I'm sorry.'
'What for?'
'For not telling you sooner.'
'Well, yes. You ought to have done that.' There is a silence, unusually awkward. That in itself is enough to break Seb's heart. Val is his rock. He likes to think he is hers. They are generally a happy little household. They don't argue, don't fall out with each other, not really. They work as their own little family unit.
'We have to tell Matilda.'
'I know.' His head slumps forward.
'Do you think she's alive?'
'Yes,' he says quickly. 'I do.'
'Does anyone else?'
'I'm not sure.'
'Women like Charlie don't make old bones, Seb.'
'I know.'
She turns to Faye. 'Did you know?'
'This evening. Seb has only just told me.'

'Right, and now you're both here.'

'We are.'

'And we'll need to tell Tilly of course,' she repeats.

'I know.'

'Oh god, Seb.'

'I'm so sorry.' She shakes her head and he doesn't know how to interpret it, doesn't know what she means. 'I should have told you.'

She sits back, eyes up meeting his. 'Yes, Seb, you should.' She sighs. 'But as I sit here thinking about Matilda, and the conversation which must ensue, I fully understand why you didn't.'

'You do?'

'I understand, Sebastian, but I'm not happy with you.'

He nods.

'Will you find her?'

'God, I hope so.'

'Tell me everything.'

Normally Seb doesn't share details of specific cases with Val. Normally he tries his hardest to leave his work outside of the house. In effect, he'd tried to do it again this time. But this was Charlie. This was different.

'Sid and Charlie met in London somewhere but seemingly he lived round here when they were both kids.'

Val frowns. 'Darnell, his mother's name is Rita?'

'Yes, you knew them?'

'Vaguely.'

'They've been arrested together twice, once for shoplifting and once Sid was arrested for drunk and disorderly, Charlie mouthed off to a police officer and was taken in and charged too.'

'Dear me,' Val says, and Seb tries to imagine if it was Tilly, and has a small moment of abject terror when he recalls the things he's heard about addiction's genetic component over the years. He squashes it down, that particular fear isn't for now.

'Sid's mum, Rita as you said, lived in a flat here. When she passed away recently, Sid let his sister use it temporarily. His sister and he don't have the same mother and actually the tenancy passes to Sid.'

'He what, inherits the flat?'

'He inherits the tenancy, but as it's a two bed, I feel like he might have been moved on at some future date. So far he's paid the bedroom tax.'

'And the rent?'

'And the rent,' Seb agrees, taking a deep breath and flicking a glance to Faye, who takes his hand in hers, squeezes his fingers. It gives him just enough strength to carry on.

'It looks like Charlie and Sid were trying to get clean, certainly Charlie was.'

'How do you know that, Sebastian?' Val asks, and Seb can hear mirrored in her voice the same dangerous thing he knows he feels. Hope. Hope when it comes to Charlie can be utterly devastating.

'She had a social worker and had been actively participating in a rehabilitation programme, collecting methadone and attending group meetings, some one-on-one sessions.'

'And this Sid?'

'He collected the methadone.' Val nods, well versed enough in the shit show that having an addict kid is to understand the implication of one partner still using.

'And he was dealing?'

Seb goes on, 'Yes. From what we can see, financially they were struggling, and there was a rent payment that went into arrears, which is when one or the other of them, we think Sid, struck a deal with a local guy.'

'I see, a dangerous person?'

'Exceptionally.'

'Do you think they might be involved?'

'In Sid's death and Charlie's disappearance?' Val nods.

'I don't think so.' Seb sighs. 'It's what I thought, what I assumed I suppose, but there'd be more evidence pointing that way.'

'And there's not?'

'No. But another young woman is missing and we also have a second murder.'

'Goodness me.' Val presses a hand to her chest. Seb can see beads of sweat on her face. He hates doing this, can only imagine how much worse this conversation is going to be with Tilly. 'They're linked?'

'I think so.'

'Do you know how?'

'Not exactly.'

'Could the women have gone off together? Charlie and the other one?'

'It's possible,' Seb says, 'though they went missing at different times.'

'How are they linked?'

'Both addicts, both mothers. Neither of those things is uncommon, in the circles they move in.'

Val nods. 'I see that.'

Faye stands, goes to the sink and pours Val a glass of water. She puts it down beside Val, who smiles at her. 'Thank you, dear.' She takes a sip, then looks at Faye again. 'This must be hard on you.'

Faye shakes her head. 'Not like it is for you and Seb.'

'No,' Val agrees, 'I suppose not.'

There is a silence. The three of them sit around the kitchen table where they have shared many happy meals.

Eventually, Val speaks. 'You grieve for a child like Charlie. No way not to. If it weren't for Matilda, and you,' she reaches for Seb's hand, and he is relieved to feel her touch, relieved to know that he is forgiven, or perhaps the anger he'd anticipated wasn't forthcoming after all, 'perhaps I'd still be running around after my daughter, trying to fix what is unfixable without her consent. We made the right call with her.' She says this to Faye and to Seb. 'Neither one of us wanted to send her on her way… it was one of the worst days of my life.'

Seb feels tears prickle behind his eyes and blinks. He can see her, Charlie, small and messed up, glaring from her mother to her husband. She'd been mad that day, the kind of madness born of unsated addiction. Seb had done his best, he reminds himself. He'd tried his hardest. He'd tried to ignore infidelity, fear and cruelty on her part. But he couldn't ignore it for Tilly. At first they'd really tried to keep up contact for Tilly's sake, but it became obvious fast that Charlie was unsafe and they had to draw a line.

'We didn't send her away, Val,' Seb reminds her, 'we gave her a choice. Tilly or the drugs.'

Val sighs. 'I know, and it had to be done, but goodness me, Seb.' She pauses, probably like him reliving that awful moment. 'We're going to have to talk to Matilda,' Val says.

'I think so, yes,' Seb agrees.

Val reaches across the table again, takes his hand in hers. 'We needn't do it tonight, she's not here and perhaps another twenty-four hours will give us some hope.'

'Perhaps,' he says.

'I need to get some sleep,' Val tells him. He glances at the clock; it's not even nine, but he knows what she means is she needs some time to process it.

—

Seb and Faye are sat on the sofa, glasses of wine in hand, though neither have really touched them. She asks him questions about the past, and at first, he answers slowly, carefully. Eventually, as he almost always finds talking to Faye, he opens up, and as he does so, he thinks about how talking about things really can help. For a man used to keeping things to himself, this has been a revelation.

Faye herself was a revelation.

'How do you think Tilly's going to take this?' he asks her now.

She leans her head to one side and her bright red hair dances around her waist. 'I think it will be tough, but life can be tough, that's reality.'

'I want to protect her from that.'

Faye leans across, pressing her hand onto the top of his arm. Her slim fingers are warm and comforting. 'You have, Seb, and you do, but you can't hide her away from problems. This is her life, Charlie is her mother and that is something she needs to deal with. You can be there to support her and to see her through as she transitions into adulthood, but really that's all you can do.'

'God.' He sighs.

'Seb, you've done a great job with her, and she has Val too. Her life is stable, her home is a safe place, these things will hold her.'

'You think so?'

'I know so,' she says. 'The kids I work with, the ones in real trouble, are the ones who have no safe adults.'

'I don't know how you do it.'

She smiles. 'I don't know how you do your job sometimes. Especially now.'

'I shouldn't be on the case.'

'I thought that. How come you are?'

'I have brownie points with Jackie and the main thrust of the investigation is murder.'

'Could she get into trouble?'

'It's possible.'

'Then you need to do it right, which means putting aside personal feelings as much as you can.'

'I'm trying.'

'If you can't and you feel overwhelmed you need to hand it over.'

'Yeah, no, I know,' he agrees, though he has absolutely no intention of doing that.

CHAPTER THIRTY-THREE

CHARLIE

I've spent the day, or what I assume is daytime, feeling anxious. The disembodied voice pulled me from a thin restless sleep to tell me breakfast and medication had arrived. I think not taking the pills accounts for the unsettled rest, but I won't start taking them again. I'm not clucking, my body doesn't hurt and my skin is dry, not swamped in sweat. I try and focus on letting that feeling wash over me and wonder, not for the first time, what it is that they've been giving me. Something strong. Strong enough to take the edge off, and my edge is big and sharp. But since I started flushing them away, my thoughts no longer feel fuzzy.

I do however feel tried, and after walking the room restless and bored for what feels like hours, I lie on my bed and give in to sleep. I'm woken up by a voice, not over the speaker but close by.

'Hello.'

I almost jump out of my skin; certainly I come close to falling off the damn bed. Instinctively I pull the covers up over my body, though what protection I think they'll offer me is a mystery. I turn and see a woman across the other side of the room. She too is in a hospital bed with collapsible sides and wheels on its feet. I look at her, she looks at me. She looks rough, skin, bone and lank greasy hair, and she looks frightened.

'Who are you?'

'Laura,' she says. Her voice is crackly, popping paper dry. I pull myself up to sitting. Wondering how long I'd slept for and how quiet they must have been bringing her in here.

She scootches to sitting up, she's in a thin hospital gown and her shoulders poke through the material like spikes. Alongside her bed just like mine is a wheeled table. She reaches for the plastic cup of water.

I watch her drink and realise that despite the dark circles and sallow skin she is very young and familiar.

'There's pills too.' I point at the small paper cup.

'What are they?'

'I'm not sure.'

'Are we in a hospital?' Her teeth are chattering slightly and it's not from cold, it's the hunger pangs. She's clucking, I think. Her need for a fix was probably awake before her body was. I swing my legs round and sit on the edge of my bed. My eyes flick to the bottom of hers. Wheels, hospital beds. A clinical white room and yet... locks on the door, a disembodied voice through a speaker system. People with masks on who speak to each other but not me. I look at the corners of the room where the red lights blink. Cameras.

'I don't know, but the pills will help,' I tell her, because her jittering is giving me a fresh wave of anxiety.

She takes them, gulping the water.

'How long have you been here?' I ask her.

'Not long at all. I was in a different room yesterday. I think I might have overdosed?' She says it like a question but I, of course, have no answer.

'I was out. I picked up, stopped at the park,' she says, frowning. 'Then I woke up here.'

'Did you use?'

'Yeah, I was going to wait until I was home. I wanted...' Her voice trails off. 'Did I overdose?'

I shrug. 'Maybe. What's the last thing you remember?'

'The park, lying down, looking at the sky.' She frowns. 'Maybe I went home, or I intended to, it's unclear. Then... here, different room.'

'I heard you,' I say.

'You banged on the wall?'

'Yeah.' OK. She was brought in after me, she is also an addict, she is being given what I was given. Now we are both here together and... she looks familiar.

'Where's home?'

'Um. Thamespark, the Hartsmead.'

I squint. 'I know you.'

She looks back. 'You're Sid's girlfriend?'

I nod, feeling a pang at the thought of him. Is he worried? Has he even noticed I'm gone? I try to think back to where we'd been. At the flat. A warm cosy place when we'd moved in. Soon to be trashed. It became a shithole, like everywhere Sid and I set up camp. I remember him scoring, a big delivery. The deal struck between Gordon, who was shrewd, and Sid, who was not. Sid assuring me that we needed the money, and we did, that the deal was a means to an end. That it needn't derail us. We could get clean; in some ways it was better still as we'd sell without dipping into it. That of course isn't what happened.

It became a doss house fast. We used more than we sold. There were lots of people in and out to pick up. Before I knew it I was using too even though I'd had a whole week where I hadn't, where I'd managed not to. A whole week of methadone, Hope Springs, and trying so hard to talk Sid into joining me. I'd known as soon as we arrived back here in my hometown that there was a clock ticking over us. A deadline on our relationship that I'd have to draw if I ever wanted to get better. If I ever wanted to be less of an arsehole. And I had wanted that. When Sid mentioned the flat, the town, I'd seen it as a sign.

I don't believe in god, had seen enough moments devoid of humanity and compassion to know no such thing existed, but I thought that maybe things came up for a reason. When he'd said Thamespark, I'd gone over us meeting, our chaotic lives and thought maybe... maybe this is it. Maybe this is my chance.

I am a terrible mother. But I do love my daughter, and recently, the drugs with their blanket of oblivion hadn't worked quite so well at vanquishing all the memories. I'd been thinking about her, dreaming about her and wondering what if, what if I got myself together? What if I saw her? Would she forgive me? I don't know. I've never forgiven my father, though as I've sunk lower and lower I've started to understand him. I'd run away from Tilly, run away from Seb, in some warped way to spare them from the disaster of my life, but is that any better than him? My dad.

'Did you do it?' Laura's voice breaks into my thoughts, snapping me back to here. This weird situation we both find ourselves in.

'Do what?'

'Kill Sid?'

I frown at her. 'Of course not, why would you ask that?'

She shrugs, her skin is pale and clammy and I note that her breathing is fast, like little gasps rather than a steady inhale and exhale. 'Figured maybe you'd taken the drugs, knifed him and run.'

'The drugs?'

'Yeah, Gordon's stash, the missing one that you owed on.'

'We... he sold most of it as soon as it came in, did he not pay Gordon?'

'No, and Gordon is livid.'

'I...' My voice trails off. 'Did someone hurt him, Sid?'

'Yeah. Shit,' she says, adjusting herself on the bed, 'don't you know?'

'No, is he OK?'

Her face tells me what I already know... did you kill him... she'd asked. 'He's dead?' I say, knowing because she'd just said so, hadn't she? Did you do it, she'd said. Kill him. Oh god. Sid. A wave of pain swamps me. Sid was an idiot, Sid was a liability and a barrier to me making the progress I'd dreamed about. But we'd lived together on and off for years now. I'd known him vaguely since we were kids. He was a broken person but not a bad person and I'd encountered plenty of those over the years.

'I'm sorry, I...' She breaks down into a coughing fit. I slide out of my bed, standing up, and as I do I realise I feel steady on my feet. Healthy, solid, stronger than I have for years. But my heart hurts and my first thought is... *I know what would fix this.* I blink back tears. For Sid, for me. He'd have been the only person who'd have noticed I was gone.

I head over to her, hand her the plastic cup filled with water and make her drink some more.

'Thanks.' She gives me back the cup, her hand shaking. 'I guess you didn't do it then.'

'Do it?'

'You didn't kill him. Sid.'

I frown. 'Is that what people think?' My mind is racing, my emotions a step behind my thoughts.

'I don't know.' The words come out on a sigh, and she flumps backwards onto the propped-up pillow. 'I went in to the drop-in centre in town and someone told me about Sid. They said the police were looking for you in connection with his death. I meant to ask my social worker about it.'

'Who's your social worker?'

'Sam Martin.'

I inhale. Sam, the harassed-looking woman with the shiny hair and sharp eyes. Really kind. 'I know Sam.'

'Oh yeah?'

'She's my social worker too.'

'Really?'

'Yes,' I say. 'Does she think I did it?'

Laura shrugs. 'Don't know. Probably not. Even if she did she'd still have your back, she's good like that.' Laura breaks down into another coughing fit.

'Why do you have a social worker?' I ask.

But she turns her head away, and as she does so, her eyelids start to droop. I step back to my own bed, heart pounding, my mind offering up a million memories, none of them good. Sid. Silly, ridiculous Sid. Kind but broken. Easily manipulated, often by me. Dead. Knifed in the shitty flat.

Laura's breaths become longer. She's asleep. I stand, head to the door and try the handle. Nothing. I look into the corners of the room, staring directly at each blinking camera.

CHAPTER THIRTY-FOUR

Overwhelmed hardly covers it, Seb thinks as he walks up the steps into the station, the conversation between himself and Faye then Val playing over and over in his mind. He'd seen the horror on his tough mother-in-law's face. Seen the look of utter desperation. He felt it too, of course he did, though he thinks it is probably worse when it's your child, isn't it? He momentarily imagines it's Tilly and the thought makes him so sick he pushes it away. Tilly had come in and thankfully gone to bed shortly after. Seb had stolen a hug, delighted when she didn't pull away and then struck all over again with guilt.

'Morning.' Lucy is just behind him as he signs in at the front desk. 'You OK?' she asks in the same way she has for the past few days, head cocked to the side in sympathy. He hates it, the look of concern, but is equally grateful to know she cares. As do Ken, Harry and Finn. Maybe even Jackie, in her own way.

'Yes,' he says, then adds, 'I, uh, spoke to Val.'

'That must have been tough.' They are walking into the cramped stairwell now; there had been talk of a lift for years, but considering they'd be lucky to get a fresh lick of paint that seemed unlikely. They were only two floors up at least.

'It wasn't my best.' He gives her a smile to take the sting out of the words. To let her know that yes, it's shit, but he can manage.

Harry stands as they come in and walks towards Seb.

'All right, guv?'

Seb nods. 'Yes, you?'

'Yeah. I think I, we,' he gestures at Finn, who is at his desk, hand raised in a quick hi, 'found something.'

'OK.'

They all crowd around Finn's desk. Seb squints at the screen; on it is a case report.

'Do you want to summarise?' Lucy snaps. 'Some of us haven't had any caffeine yet.'

Seb frowns. 'Didn't you have a cup at home?'

She grins. 'I didn't come from home.'

'Oi Oi.' Harry, who she slaps on the arm.

'Yes, all right,' Seb says. 'Summarise, Harry.'

'Another case a year ago, a local small bit dealer, Darren Oliver, found overdosed and with his throat cut.'

'Just like Sid.'

Harry nods. 'Quite, just like Sid.'

'But,' Lucy interjects, 'drug dealers get killed a lot and knife crime is the nation's favourite.'

Seb winces at that, though he can't deny it. Knives are the weapon of choice among the local criminals. It was like a disease, starting in London and spreading out like fingers making a grab for victims.

'Yes, but his partner,' Harry puts this in quotation marks, 'local prostitute Clare Parker, went missing at the same time.'

'Was she found?' Seb asks faster than he'd intended and with a slight tinge of panic.

'Um.' Harry looks at Finn. Finn says, 'She was found a month later, I'm afraid to say she wasn't found alive.' Finn flinches as he says the words and Seb knows that he and Harry must have discussed this. Known that they will understand this news is devastating for him to hear, and it is. His voice is calm and even, thank god, but his insides are like jelly and his heart is hammering.

'How?' Seb asks.

'An overdose.'

'And where had she been for the weeks she was missing?'

'Well,' says Harry, 'this is where it gets a bit odd.'

'OK...'

'She was in good shape.'

Seb blinks. 'You just said she was dead.'

'Well aside from that.' That gets a quick laugh from Lucy, who immediately says, 'Sorry, it's the way he said it.'

Seb can't disagree; Harry has an uncanny knack for clumsy bluntness. It's why he'd never make it too high up the ranks and why Seb made sure he was mainly office based or accompanied by someone who could step in when needed. Harry was, however, a diligent and effective researcher, and he and Finn made a formidable team. Finn was technically brilliant but socially awkward. One thing Seb loved about the small team he'd cobbled together was that they all had different functions, different strengths that complemented each other.

'So aside from death...' Seb prompts.

'Well, she'd been living a hard life, lost her kids, low-level addict, but had had a couple of attempts at getting better.'

'Like?'

'What?'

'Attempts like what?'

'Oh, I see. She actually went into a rehab.'

'Which one?'

'St Carmella's,' Finn says. 'She was there for twenty-eight days, had a detox.'

'Then?'

'Came out, took up with Darren and started using again. Then he was dead and less than a week later, she went missing.'

'OK.'

'Whilst she died of an overdose, it looked like she'd got clean again whilst she was, well, wherever she was.'

'Can they be sure of that?'

'Not one hundred per cent – ninety-nine, as Martina might say. Like I said Clare Parker's death and cause of death aside, she was physically well, she was clean, well fed and there was only one recent set of track marks and that was from the dose that killed her.'

'So what, she went off, got well, then relapsed and showed up where?'

'Outside A&E.'

Seb frowns. 'Why?'

'Exactly.'

'Who were the suspects in Darren's case?'

'Quite a few. His brother Michael – Darren had robbed him and his parents. Had been seen threatening to kill him. Local guvnor of the Wheelwright Arms, Greg Anderson, claimed Darren robbed the till, and Gordon, to whom he owed money.'

'What came of that?'

'Nothing – he was abroad at the time and there was proof of it.'

'But, like he said, if he wanted to off someone he wouldn't go near it himself.'

'True,' Harry agrees.

'But we don't like him for Sid,' Lucy says, 'and if we're saying this case is linked...'

'There's a lot of similar ties for it to be a coincidence.'

'There are,' Seb says. 'How long had Clare been dead when she was found?'

'Less than a day.'

Seb swallows. 'So working on the assumption the same person who killed Darren took her, she was alive for how long after his death?'

'Weeks, almost a month,' Finn tells him.

'Right.' Seb's heart picks up. She was kept alive, for some reason. 'Any other suspects?'

'In Darren's death, initially her, Clare.'

'Right, have we found any footage yet of Laura?' The team had been scouring for CCTV going on the titbit that Laura argued with someone and got into a car.

'No,' Finn says, 'most of the cameras are defunct, but I've widened the search to surrounding areas, so fingers crossed.'

'Fingers crossed indeed,' Seb agrees. 'Right, let's wade through paperwork, shall we?'

—

Seb spends the next hour pouring over Clare Parker's case notes. A sad and not unusual story. Her own childhood blighted by domestic violence and abuse. A juvenile record, a stay in prison at nineteen by which time she had two children. She got the kids back after she was released, seemed OK for a few years, then she met Darren. A year into their doomed relationship, the kids were taken away, and by this time Clare was turning tricks. She and Darren were using more than they were selling. They were in trouble, and neither would have made old bones, but still. Murder and an OD? Or both murders, his mind offers up.

He stands and gets his team's attention. He adds a printed photo of Clare alongside Laura and Charlie's, studiously avoiding his ex-wife's eyes while he pins it to the broad. He puts a mug shot of Darren, who looks like a real charmer, complete with skinhead and terrifying scalp scar, next to Sid and Amanda.

'Charlie, Laura, Clare. All addicts, all known to social services. All three had kids who they had lost one way or another, right?'

This is met by nods and Seb goes on. 'Laura's mother has custody of her children, Clare's are with her parents, Charlie, well Tilly is with me and Val.' He pauses, swallows and continues, 'All three women had made some noise or indication that they wanted out of the lifestyle.'

'Don't addicts do that all the time?' Lucy asks.

Seb nods. 'You're not wrong, but each of these women tried to some degree, even if it was half-arsed.' He thinks of Barry at Hope Springs talking about Charlie and acknowledging that as long as she was with Sid it just wouldn't matter. 'More importantly, it's a pattern, isn't it. Let's look at the murder victims. Sid, Charlie's dubious partner in crime, Darren, Clare's, Alan Humphreys is Laura's ex, the one Sam said threatened her. I've contacted his family by the way, he's in Australia, so hopefully he won't be at risk there.'

'That's good, I guess,' Harry says.

'Amanda is the odd one out here,' Lucy says.

'She is, though she was in the flat when Sid was killed and I know we've never been sure if she was the one who made the call, but if she saw something, or someone...'

'That would make sense,' Harry says.

'Seb, what do you think the women are being held for?'

'I think someone is trying to get them clean,' he says, trying out this theory without hesitation and thinking, *yes, that's it.*

CHAPTER THIRTY-FIVE

SAM

'The detective called *me*,' I tell Mark, who is frowning so hard it looks like his forehead is about to split in two.

'But you're the one who approached him, about Laura.'

'Yes, but the fact he's also concerned says maybe my gut instinct is right here.'

Mark sighs, and his face smooths out. He no longer looks pissed off so much as exhausted.

'Look, if she's in trouble, it's good that he's looking for her,' I say, 'surely.'

'She's always in trouble.'

'You know what I mean.'

'So you need to go into the station again?' Mark asks, which is the real problem here.

'I do, yes.'

'What about your morning schedule?'

'It's an admin morning anyway.'

'Which you're behind on,' he reminds me. I bristle at that – we're all behind on admin, all the time. We have a tremendous amount of it now, mostly pointless box ticking. Along with our ever-unwieldy caseloads, it's yet another thing that makes our job almost impossible.

'I'll catch up,' I sigh.

'Yeah, when?'

'By the end of the week.'

'You'd better.' He leans forward, eyes going back to his computer. I am dismissed and I got my way because really, what choice did he have? Mark doesn't outrank a homicide detective.

'Mark, all of the missing women and at least two murder victims have links to us here at social services.'

He looks at me wide eyed and I realise he's so overstretched, so jaded that he hadn't quite let that sink in. 'I... you're right, it's just...'

'We have a lot on, I have a lot on, and this is another extra thing?'

'Yes,' he agrees.

'I'll work overtime.'

'You always do,' he sighs, 'and I do appreciate it.'

'I know, but this needs to be resolved, hopefully fast and without too much press involvement.' The two words that always shit him up land exactly where I hoped they would. He nods and I'm dismissed, but no longer the focus of his anxiety, at least.

I leave the office. Outside it's overcast but warm. I start to walk, deciding that will be quicker than driving and trying to find a parking space in town. I call Alex and he picks up on the second ring. 'All OK?'

I laugh. 'Not even hello?'

'Well, you're at work I assume?'

'I am. I'm walking at the moment though.' It's busy outside and I weave my way through throngs of people who, I suspect, are off to work just like me, heads down and in a hurry.

'So just calling to say hi?'

'Well...'

He laughs. 'And Caroline left me a note saying you came by ours last night?'

'Yeah, she said you were working late?'

'I was, yes.'

I leave space for him to expand but he doesn't. Instead he says, 'Go on then.'

'It's Laura.'

'She's still not shown up?'

'No, and the detective is worried too.'

'Really?'

'You sound surprised.'

'I am. Women like Laura go missing all the time.'

'Yeah, no, I know, but we've also got two murders and the detective mentioned something about an old case.'

'An old case?'

'Yes, I don't have any details but I'm going to see him now.' I hear a voice at Alex's end, his muffled answer in turn.

'Sam, I've got to go.'

'OK, speak later?'

'Come for dinner.'

'Yes please.'

'I'll let Caroline know and you can fill me in on this.'

'Thanks Alex.'

—

The detective looks stressed. His demeanour is calm and professional but I can see the clench in his jaw, the tightness of his shoulders. Addiction, I've heard time and time again, is an illness. One where all members of the family are affected. Pity the children, spouses and friends of those who are afflicted with it. I know better than most the devastation it can wreak. I know too how sorry Charlie was for walking out on him, for leaving her daughter. And how that guilt was nowhere near enough to stop her going out and doing it again anyway. It's brutal and undignified and it takes no prisoners.

'Thank you for coming in,' he says.

'No problem. You said there was another case?'

'Yes,' he agrees. We're walking up a set of stairs that run adjacent to the station, eventually hitting the open plan office. The smiley young sergeant says hello and the detective takes me away to a side room. Not the family room this time – I noted the door was closed so maybe someone else is using it. In contrast, this room is a horrible dingy space that is probably used for interrogation. A room made to unsettle the people in it. My head aches, a dull pressure worming behind my eyes. I'm exhausted, I think. I didn't sleep well at all. My dreams were full of my mother and my father. I'd woken after fitful broken hours feeling worse than if I'd just stayed awake. I'd see Alex later and perhaps ask him for something to help me sleep. He was always wary of prescribing such things but knew all too well that insomnia could make me less than functional.

'Clare Parker.' The detective gets an image out of a thin file and slides it over to me.

I frown. 'Yes, I vaguely remember her,' I tell him.

'One of your clients?'

I shake my head. 'No, but I knew her.'

'Knew her?'

I shrug. 'By face and name. She was very young.'

'Only twenty-two when she died.'

'God, how did she die?'

'An overdose.'

'That's sad,' I say, 'but why do you think it's connected to Sid?'

He pulls out a second picture. 'This was her boyfriend, Darren Oliver. He was killed.'

'Gosh,' I manage.

'Low-level dealer. Clare was his girlfriend, he terrorised her.' He opens a file, pulls out a photo and slides it across to me. A man, young but with a hard face. 'His throat was slit.'

'Oh,' I say. 'Just like Sid and Amanda.'

'Right. Clare Parker went missing around this time.'

'Did they die at the same time?'

'No, her body turned up almost a month later.'

'Had she been missing the whole time?'

'Yes, and alive until the day she was found.'

'That's...'

'Weird?' the detective says, and I nod. 'Weirder still, just like Charlie and just like Laura, she'd been trying, and failing to get her act together.'

'That's not uncommon.'

'No, but all three have gone AWOL. Another weird thing – when she was found she was healthy aside from the overdose which killed her. It looked like she'd managed to get herself together, if only briefly.'

I frown, trying to take in what the detective is saying. 'Where was she then?'

'That is the million-dollar question, and judging by the look on your face you have no idea either.'

'No. I...' My phone vibrates on the desk between us, making me jump. I glance at it. Barry. I let it ring out, murmur 'Sorry' to the detective, and it starts ringing again. 'It's Barry,' I say, frowning at the phone, 'from Hope Springs.'

'Maybe get it, ask him about Clare?'
'Barry, hi.'
'Sam, it's Tiny.' I can tell by the tone of his voice that it's nothing good. And that sends a shiver down my spine.

CHAPTER THIRTY-SIX

Seb tells Harry to drive Sam to the hospital and he and Lucy follow only moments behind.

'So tell me again what's happened?' Lucy says.

'Tiny was found at the edge of the Hope Springs plot.'

'How much land do they have?' Lucy asks him.

'Loads.'

'What was he doing out there?'

'That's the thing; no one seems to know.'

'He works there, right?'

'And lives there too.'

'Well,' Lucy shrugs.

'Yeah, no, I know, but Barry says he went for lunch and was due back but never showed. He'd overdosed on insulin and as he's diabetic that's unusual.'

Lucy frowns. 'He has some special needs, according to his report?'

'Yes, but he's savvy enough to take care of his illness and always has. If Barry and a co-worker hadn't found him, he'd have died for sure.'

'When will he wake up?' Lucy asks.

'Doctors seem unsure, but I guess we'll know more once we arrive.'

Sam, Barry and Debbie are all in the waiting room when Seb and Lucy arrive. Barry looks clearly shaken up; his wife is next to him, arm slung across her husband's shoulders. Sam's face is set in its usual scrunched-up stress lines. She stands as Seb comes in. 'He was worried about Laura.'

'I know, you said that.'

Barry stands, holding his hand out. The man's dark skin has a definite grey tinge and he looks frightened. Seb shakes his hand and Debbie murmurs, 'Hello detective, sorry about the circumstances.' Her eyes are red rimmed, she's been crying.

'You found him?' Seb says to Barry.

'I did, yes. Well one of my staff did actually, but we were all looking. Yesterday he didn't come back after lunch, then the day went on, it got dark. I messaged his phone and got a message back.'

'You what?'

Barry nods. 'I know.' He holds his phone out to Seb. Seb scans two messages Barry had sent. At nine p.m. a message comes back:

> Am okay with a friend.

'Which friend was he with?'

'Well that's the thing. His friends are Laura, who is missing, isn't she? Everyone else was at Hope Springs. And the information was so scant.'

'But by the same token,' Debbie says, 'you can understand why we didn't act then.'

'Yes, it's understandable,' Seb says.

Barry goes on, 'I couldn't sleep for thinking about that message. Why no further detail? I was up early, and I tried to call, but nothing. This time all I got was voicemail. I, uh, let myself into his room. I knocked first,' he adds.

Seb shrugs. 'You were concerned, I get it. Did you notice anything unusual?'

'His medication box – the insides were strewn about the place.'

'Is than not normal for him?'

'No.' Barry shakes his head.

'It might sound minor,' Debbie says, her voice soft, 'but Tiny was a neat freak. Honestly, it's a running joke, everything in its place and whatnot. It's one of the things that makes him so good at his job.' Her voice hitches. Barry takes her hand squeezes it.

'So you were in his room, which is on your property?'

'Yes, he has a self-contained studio out over one of the residential blocks. We should have called you then perhaps,' Barry says. 'Anyway, Debbie had to start work. I should have too but I started walking, decided I'd check everywhere and asked Connor to do the same. We found him and it was dumb luck really because he was in a patch of fairly deep woodland.'

'And how's he doing?'

'They don't know.' Barry says. 'If I'd just looked last night…'

'We have no idea how long he'd been there, Barry, and this isn't on you.' Debbie's voice is smooth but the scrunch of her forehead tells Seb she's worried for her husband.

A doctor comes in, sees the extra people and frowns. Seb and Lucy flash their badges and the frown deepens. 'Is this a police matter?'

'Do you think his condition is accidental?'

'He wouldn't be the first diabetic to get his dose wrong.'

'He never gets it wrong,' Barry snaps.

'He was worried though,' Debbie says, 'about Laura,' by way of explanation.

The doctor runs a hand across his face. Seb thinks he looks tired, and also isn't likely to be interested in how this happened so much as what needs to be done next.

'Will he come round?' Seb asks, and sees Barry crumple back into his chair, Debbie beside him, arm stretching back out around her husband's broad shoulders.

'I hope so,' the doctor tells him. 'If he'd been left without treatment for much longer he wouldn't have made it.'

'God.' From Barry, the word comes out on an exhale.

'We will stabilise him and then we'll wake him slowly.'

'When can we talk to him?'

The doctor shrugs. 'When he's awake and if he's up to it.'

'You can't give us a timeframe?'

'I can tell you it won't be today. We'll keep him sedated while we stabilise his blood sugar levels.' He glances at his wristwatch. 'Also visiting hours are over until this evening, so I'm going to politely ask that you all leave.'

'Will you let us know if there's a change?' Debbie asks.

'I will, yes, and you, Barry Sharpe, are listed as his next of kin.' Barry nods. 'I'll be in touch.'

They all walk out of the hospital together. Barry and Debbie leave to return to Hope Springs and Seb says to Sam, 'He's very close to Tiny?'

'Oh yes.'

'And Debbie?'

'Debbie too.'

'Do they have children of their own?'

'Debbie has two children, adults now, but they are no contact.'

'Oh?'

'Yeah,' Sam says, 'it's sad. She went and got clean, but by the time she got out of rehab their father had full custody.'

'She didn't get on with him?'

'By all accounts, no. I think they tried initially and she had supervised visits. I don't know the ins and outs but once they were old enough to make their own decisions they decided not to see her.'

'That's harsh,' Lucy says.

'If she was drinking and using around them they likely had a million reasons not to want to see her,' Seb says, more sharply than he intended.

'Yeah, I know, but she's done well now and she helps a lot of other people,' Sam says. Seb thinks about what she'd told him about her own mother. A woman who never improved and who had damaged Sam and Alex.

'That's true,' he says.

Sam looks up at him, shielding her eyes from the low sun. 'Anyway, Tiny goes looking for Laura and ends up here. Another coincidence?'

'Seems unlikely it's not connected. But his search didn't take him very far, did it.'

'No,' Sam says, frowning.

'Who else is there at Hope Springs?'

'Who could have done this?'

'Yes.'

'God, I'd like to think none of them. But the community there is very transient of course. Loads of people in and out and Barry and Debbie will give a day's work to anyone willing to undertake it.'

'A lot of high-risk people?'

'Yeah, I guess.'

'Hmmm.' Seb turns to Lucy. 'I think we need to go and see who was there yesterday.'

CHAPTER THIRTY-SEVEN

Seb and Lucy make a pit stop for food and coffee. They find a corner of the hospital cafe to regroup in. It's mostly empty and Seb calls into the station, putting the phone on speaker and updating Harry, Finn and Ken.

'What did you pull on Tiny?'

'Real name Marcus Crest, in and out of the care system as a child. Mother had learning difficulties and spent a lot of time institutionalised. Marcus got in with a bad crowd who used him for his size. He was arrested as a minor, he was just seventeen, and came to Hope Springs, which was newly set up.'

'Year?' Seb asks.

'2016.'

'So he's twenty-five?'

'Yes. Knew Laura Doyle through one of the care homes. Whilst Barry helped Marcus, Tiny – Tiny tried to help her to no avail.'

'He's the only permanent resident at Hope Springs?'

'Actually, no, two men older than Tiny have both been there for several years.'

'Names?'

'Owen Sanchez and Timothy Stanton. Both have records, mainly minor offences, though Timothy has a history of violence. Owen was there from the beginning, I believe.'

'Violence?'

'Domestic abuse.'

'Right. Thanks Finn.'

'No problem. You heading over there?'

'We will, yes. Debbie and Barry have just left; we'll give them a chance to get back and follow closely behind.'

—

They end up pulling into the car park almost directly behind Debbie and Barry, who step out of the car, squinting at Seb and Lucy in the low autumnal sun. Barry looks awful. Debbie smiles at them but it looks forced. 'We weren't expecting you quite so soon.'

'We stopped for coffee, hoped to give you a chance to get back.'

'Ah, we did the same, great minds. Come in.'

They follow the couple through. A woman with a high ponytail pulled so tight it makes her skin look stretched smiles at them. 'Hello.'

'Carly,' Debbie says. 'Not sure you've met Detective Locke and um…'

'Detective Sergeant Quinn,' Lucy says.

'Sorry,' Debbie murmurs, 'I'm usually good with names.'

'She is,' Carly agrees. 'How's Tiny?'

Debbie shakes her head. Carly's eyes flick to Barry, who says, 'He'll be fine,' but with little conviction.

'Right,' Carly manages. 'Gosh.'

'Is Timothy around?' Debbie asks Carly.

'Out back I think.'

'Would that be Timothy Stanton?' Seb asks.

'Oh, yes, do you know him?'

'We know of him,' Seb says.

'Ah,' Debbie says. 'Come through into the smaller office, yes?'

Seb follows her. Barry slumps into a chair in the common room. Seb nods at Lucy, a signal to stay with Barry.

In the office Debbie quietly shuts the door. 'You know of Tim's previous troubles?'

'Battering his ex-wife?'

Debbie flinches. 'Would you believe me if I told you he was a changed man?'

Seb shrugs. He's sick of hearing about it, if he's honest. These people who behave awfully but can't help it because they are 'sick'. There was a time when he'd clung to that idea like a drowning man reaching for a life jacket. Long before he started hearing Charlie's endless excuses for what they were. Lies. Good ones, ones she meant ones he was sure. But ultimately ones she couldn't keep.

Debbie sighs. 'Hard to believe it when it seems so hollow,' she says, as if reading his mind. 'Let me call him in?'

'Sure,' Seb says. 'And Owen Sanchez, if possible.'

'Owen's not here today or tomorrow, I'm afraid, but I'll send him your way once he's back.'

'Where is he?'

'At a conference.'

'For what?'

'Advances in medication for anxiety and depression.'

'A medical convention then?'

'Of sorts, yes.' She smiles.

'You were a nurse?'

'I'm still fully trained and qualified. It's certainly helpful in this line of work.'

'But you have a doctor on site?'

'Oh yes, I can't prescribe, and I updated my training after I sorted myself out.'

'But you like to stay up to date on what's happening in the medical world?'

'More Barry than me, actually. He's always hopeful. He lives for the success stories.'

'Right.'

'Anyway, let me go and get Tim.'

'Thank you. If you wouldn't mind sending Lucy in to me, we'll talk to him here?'

'Of course,' Debbie says. She smiles at Seb, but Seb can see that the expression is strained. They are worried about Tiny, and probably unsettled having Hope Springs looked at through this lens.

—

'How's Barry doing?' Seb asks Lucy as she comes in.

'He's quiet, didn't say a lot. Debbie says she's gone to get Tim?'

'That's right. Owen's at a conference.'

'Oh yeah?'

'Apparently so. I made a note of it sent it to Finn to check. He's just messaged to say it's running.'

'What's it about?'

'Medical approaches to treating mental illness.'

A knock at the door. A tall thin man with long ratty brown hair tied in a ponytail comes in a step behind Debbie.

'This is Tim. Tim, Detective Locke, Detective Sergeant Quinn.'

Tim nods. Debbie stands for a moment and Seb tells her, 'We're OK from here.'

After she leaves Seb gestures to a seat and he and Lucy settle into what he thinks are called tub chairs. They are slightly too low and his legs spread out in front of him. Lucy on the other hand fits perfectly. Tim has the same issue as him. 'Did Debbie tell you why we wanted to talk to you?'

'She said it was to do with Tiny?'

'That's right. You know what's happened?'

Tim frowns. 'He took too much insulin. Debbie says he's in a coma but should be OK?'

'Hopefully yes.'

Tim nods, his eyes straying to the window. 'That's good.'

'He was looking for Laura Doyle.'

Tim turns to meet Seb's gaze. 'She'll likely show up.'

'You think she's gone somewhere of her own accord?'

Tim shrugs. He is wearing all black, skinny jeans, a short-sleeved tee. He has an assortment of badly done tattoos on his arms, mostly blue aside from one red rose. Thickly lined and clumsy. 'Probably. She normally does.'

'You know her?'

'I know most of the people who come in here.'

Seb nods. 'That's right, you live here.'

'Ever since I left prison.'

'Where you were put for assault.'

'I was, yes.'

'You beat your ex-wife so badly she was hospitalised for a week.'

His lower lip twitches and he looks down at his hands. 'Don't even remember doing it.'

'Doesn't make it better.'

'No, makes it worse in some ways. She has to relive the horror while I get away with knowing nothing about it.'

'You regret doing it?'

'Every day of my life.'

'Are you in contact with her?'

'No, my amends to Lillian is to stay away. I wrote her a letter, apologising, saying I'd be happy to do it in person but understood if she never wanted to see me again. She chose the latter.'

'What would you have preferred?'

'I'd have preferred to not have done it, to not have become the sort of person who would.'

'You're a changed man, Debbie tells me.'

'I'm trying to be.'

'How did you end up here?'

'Barry goes into prisons, holds recovery meetings for those who are interested. I went every week, got clean, got clear-headed. He said come see him when I got out, I did.'

'And he employed you here?'

'He and Debbie did, yes.'

'What do you do exactly?'

'Bits and bobs, site maintenance, odd jobs. I hold meetings, help out at the clinic.'

'That's with Debbie and Dr Alex Martin?'

'Right.'

'Good success rate?'

'Not really.' He grins.

'So why bother?'

'Because occasionally it sticks.'

'So Laura.' Tim blinks at the sudden change of direction. 'And her ex.'

'Awful man.'

'Or a sick man, like you were?'

'No,' Tim shakes his head, 'that guy's mean sober as well as not.'

'Right.' Seb sees real anger on Tim. 'His rap sheet is certainly colourful.'

Tim's nostrils flare. 'And Laura with her kids to think about.' He shakes his head. 'He's long gone at least, went to stay with some relatives in Australia. Good riddance.'

'She attended some of the meetings here?'

'Oh yes.'

'Same ones Charlie came to?'

'Don't think they were in one together.'

'But Debbie tells me both women wanted to get clean.'

'Wanted but didn't manage, despite all of us trying to help.' He looks out of the window again.

'You knew them both?'

'Laura more so, she's been attending group on and off for almost a year, the whole time I've been here. Charlie I've met a few times.'

'You like Laura?'

'Yeah,' his voice is soft now. 'You could see the good in her.'

'Tiny is her friend?'

'Yeah. I mean probably he has a crush on her.' Seb notes a hint of something there when Tim says that, amusement? Jealousy? Scoffing?

'Did she feel the same?'

'Doubt it.' He snort-laughs.

'Oh?'

'Tiny's nice, sweet even, but not the brightest button, know what I mean?'

Seb nods agreement but decides that he doesn't care much for Tim. He's saying the right things, expressing his regret, but Seb isn't sure he totally means it.

'Did you see Tiny yesterday?'

'Probably in the morning.'

'Probably?'

'I was working on the outbuildings.'

'Which ones?'

Tim blinks. ' 'scuse me?'

'Which outbuildings?'

'Um, numbers four and five,' he says, but it comes out like a question. Comes out as if he's been caught out lying.

'So probably you saw Tiny but you're not sure?'

Tim does that shrug again. 'I mean I see him every day you know, he was here so was I. We would have crossed paths, nodded, but I don't remember exactly where or when.'

'He was here until lunchtime. He spoke to Barry.'

'Yeah, well he's Barry's golden boy.' That jealousy again.

'Heard they were close.'

'Tiny will do anything for Barry.' Seb files that away. He likes Barry, but Barry had access to all the victims, Barry was trusted by them and everyone else. They had accounts of the missing women at least in Clare Parker's case talking about more experimental means of recovery and Debbie had told Seb just this morning that Barry had an interest in such things.

Tim glances at his wristwatch. 'Anyway, day's getting away with me.'

Seb smiles. 'Of course. If you think of anything else…' He holds out a card.

'I'll be in touch.' Tim takes it, leaves the room and is gone.

Lucy raises her eyebrows at Seb, who murmurs, 'Let's get out of here.'

CHAPTER THIRTY-EIGHT

CHARLIE

The girl, Laura, is sweating buckets. It's been hours since anyone has been in, hours now since she had the last lot of pills. I'm hungry, which is nothing new and easy to ignore. I'm also aware I too haven't had the pills but that I don't feel too bad at all. Laura, on the other hand, is suffering. I wet a flannel in the small bathroom, bringing it back out and using it to wipe her brow. She's where I was when I arrived. What had she said? *I used, then I was here.* I keep forcing my mind back to my own arrival. The same pattern. I'd been doing quite well for a week? More. I'd been medicated heavily, going in to Hope Springs to see the doctor, who was helpful and non-judgemental. Not only did he happily prescribe for me, he also sat and listened. He told me to take things one day at a time, to focus on the end goal.

Tilly.

I blink away tears, murmur soft words to Laura and think the last time I did this for someone, mopped another person's brow, it was probably hers. My daughter. Laura slips into restless sleep. I go back to my own bed and watch her from the other side of the room. I have no grasp on time here in this windowless room. I have the sense that quite a few days have passed since I got here. Laura has been in this room with me for over twenty-four hours. I think she'd been next door for one day, maybe two. Maybe even three. Her arrival had coincided with me coming through withdrawal. And I have done that, I think with a moment's fleeting triumph. Short lived, because what good is that while I am here? Locked in an airless dungeon. What is the plan for me? Who is holding me – us – here?

Laura wakes up, coming to with a gasp, eyes wide. Her body bending over double.

I'm off the bed, going to her. 'Look at me,' I say as her wild unfocused eyes scan the room, finally settling on me. They are glassy, but I think she can see me. She lets out a whimper, her stomach makes an awful sound and she starts gagging.

'Come on.' I pull her to standing, knowing what's coming next as I haul her into the bathroom. She hits the tiles, the sound of her knees making an impact so loud it makes me wince. She'll be bruised, I suspect. More to add to the collection of them. Her body littered in stories of a life poorly lived, her thin limbs covered in yellows, blues and purples.

A plume of awful-smelling bile shunts from her into the toilet bowl. Once, twice, three times. Her stomach, I suspect, will feel like it's been razorbladed.

'It's OK,' I murmur, holding strands of greasy hair back from her clammy face. It's not OK, not for her. She'll be at the stage where she feels like every single nerve in her body is on fire. Where her bones ache and her mind is a slippery unstoppable thing. I'd done this with the tablets, whatever they were, and it had hurt. She will be absolutely wretched. When she's finally spent I say, 'Lean on me, I'll help you back to bed.' We move as a pair, making slow juddering progress, her leaning against me. I lay her down on her wheeled hospital bed, noting that the bedding is damp and doesn't smell great.

She falls into sleep again, or more realistically, she passes out. But she's restless and fidgety, crying out, limbs flailing.

I watch her, but at some point I must drift off because I come to and hear the low murmur of voices. Two people are in here, bending over Laura. Laura is whimpering. The door to the room is open. The people have their backs to me. I sit up, quiet, quiet, and stare at the door. The lights in here are low; the corridor outside, however, is brightly lit, and I see a trolley with various small shelves. It's metal. The walls are plain white textured concrete. I can't see any evidence of natural light, just bright fluorescent. Like in a hospital? Maybe. I can't make out what is on the trolley but I think it's like the one I see sat in the middle of our room. A sight I have become used to. A tray of food, normally covered. Alongside it, the small cardboard pill pot, a large two-litre plastic bottle of water beside it.

The door, the open door. I turn quietly, my feet meeting the linoleum floor.

One of the masked figures turns to face me. Dark eyes glint in the dim light and my heart sinks.

They finish whatever it is they were doing to Laura. My hand instinctively reaches into the crook of my arm, the last place a needle stabbed. One of theirs. Laura's breaths are long and even, her face, which had been twisted and contorted in pain, is calm now. A bundle of sheets and blankets are next to Laura's bed and one of the masked people leans down to pick them up. They move to the corridor, putting the dirty bedding on the bottom shelf of the trolley outside. The second figure turns, sees me and meets my eyes. I feel my breath held. My heart pounding.

Was that my chance? That I have just missed? Could I have made it?

It ceases to matter. The door whumps shut. The dim light in our room turns up, revealing the tray, and although I'm hungry I'm also pissed off. I ignore it, turning to face the wall and forcing back tears.

CHAPTER THIRTY-NINE

'Clare Parker was only twenty-two when she went missing,' Harry says.

'How old were her children?'

'Six and four, so she started when she was a child herself,' Harry says, and then remembering perhaps what Seb's own situation had been, he quickly adds, 'But...' before trailing off.

Seb smiles. 'It's OK, Harry, it's very young to be a parent.'

Harry nods, turning to Finn, who steps in. 'We got an address for her mum and dad, Lynn and Mike Parker.' He presses some buttons and Seb's phone pings. 'I've sent it to you. We've called her, and they're both in and said they'd speak to you.'

'OK, great.' Seb goes to stand up.

'Jackie wants to see you first, son,' Ken tells him.

'Oh,' Seb says. 'Right. Lucy, I'll be right back.'

'No rush.' She looks tired, and he makes a mental note to discuss late nights during cases with her. Awkward but perhaps necessary? They are a young team, and while he doesn't expect them not to have lives Lucy has a habit of pulling all-nighters. She's nothing but professional, but it will start to take its toll and he needs them to be sharp, especially mid-investigation.

'Hello,' he calls into Jackie's open office door.

'Don't loiter.'

He steps inside, closing the door behind him. 'Just checking I wasn't disturbing you.'

'No, sit.'

He does. She stares at him, resting her sharp-featured face on steepled fingers. 'Ken told me about the handyman, Tiny.'

'He's in a coma.'

'His own doing?'

'I suspect it's not, no.'

'Thoughts?'

'Everything leads back to the centre.'

'Hope Springs?'

'Yes.'

'They do some fine work, so I've heard.'

'They do. They run various drop-ins, take people in, help with form-filling and even run meetings in prisons.'

'But you want a warrant to search their premises?' Seb had called and left her a message to this effect. He hadn't run it past the rest of the team yet – he'd wanted to see how Jackie might respond first.

'I do.'

'Which is going to piss them off.'

'They deal with people with complex needs, so I think I'll need one even if they agree amicably.'

'But you haven't broached that yet?'

'I'd prefer not to give warning,' he says. What he wants is to go in, say he'd like to search it, get told no and be able to produce the warrant.

'Tell me why.'

'Everyone is linked to them. Charlie, Laura and according to what we've found out, Clare all used their services. Sid and Amanda have attended meetings there.

It's on Clare's notes that she mentioned experimental treatment of some kind. Today I get told one of the men I'd like to speak to is at a conference discussing just that kind of research.'

'You've spoken to Clare's parents?'

'Next visit.'

'Do that and come back to me.'

'You're not saying no.'

'Not yet,' she says, way too cheerfully. Seb manages to avoid rolling his eyes. Instead, he says, 'Thank you, ma'am.' To which Jackie grunts and tells him, 'Close the door on your way out.'

—

Clare Parker's parents, and children, live in a small cottage not entirely dissimilar to the house Seb, Val and Tilly live in, though Seb doesn't see an extension here. They have an almost separate granny annexe for Val, which had been the property's main selling point. Though Val spent the majority of her time in their kitchen – far too much over this past week, Seb thinks with a pang of guilt.

The door opens before Seb and Lucy have a chance to knock. A plump woman with bright blonde hair like her daughter and wide dark eyes answers. 'Police?'

'I'm Detective Inspector Locke this is Detective Sergeant Quinn.' They flash badges. Seb adds, 'It was me you spoke to on the phone.'

'Yes, come in please.' They follow her through to a kitchen just big enough to fit a round table in, which she gestures for them to sit at. 'Mike will be down in a sec, let me get you tea? Coffee?'

Seb spies a pot on the counter. 'Coffee please.'

'Me too,' Lucy murmurs.

Lynn Parker pours cups out, adding a fourth to the table just as the kitchen door opens. A tall man, dark hair, a harassed-looking face that softens when he throws Lucy and Seb a sad smile.

'Hello.'

Once they are all seated Seb says, 'Firstly, I'm sorry for your loss and sorry to bring it all up again.'

'Never mind that.' Mike leans forward. 'Nothing can bring Clare back, but it's always stung that no one ever paid for it.'

'Her death?'

'Yes.'

'You don't think the overdose was accidental?'

Mike and Lynn exchange a look that Seb can't quite read and Lynn sighs. 'We don't, detective, no. Never have. Even at her worst, Clare was self-destructive but generally careful with it. Especially after she had the kids.' Her eyes flick to a photo on the left-hand wall. Seb's eyes follow. Clare's children, well into adolescence now.

'She loved them,' Mike says. 'Despite all her flaws, she loved them, and they loved her.'

'Perhaps you think we're being naive, detective, but Mike and I always believed she'd pull through. That once she was out of Darren's control she'd see the light, sort herself out and come home.'

'We'd have welcomed her,' Mike adds. 'We got things wrong with Clare but we loved her.' He pulls himself up as he says this.

'What do you mean you got things wrong?' Seb asks.

'It's a long story,' Lynn says.

'We're not in a rush,' Seb tells her.

Lynn sighs. 'She was our only child, and we had her late. She was unexpected, very welcome.' She smiles at Mike, who takes her hand in his, squeezing it. Seb had seen things like this rip families apart. In this case, they seemed cemented together by the tragedy. He's glad, especially for Clare's children. He can feel the love in this home. Knows from his own experience that while you can't shield them from pain, you can provide stability, and that is worth a lot. The important and often underrated key to happiness.

'We spoiled her, doted on her, and she made it easy. She was a sweet child, and she grew up to be a sweet teenager too. But it was around what, Mike, year nine?'

He nods. 'Yes.'

'Year nine, she started acting differently. Rude, obnoxious.'

'We figured puberty, you know, you hear all about the teenage moods, and we're old enough to remember Kevin the Teenager,' Mike says with a smile.

'But it got worse. She started—' Lynn pauses. 'She cut her legs with razorblades, she wasn't sleeping, she started bunking off school. We went through her phone and she was being bullied.'

'It was awful,' Mike says. 'A mixed group, boys and girls. No reason other than they thought she was weak, but one of them, a boy, convinced her to send him some pictures.' Mike shakes his head. Lynn takes over. 'They were nudes, and he posted them everywhere. It... It destroyed her.'

'What did you do?' Lucy asks.

'Took her out of school, enrolled her in a small independent that we could ill afford. But her old school, they wouldn't act. Said the images were shared out of school time. The police did what they could, which wasn't much.' Mike shrugs. Seb knows how hard it is for charges to be brought in cases like this. It's getting better, but tech and linked crime have moved faster than the law.

'For a while, she improved, though she never went back to being happy and carefree, and I suppose knowing the images would always be out there somewhere was too much. She didn't make friends at the new school, but she didn't make enemies either. The staff knew what had happened and were supportive.'

'She would have been fine eventually,' Mike says, 'but then she met Darren.'

Seb listens to Mike and Lynn tell him and Lucy a familiar tale. Clare moved out, they had the children quickly, Clare started turning tricks, both she and Darren were using.

'She left him, you know, came home with the children,' Lynn says. 'We were hopeful, but then one morning we woke up, the kids were here, she was gone. Left a note saying she loved him.'

Mike shakes his head. 'It wasn't love.'

'No,' Seb says. 'I don't suppose it was.'

'She came back three months later and she was a mess. We took her to our GP, she was given a social worker.'

'Do you have a name?'

'Anne Marie Olsen. Retired now and honestly fairly useless.'

'Sorry to hear that,' Seb says. He doesn't suggest Clare was difficult to help, though he suspects she was.

'She tried her best, love,' Lynn tells her husband.

'It says in our notes that she was showing signs of improvement?'

'She was. She went onto methadone, attended some meetings at a local drop-in centre. It's like a community project.'

'Hope Springs?'

'That's right. The social worker recommended that. That was a good move. It was... calmer for a while, and we felt better, didn't we, love?'

'We did,' Mike agrees. 'She was here with the children and you could entertain the idea that there might be hope for her yet.'

'Do you know how involved she was at Hope Springs?'

'Um,' Lynn chews her lower lip, 'she helped out sometimes, did some work in the kitchen. Saw the GP there for her prescription, attended meetings – a woman ran those I think.'

'Debbie?'

'That's it, terrible her name slipped my mind, she and her husband were wonderful after Clare was gone.'

'Oh really?'

'Yes, well mainly Barry – he popped by a few times, dropped some information in about what we would and wouldn't be entitled to, benefit wise. Clare liked him a lot, spoke about him very fondly.'

'That's nice,' Seb tells her, but in his mind he's thinking about Barry, the man involved with every single victim. A man who'd never given up hope, and Seb himself knew how dangerous that hope could be. How crushing when it was eroded. How infuriating the people you were trying to help could become.

'So she went back to Darren?'

'Disappeared for a weekend, came home worse for wear and bruised.' Lynn shakes her head. 'She was gone that Monday morning, told us she'd been speaking to someone in the recovery community and they said they could help.'

'Did you get a name?'

'No,' Lynn says, her voice breaking. 'She said he, but nothing else and... It was Monday morning, I had to get the kids to school and... I was cross with her.' She blinks away tears, looking down at the table beneath her hands.

'Understandable,' Seb says.

'I didn't know it would be the last time we'd ever speak.'

CHAPTER FORTY

SAM

Alex is waiting for me outside of my office.

'I walked to work today,' he tells me by way of explanation. 'Figured you could drive me home as you're coming for dinner.'

'Oh, yeah of course. Mind if we stop at mine first though? I've got some bits I need to drop off.'

'Yeah, fine.'

I park up and Alex follows me in. He'd spent most of the short journey here yawning and he yawns again now, sat on my sofa, his long legs out ahead of him.

'Tired?'

'I am, yes.'

'Caroline said you'd been working late?'

'Studying.' He yawns.

'What are you studying?'

'Some new research.'

'About?'

'Addiction treatments and some data on rates of recovery.'

'How's it looking out there?' I try and inject some humour into the question but it falls flat.

He sighs. 'Same as always. People are more likely to get well if they have a reason though.'

I put a few files down on my kitchen table. I'd pulled both Charlie's and Laura's. I remembered a conversation with Laura some time ago about some sort of trial and wanted to go over my old notes. The stack also includes the information the detective gave me about Clare Parker. She'd been with Anne Marie, who left. I took over most of her caseload, and had Clare not met an untimely end, she probably would have been one of my clients.

'Barry's in a right state,' Alex says.

I sigh, sitting on a chair at my table. It's a folding chair, flimsy and uncomfortable. A sign of how little time I spend eating here. I shift and my bones moan. 'Can you blame him?'

'No, but he does take things personally.'

'Tiny is like a son to him,' I snap. 'It is personal.'

'Yeah, no, I know that, and I like Tiny too.'

'Yes, I know. Sorry.' If Alex looks tired, I know I'm exhausted, anxiety ridden and snapping at him for no reason.

'Look, why don't you shower, pack an overnight bag and stay with us tonight.'

'Worried about me?'

'Always.'

I think about that as I get in the shower. Always. I can't imagine how tough it must have been for my brother to lose both of his parents, his mother in the worst possible way, and then to have to take responsibility for me. I wasn't an easy teenager either. I was so brittle with my own grief that I don't think I really considered his. Not until much later.

I dry off and pack a small bag. When I head back out into the living room, I see Alex standing at the fireplace holding a picture. It's our parents and us. An image so sickly sweet it feels like a mirage.

'She was drinking even then you know.' He's talking about Mum.

'She was fine then.'

'She wasn't, she was never fine.'

'Before Dad…'

'Dad held her together; Dad was the one who kept everything going.'

'He loved her.'

'He did, yes, and look where that got him.'

'His cancer wasn't Mum's fault.'

'You don't think stress affects health?'

'I…' I trail off. We've done this a million times before. It's a circular argument. I have forgiven our mum. Alex can't do the same.

'I don't want to argue,' Alex says.

'Me neither.' And I don't; I don't have the energy for it, not with him.

'Then let's not. I know this stuff affects you, and look, I'm sorry about it all too. I liked Charlie, and Laura for that matter.'

'Do you remember Clare Parker?'

He frowns. 'Clare… oh god, yes. OD'd.'

'I only just found that out, actually,' I tell him. 'And her boyfriend was killed.'

'That's right. Dan?'

'Darren.'

'Darren.' He nods. 'I remember him, terrible person.'

'He died the same way as Sid.'

That gives Alex pause. 'He did?'

'Slit throat.'

'But that was a while ago?'

'A year.'

'What's that got to do with Charlie or Laura, or Tiny for that matter?'

'The police think it was the same person.'

'Who killed Sid?' He's frowning.

'And Amanda. Clare went missing too before she died.'

He scrunches up his face even more, putting worry lines across his forehead that are already on the way to being permanent. 'That's right.' He shakes his head. 'Such a shame. As I recall she had two children?'

'Yes.'

'Do they have any leads?'

'Not exactly. They were all linked to Hope Springs, all under some kind of social care.'

'Lots of people linked to Hope Springs don't make it, Sam.'

'Yeah, no, I know.'

He sighs. 'I liked the detective, though we only spoke briefly.' I know they'd spoken to him between clinic sessions. I suspected they'd be back to talk to him again soon. 'But he's really close to this, isn't he.'

'What are you saying?'

Alex shrugs. 'I don't know, maybe he's looking too deeply for connections that are tenuous at best.'

I shake my head now. 'No, I feel the same.'

He gives me a smile and I know what he's saying without words. I'm too close to this too. I'm about to open my mouth and argue when he says, 'Come on, let's go and eat and try and have a night off of worrying about this.'

'Yeah, OK.'

I grab my overnight bag, Alex picks up his briefcase and we leave.

CHAPTER FORTY-ONE

Seb opens the door and is greeted by Mimi meowing and winding herself around his ankles, and wonderful smells emanating from the kitchen, where he heads now. 'Something smells good.'

'Nan baked,' Tilly says, looking up from a sketchpad. She spends a lot of her free time sketching out plans for set designs and thinks this is what she wants to do later on. Seb loves that she's talented and loves that she puts the work in. Really, he just loves her. He goes over now, leaning down and hugging her. She squeezes him back. She is over the tiredness of her birthday and sleepover, and taking a break from the usual teenage gloominess. Shame he was going to have to shatter it. He and Val had decided to wait until the next time they were all in, and that time was now. He'd texted as he left work to remind her, as if she could forget, and now here they were.

'Dinner first, Sebastian.' Val puts a bowl of stew in front of him. He eats and realises he's starving. It has been a busy few days and also a fraught few days, and it isn't over either.

When he's done, Val moves his plate, putting it in the dishwasher. It's quiet in the kitchen; he can hear the ticking clock, Mimi purring and the faint scratch scratch scratch of Tilly's pencil as she sketches. Her face is scrunched up in concentration and his heart lurches.

Val catches his eye above her head and nods.

It's time. God.

'Tilly.'

'Dad.' She looks up, grins, goes back to her pad.

Val takes a seat beside him. 'Matilda, can you stop for a moment.'

'Matilda? Must be serious.' She grins at Val, lays down her pencil and looks from her nan to her dad. The smile falls. 'What's the matter?'

'It's… I've been working a case.'

'Well duh, you left my party sharp enough for it.'

'I did, and I'm sorry.'

'It's fine, Nan let us have pancakes for breakfast anyways.'

'I… what?'

Val shrugs. 'It was a one-off.'

'Anyway, that's not important.'

'You're always stressing the importance of a healthy breakfast, Dad.'

'Well, yes, but…'

Tilly is grinning; she's making fun of him. Any other time and he'd love this, bask in it, drag it out. Raising her, being her dad, is the bright point of his life. Her teenage years have been hard so far because she has started pulling away. Normal, he supposes, but it means that usually when she is like this, smiling and jokey, he tries to prolong it. But not today.

'The case involves Charlie,' he says. Blunt and quick. A wound he has to inflict, and he sees the effect of it immediately. Tilly's face, so like her mother's, is frozen in a smile still but her shoulders sag, her eyes widen.

'Is she…'

'She's not dead. Or I don't think so. She's missing.'

'She's been missing for years,' Tilly says, smile gone, voice hardened, air quotes surrounding the word 'missing'. 'That's nothing new.'

'No. But this time her... partner was killed.'

'Killed as in murdered?'

'Yes. She hasn't been seen since.'

'How long ago?'

'Just under three weeks.'

'Why is it your case?' Her eyes narrow. Tilly is young, silly and naive because she's a child still, mostly. But she's not stupid.

'Charlie and her... the guy were here. In Thamespark.'

Tilly makes a sound that could be a sort of laugh but is devoid of humour.

'She was... she came home?'

'She came back to Thamespark. The town.'

'Did she come here?'

'Not as far as I know.'

'How long was she here?'

'Months. Just under three.'

'Oh.' He can practically see her thinking. Her mother, who she professed not to care about, had been here. In the area. For months. She hadn't come to find her only child. Or him, or Val.

'I have good reason to believe she came back here with the hope of sorting herself out.'

'Sorting herself out?'

'She was trying to get clean.'

'Trying but... failing?'

'It's a hard thing to do,' he says, the excuse sounding weak even to him. Because it is weak, it's not good enough. Tilly deserves better.

'Why now?'

'I don't know.'
'Who killed him, her... whatever?'
'I don't know yet.'
'You think they have M... Charlie?'
'I think it's a strong possibility.'
'Should you even be working this case?'
'Probably not.'
'But you are?'
'I am.'
'Will you find her?'
'I'm trying.'
'Right.'
'I know this is tough.' Val leans over and takes Tilly's hand. Tilly pulls it away and shrugs.
'It's fine, it's not much different to how it usually is, is it? We normally don't know where she is so...' She shrugs again.
'But Tilly...' Seb says.
Tilly stands, making the chair she'd been sitting on scrape backwards. 'I'm tired,' she announces.
'Don't you want cookies?' Val asks Tilly pauses, smiles at her and leans down, giving her a quick hug. 'I'll get some later.'
'Tilly.' Seb goes to stand.
'It's fine, really.' And she is gone.
They hear her door close. Val and Seb look at each other.
'It could have been worse?' Val says.
'It was quite bad.'
'She didn't freak out.'
'I think I'd have preferred it if she had,' Seb says. Tilly's tantrums can be astronomical at times.
'Give her time.'

Val stands, squeezing Seb's shoulder and leaving him alone with his thoughts, the most burning of which is – bloody Charlie. Old resentments, ones he thought he'd put to bed, rearing their ugly heads again. He wasn't a grudge-holding man but he could never imagine fully forgiving Charlie for what she'd done. Not to him, but to Tilly.

He and Val had made a nice life for themselves and for her but the absence of her mother, the awfulness of the reasons why, must eat into Tilly, they must have an impact. And just like that the anger is gone, replaced with sadness, because all he's ever wanted was to protect her from pain, but maybe that's never how life works. All he can do is be there for her if and when she needs him.

CHAPTER FORTY-TWO

Tilly had been up before Seb left. Unusually early for her. She'd told him she was going out with Kai later. Kai is, Seb suspects, Tilly's boyfriend, though she had so far been careful not to label him as such to Seb or to Val.

'Oh, you're meeting early?'
'We might go to Brighton for the day.'
'Right.'
'It's sunny.'
'It is. I'll transfer some money to you.'
'Thanks Dad.' She'd smiled.
'Are you…' That got an eye roll.
'Dad, I'm fine. I hope you find her, of course, and I'm sure you will.' Tilly shrugs. 'This is what she does.'
'If you weren't fine…'
'I'd say. Bye Dad.'

He even had a hug and had held her, inhaling the familiar scent of her, some cheap perfume named after a pop star, which is super sweet, and coconut shampoo.

'Bye Tilly.'
'You all right, guv?' Harry asks now.
'Yes, sorry, you were saying.'
'Hope Springs. Barry has a juvenile record.'
'Oh?'
'Yup, attempted murder.'
'Who did he try and kill?'

'His dad.'

—

'When will the warrant be ready?'

'Hopefully later today,' Seb tells Lucy.

'We could wait until then to talk to Barry?'

'We're here now,' Seb says as they get out of the car.

'I guess.' Lucy trails in behind him.

They are inside. Debbie is talking to the receptionist and looks up with a frown. 'What is it?'

'We'd like to talk to Barry.'

'He's not here right now.'

'Where is he?'

She sighs, eyes flicking to the woman on reception who is looking between Debbie and Seb and Lucy with thinly disguised curiosity.

'Not here.' She inclines her head to a door on the other side of the open hallway.

They end up in a large room. The door on the other side opens and Dr Alex Martin comes out, a stack of papers in hand. 'Oh, hello, detective.'

'Dr Martin.'

The doctor looks at Debbie. 'All OK?'

'They're looking for Barry.'

'Ah.'

'Where is he?' Seb asks Debbie for the second time.

'I'm not sure.'

'You're not sure?'

She sighs, sinks into an armchair. Gestures at two across from hers. There is a low coffee table between them.

Dr Martin puts the paperwork down on a side table, glances at his watch and takes a seat next to Debbie.

'Wasn't he at the hospital?' he asks her. His voice is gentle and low. A good bedside manner, Seb thinks fleetingly. He'd thought the same when they met; even though he'd been busy and stressed he'd also been gentle, especially when he acknowledged Seb's connection to Charlie.

'Not when I left, no.'

Dr Martin says to Seb, 'Barry has been struggling since Tiny – well, it's understandable of course.'

'Right,' Seb says, his sympathy wearing thin. 'But where is he?'

'Well that's just it,' Debbie says, turning damp, wide eyes on Seb. 'I haven't seen him since last night.'

'And last night?'

'We were both at the hospital. Honestly, he's… not himself.'

'Not himself?'

'I mean, he's…' Her eyes dampen again, she is on the verge of tears. 'He's beside himself.'

'Which is unusual for him?'

'You've met him,' Debbie says. 'Barry is even tempered and fairly relaxed.'

'He has a history of being less than even tempered though.'

Debbie frowns. 'He had a difficult childhood and years of addiction, detective, but he has overcome his past.'

'Has he?'

'What are you implying?'

'He attacked his father with a knife.'

'He was a child, and he was defending his mother.'

'Who overdosed just six months later, whilst Barry was in juvenile detention?'

'Yes,' she says, raising her chin in challenge. 'What are you getting at, detective?'

'I'm saying Barry didn't mention this.'

'You didn't ask,' she snaps, then sighs. 'It's not something he likes to dwell on, I'm sure you can understand that. You can't possibly think there's a link between that and,' she waves her hand around, 'this.'

'This? Two missing women, three maybe four murder victims.'

'Four?'

'I strongly suspect Clare Parker's death to have been foul play. So that's Sid, Amanda, Darren and possible Clare.'

'Really?'

'Yes.'

'And you think Barry may be involved? For what reason?'

'His own mother was an addict, and as you've said he's interested in experimental treatments for recovery – maybe he thought he was helping, and maybe he doesn't like it when people don't want to be helped.'

'That's preposterous.' From Dr Martin. 'Barry is a good man, a kind man.'

'Great, when you see him send him my way and he can tell me all about it.'

Lucy puts a hand on Seb's arm; he ignores it but knows that he has probably gone, if not too far, then certainly close.

'If you hear from him,' Lucy says, 'please contact us.'

CHAPTER FORTY-THREE

CHARLIE

She's asleep finally. I dried her duvet out for a few hours. Her sheets are still damp with her own sweat but as that's continuing, I see no point in moving her. She slept fitfully and I sat by her side, holding her hand, smoothing the hair out of her eyes. The tray from yesterday is still in here and it's giving off an unpleasant smell, which is mingling with her pungent stench.

I stand and stretch my arms over my head, looking around the small room as I go. Cameras in each corner. There's even a blinking eye in the small bathroom. No facility I've ever encountered would have let Laura in in such a state without supervision. I suppose, in the end I'd supervised her. Certainly I'd taken care of her. I pause, looking at her small prone body now; she looks impossibly young with her eyes closed, her face smoothed out. Kneeling beside her, patting her face with a damp washcloth, had reminded me of doing the same for Tilly. Before everything went bad – or more to the point, before I went bad.

Sid was dead. I'm still trying to get my head around that. I didn't love him. Hadn't loved another human being since Tilly and Seb, not really. But he wasn't a bad person and he treated me better than plenty had. I'd known shortly after we arrived back here that our days together were numbered. In my head I'd thought, get to Thamespark. Get clean, get respectable. See Tilly.

I wonder now if Seb knows I was there, if Tilly knows and thinks I didn't come to find her.

Seb is a murder detective and Thamespark is a small town. He'll have at least heard about Sid by now.

Laura moans, turning over, and sits up with a gasp.

'Hey,' I say.

'Charlie.' She says my name with relief. I pour her water, now warm, and sit on the edge of her bed, holding the cup to her lips. She goes to chug it and I tell her, 'Sips only.'

'Thanks.' She flumps back on the pillows. I know from experience that just sitting up will have taken a lot of energy out of her.

'How are you feeling?'

'Awful, but maybe a bit better?' She says it like a question.

'I think you did the worst of your detox in another room.'

'Yeah, maybe.'

'Can you work out how long you've been here?'

'No.'

'What was the other room like?'

'I...' She pauses, swallowing thickly. I help her sit up and drink again. 'My throat hurts.'

'Yeah, everything will hurt for a bit.'

'Does it stop?'

'It has for me.'

'You're clean?'

'I guess I am.' I smile, but it's fleeting. I'm clean, great – but I'm a prisoner too.

'We're not meant to be here, are we?'

'What do you mean?'

'This place, it's not a hospital, is it?'

'I don't think so.'

'I heard them, the people here talking.'

'Oh?'

'Yeah, I mean I was pretty out of it, but I think they said your name, maybe mentioned someone – a detective?'

'Oh.'

'I guess the police would have been looking into Sid's death, maybe looking for you.'

'Maybe,' I agree. The police, in the town where Seb worked. Even if he wasn't directly involved he'd hear about it. About me. My heart clenches, a tight first of bitter hurt and regret. Even if it wasn't him, he'd know by now, it's a small team. He'll know I'm in Thamespark, or was if I've been moved somewhere else. Maybe he saw where Sid and I were living. Oh god. He might have stepped into that disgusting place. The flat had been nice when Sid's sister was there. I'd met her briefly, she'd smiled thanks to Sid, who was a pillock but could be kind too. Who could be the kind of man who wanted his sister to be safe. He was not, however, the kind of man his sister could have left her children with, and when we met, she had shielded her children from us with her body. And who could blame her. We'd trashed the place of course, exploding into the space like a dust storm. We'd filled it with warm junkie bodies and bad vibes. Seb will have seen it all. He'll have seen Sid. I wonder if he knows yet who killed him. I wonder if he thinks it was me?

'What else did they say?'

'I didn't catch all of it but they said they had to move me. That wherever I was wasn't secure.'

Laura coughs and I hold out water to her. 'Here,' I say, helping her sip it and thinking, *this is who I should have been*. This is how I should have been with my own kid. I blink back tears, trying to make sense of what she's said without freaking her out any more.

CHAPTER FORTY-FOUR

SAM

'You can't seriously suspect Barry.' I almost laugh but I'm stopped when I see the look in the detective's eyes. That's exactly what he thinks. 'God.' I say the word on an exhale. It's busy today, I have more notes to write up than I care for. My work has suffered with the background worry of Laura, Charlie, Tiny, deaths and now... this.

'Barry is one of the best people I know, detective.'

'With a history of violent crimes.'

'Sure, but Barry turned his life around before he hit twenty-five. He and Debbie have been running Hope Springs for years. They are stalwarts.'

'All roads lead back to Hope Springs.'

'All roads lead back to Gordon too.'

'He has an alibi.'

I scoff at that. 'He wouldn't get his own hands dirty.'

'That's true,' Seb says. 'I also don't think he'd cause aggravation over this and he had no reason at all to go after Amanda.'

'Neither has Barry.'

The detective shrugs. 'Unless she saw something or someone at the flat.'

'Then why didn't she just say that to you in the first place?'

'She was pretty out of it when we found Sid,' Lucy says. 'To be honest we couldn't get much information out of her at all, and then we were told to stop questioning her as she needed medical assistance. She didn't hang around long enough to get any and we were looking for her to talk to when she turned up dead.'

'Barry liked Amanda, and Charlie and Laura. He's helped them all one way or another.'

'I know,' the detective says. 'Look, all I'm doing is giving you a heads up. If you hear from him, or hear where he might be, please let us know.'

'Yes,' I murmur. 'I will, of course.'

After he leaves, I step out to the stairwell and call Alex.

'Yes?' he says, voice curt. He's at work.

'You're busy?'

'I have literally a minute. What's wrong?'

'Nothing.'

'Not true.'

I sigh. 'It's Barry.'

'Is he back?'

'You know he's missing?'

'Debbie mentioned it.'

'Oh,' I say. 'Is she worried?'

'Not unduly. She thinks he's just taking some time out to cool off. The thing with Tiny has hit him pretty hard.'

'Understandable,' I murmur. 'But unlike him to disappear, where would he go?'

Alex sighs. 'Well, that's the thing that's getting to Debbie. She has no idea.' I hear voices in the background. 'Sam, I have to go, will I see you later?' He'd said I could stay with him and Caroline for a few days, which sounds nice, but I'm tired and out of sorts.

'Maybe.'

'OK. Let's speak later anyway.'
'Will do.'

—

Mark comes over to me as soon as I step back into the office. I manage to avoid sighing and am glad when he looks at me with concern. 'Are you all right?'

'Do I not look it?' I smile.

'You look tired.'

'Ha, yeah, maybe I am. It's been a bit of a week.'

'It has, yeah. What are you doing today?'

'Paperwork mainly, but I've just realised I've left quite a bit of it at my flat.' The files I'd taken home the other day. I'd pulled loads on residents and users at Hope Springs including Laura and Charlie and had planned to go and collect them later. I had some vague idea that I'd seen some type of waiver in one of Laura's files, a medical one, and in light of what the detective had said about Clare Parker, I figured perhaps it might be relevant.

'Why don't you take it home?'

'Really?' We do all work from home but it tends to be occasional rather than regular.

'Really.'

'Thanks Mark.'

'Look, I know we don't always see eye to eye, but you're good at your job, great even, and all that aside, hopefully one day you'll take over from me and I can retire.' He's grinning as he says this but he likely means it too. Would I want to do Mark's job? I complain about him all the time, but if my caseload feels unwieldy, I imagine that overseeing various people while working a full caseload, plus all the politicking that he does, must be a huge cross to bear.

'Don't make threats,' I say, 'and don't leave. Not yet.'
'Not yet. Go, I'll call if anything comes up.'

CHAPTER FORTY-FIVE

There is a bigger than normal crowd gathered back at the station. Seb is briefing a team of beat officers about the search later today.

'We are actively searching for Barry from Hope Springs, though he is proving elusive, and most of his connections are at the centre or related to it. We need to be careful during today's search. There are vulnerable people there and Hope Springs may have nothing to do with anything. So the tone we want is firm, polite but thorough.'

They all murmur agreement and Seb tells them they'll meet back here after lunch.

They file out and eventually it's just the small team left.

'So what have we got?' Seb had tasked Harry, Finn and Ken with looking into new treatments for addiction. Harry had been looking online and making calls, while Ken and Finn had been out talking to people around Hartsmead and the encampment.

'Lots of people we spoke to said they take part in various drug trials.'

'Drug trials?' Seb frowns.

'Yes, legitimate ones. Harry has looked up several companies who have reached out to Hope Springs. There isn't a lot of information in the public domain about experimental tests for addiction recovery.'

'Oh,' Seb says, and Harry grins. 'But thanks to our techno wonder kid I have found a few places offering it and I also found a contact for the conference that Owen was attending.'

'Brilliant.'

'Yes – better still they're local. Better Life they are called, run by one Will Shea.'

'That's brilliant.'

'He has free time this afternoon if you can make it before the search.'

'We'll make it. Thanks Harry.'

Harry nods and says, 'We had some interesting conversations with a few people about Hope Springs.'

'Oh?'

'Yes, mostly they are well thought of, though Tim has a reputation for being hard line and also quite patronising.'

'Patronising how?'

'Talks down to people, preaches, same with Owen apparently.'

'Barry?'

'Well liked.'

'But he brought Owen and Tim in?'

'Unclear. Seemingly Debbie gets final say on who lives there. She's the owner after all, it's her inheritance that pays for the place.'

'They have some private funding though?'

Harry shakes his head. 'Very little actually. They are a registered charity and have had some sizeable donations. One fairly big one from Alex Martin.'

'Sam's brother?'

'That's right.'

'He and Sam lost their mum to addiction.'

'They did, yes, and he doesn't take any payment for the clinics he runs there.'

'Wow, that's generous.'

Harry shrugs. 'He works as a consultant at a swanky Harley Street office a couple of days a week. I think that pulls in a lot of cash.'

'Does Sam know?'

'Maybe, maybe not. The donation was anonymous,' Harry says.

'Then how did you find out?'

'Like I said, techno wonder kid.'

'I can't take credit,' Finn pipes up, 'Harry followed this trail all by himself.'

Harry grins. 'Taught by the best.' The two young men exchange a smile. If Seb was less anxious right now this would warm his heart. As it is, the anxiety wins out. They are close and Hope Springs is the key, he's sure of it.

'Is Owen back at work?'

'He's on the rota this week,' Lucy says, and Seb turns to her with raised eyebrows. She shrugs. 'It's pinned up behind reception.'

'Oh, well spotted.'

'Your eyes are likely too old to see at that distance.' She smiles sweetly and that does make him smile.

'Thanks for that.'

'Anytime.'

'Shall we go and see this Will Shea?'

'Yes.'

His phone buzzes in his pocket. Faye. 'Can you give me a sec, Lucy?'

'Yeah, course. I'll meet you in the car park?'

CHAPTER FORTY-SIX

CHARLIE

The door opens with a soft whoompf which makes me think the mechanism for locking us in may be digital. A tray is wheeled in. One smallish person, face masked, hair covered, and two larger people. One big, like all over big, the other one tall but slight. Both men, I reckon. The other person could be a man or a woman. They load old plates onto the trolley, swapping things out. The tall, thin man pauses at the door.

'You look a lot better, Charlie.'

'I feel it, too,' I say, resisting the urge to charge at this person, to batter my way past him. I'd feel better for all of two seconds, but I wouldn't succeed in escaping. He sees my eyes go to the door and keeps looking at me steadily. 'Laura is sick.'

'We're helping her too.'

'Are you?'

He blinks but doesn't answer.

'You can't keep us here, we haven't agreed to anything.'

'You'll thank us for this. One day.'

'Maybe, when you let me go.' I swallow and ask, 'When will that be?'

The corners of his eyes crinkle up above the mask. 'Let's see how you do.'

The door closes and they are gone.

'I know that man.' A half whisper from the other side of the room. I snap my head around to look at Laura. She looks better than she did, though she's still in a stale crumpled hospital gown and her hair is glued to the sides of her face in thin greasy tendrils.

'Who is he?'

'It's Tim – he lives at Hope Springs.' She pauses, coughing so hard her body shakes and so too does the bed.

I pass her one of the bottled waters. 'Thanks.'

'I think I know who you mean,' I say. I sat in meetings at Hope Springs with him. He gave off a less than fuzzy vibe. I hung out with lowlives of course, I was a lowlife myself after all, but Tim had something mean about him. Eyes like a snake.

'Laura,' I say again, my heart picking up pace as I think now about the days and weeks leading up to this moment, 'tell me again exactly what was going on for you, before you woke up here.'

CHAPTER FORTY-SEVEN

Will Shea works out of a small single-storey facility. When Seb and Lucy step inside they are hit with the smell of bleach. On the front desk is a woman with immaculately groomed hair and lips that are too big to be natural. Seb tries not to stare as she takes their names, her voice a low murmur, and tells them to follow her.

She leads them through a long white corridor to a large office with a nice view of a small and very green garden outside.

'Will.'

'Thanks, Sharon.' Will stands. He is tall and muscular, wide in a way that lets you know he goes to the gym and takes it very seriously.

'You must be Detective Inspector Locke?' he says to Seb, who nods. They shake hands.

'This is Detective Sergeant Quinn.'

Will Shea turns brilliantly white teeth on her and grins. 'Pleasure to meet you both, or perhaps that's the wrong phrasing, given the context.'

Seb offers a brief smile as they all take seats. 'I appreciate you seeing us so quickly.'

Will's face settles into serious lines. Seb notes that whatever his expression, his forehead is perfectly smooth. Botox, whitened teeth, a pumped body. A man selling a brand and selling it well. Harry had shown them Will's impressive Instagram page, where he had hundreds of thousands of followers.

'This is a treatment centre?'

'Of sorts. I prefer wellness centre.'

'But people can come here to overcome problems?'

'They can, yes, but sometimes people come to us for a recharge or a break too.'

'For a tidy sum.'

Will shrugs. 'We're not a charity and don't pretend to be.'

'And you run drug trials?'

'We ran one, singular.'

'What was it for?'

'A mood-regulating medication which I guess would come under the umbrella of psychedelic drugs.'

'LSD?'

'We are using hallucinogens,' he says. 'Micro-dosing has been found to have excellent impacts on all kinds of things. It's fairly mainstream now, lots of literature supporting it.'

'And Barry was interested in this?'

'Barry?'

'From Hope Springs?'

'Oh no, not Barry, Debbie.'

Seb pauses. He says to Lucy, 'That event that Owen attended.' Lucy pulls up the flyer Harry found on her phone and shows it to Will.

'Oh yes, I know these people, a tough love approach to treating problems of addiction and lack of productivity. I was at the conference, some good speakers, interesting ideas. Mainly that in order to recover, people have to be entirely removed from their current lives.'

'Like a rehab?'

'Yes, but mandatory.'

'What do you think about that?'

Will shrugs. 'I think it would be hard to get approval, legally.'

'Right. Owen was in attendance on behalf of Hope Springs.'

Will frowns. 'Are you sure?'

'Debbie said he was, why?'

'I didn't see him.'

'Maybe you missed him?'

'Unlikely – it was a pretty small event and I know Owen quite well.'

'Right,' Seb says, 'perhaps I was mistaken.' He wasn't, though. Debbie had told them that was where Owen was, and why he'd been unavailable for questioning.

Seb's phone buzzes. He pulls it from his pocket, surprised to see the name that pops up. 'We'll let you get on,' he says, standing.

'Yeah, OK. Let me know if you need any more help?'

'We will.'

'You cut that short,' Lucy says as they step outside.

Seb holds up a hand and picks up the call.

–

'Dammnit missed him,' he murmurs, 'Barry,' to Lucy. As soon as they are outside the facility, Seb rings Barry back.

'I'm getting his voicemail.' Seb frowns at Lucy, hanging up the call. 'But he's left a message, hang on.'

He dials in and listens to the message on loudspeaker. 'Detective Inspector Locke, sorry not to have called sooner, I... I found some paperwork at Hope Springs. It was about – well I'm not totally sure what it was about.

A trial, by the looks of it, but I know nothing about it and… Look. I don't know who I can trust, but maybe you can help. Call me.'

CHAPTER FORTY-EIGHT

SAM

I get back to my flat and am surprised at how exhausted I feel. I sink into one of my armchairs, cheap IKEA ones that are genuinely comfortable, and consider sacking off my reports and instead just going for a nap. I don't. I let myself sit for a few minutes and then I stand, head into my kitchen and make a strong cup of tea. I'm in an upstairs flat in a block of two. Alex helped me out with the deposit and we'd found this new build. I'd dithered between wanting a garden and not having anyone above me. In the end, I'd decided peace was more important than a garden I likely wouldn't have time to maintain anyway. Sometimes when I get in from work, I'm agitated enough without hearing someone's TV or footsteps above my head. The man who lives downstairs has never complained and he has also done a much better job with the garden than I probably would have. He's recently added a collection of gnomes, funny little squat creatures. I find myself smiling out at them as I wait for the kettle to boil.

I have tea, I have opened my laptop and I start methodically working through the ridiculous form-filling for every case I've dealt with in the past week. I work my way through familiar but no less daunting domestic horrors. I reduce each highly emotionally charged situation into a box-ticking exercise and finally, finally I am almost at the end. When I glance at the clock, I see I've been at it for three hours. If I'd been in the office, I'd have been interrupted multiple times. As it stands, it's 4:30 and I am free for the day!

I check my phone, which I'd switched to silent, and see a missed call from Barry and one from the detective. I dial Barry and get voicemail.

I call the detective back, chastising myself mentally for not at least having it on vibrate.

He picks up on the third ring. 'Sam, hello.'

'Hello, detective, sorry to have missed you. I came home to catch up on paperwork.'

'No problem.'

'What's up?'

'I had a message from Barry which was slightly concerning, have you heard from him?'

'Yes,' I say, 'I had a missed call from him.'

'What time?'

'Hang on.' I pull the phone away from my ear and check the time stamp. 'Just after one.'

'That must have been just after he called me.'

'What did he say?'

'That he'd found some paperwork at Hope Springs about some kind of trial.'

'Trial?'

'Like a drug trial maybe.'

'Oh.' I frown. 'They don't hold them there, but I know there have been a few locally.'

'Yes, we just spoke to a Will Shea, who said he'd dealt with Hope Springs.'

'I've heard Alex mention him, I think.'

'Do you remember what he said?'

'Not exactly, no, sorry, though I'll see him later and I'll ask.'

'Appreciated.'

'Are you still planning to question Barry?'

'Yes, if we can track him down.'

'Debbie said he'd gone AWOL, she must be so worried.'

'Mmm, must be.' A pause. 'How well do you know her?'

'Debbie?'

'Yes.'

'I mean, not as well as I know Barry.'

'How come?'

'I guess because Barry runs the outreach and drop-in sessions, along with a few meetings where I send clients.' It's not that entirely though. I've never really warmed to Debbie. She says all the right things, does all the right things, but we don't gel.

'It's her place though.'

'Well yeah, but they're a couple.'

'A couple, but not married,' the detective tells me.

'Oh,' I say, surprised. 'I just assumed they were. They've been together yonks though.'

'They have, and running Hope Springs for a really long time.'

'I imagine they have different strengths.'

'Yes,' the detective says, but there's something in his voice.

'What is it?' I ask.

'Nothing, or I'm not sure yet.'

'Right,' I say feeling more annoyed than I probably should. 'For what it's worth I like Barry a lot.' I more than like Barry, though I don't need to say that explicitly. 'I know you think everything points to him as a suspect.'

'Some things do. His proximity and involvement with everyone in this case, for example.'

'You could say the same about me, detective.'

'I could,' he says, 'only you were accounted for at your office when Sid was killed.'

'Thanks, I guess.'

'Sorry, that came out more bluntly than I meant. Look, to be honest, the message from Barry makes me more concerned for his welfare than suspicious.'

'Oh.' Now my heart is racing. 'I'll have a ring round and see if any of my clients have seen him?'

'I'd appreciate that, if you have the time?'

I do, though it is a thin sliver between now and heading over to Alex and Caroline's.

'We're looking too, and we'll follow up in a few hours.'

'Yeah, OK.'

I hang up with a sigh, rub my tired eyes, open my phone and start making calls that will all either go unanswered or go on for too long.

CHAPTER FORTY-NINE

'Well?' Lucy asks as Seb hangs up the call.

'She's absolutely certain Barry isn't involved in any wrongdoing.'

Lucy shrugs. 'He might be.'

'He might, but that message suggests it could be someone else.'

'Or he's trying to deflect,' Harry pipes up.

'Also possible.' Seb glances at his wristwatch. 'It's probably time to head back to Hope Springs, the team should be there ready to start the search.'

'Yes.'

–

Debbie glares at Seb. 'Why didn't you just ask?'

'I'm asking now.'

'You're asking with a search warrant,' she scoffs, 'it's hardly the same.'

'If I had just asked, would you have let us in?'

'I would, though I might have wanted twenty-four hours, which isn't unreasonable. This is a therapeutic setting and we have people living here.'

'I understand your viewpoint,' Seb says, and he does. 'From mine, we don't want to give people here any warning for good reason.'

'You surely don't suspect any of our residents or service users?'

Seb doesn't respond. Debbie sighs and steps aside, swinging the door wide open. 'Come in, I guess.'

Seb has Lucy, Harry and Finn with him. There is a wider team of officers and they liaise at the back of the property. Seb is working off a map of the place, amazed again at how much of it there is. A large amount of acreage, which he supposes you can get if you head to the edges of the town. Thamespark is surrounded by greenbelt and woodland, a strong part of its appeal.

Seb takes Debbie and Barry's main office. Debbie trails behind him until he turns and says, 'Can you leave me to it please?'

She scowls but goes. Seb starts methodically going through paper files while Harry and Finn sit looking through the various computers that all use the same cloud system.

'Barry said he's found evidence of a clinical trial being run here, said he found paperwork to back it up. We're looking for that.'

'Well he's probably got it with him?'

'Perhaps, but maybe you can find it digitally.'

'Maybe,' Finn says, face scrunched up in concentration. 'As they all use laptops, we can always take one with us.'

'Good call.'

Minutes turn to hours and before they know it, the day is closing in around them.

Seb leaves the offices – they'd managed to go through all three of them – and heads outside to join other officers.

'Anything of interest?'

Seb is handed some confiscated drugs along with information on where on the property they were found.

He heads back inside as the extra officers pack up and leave.

Debbie is in the large shared kitchen, face pinched and drawn. 'You're finished?' she asks.

'For now.'

'Is that a threat, detective?'

'Not a threat, but we might need to come back.'

'Find anything?'

He shows her the confiscated drugs.

'Oh,' she says, her frown deepening, her eyes wide.

'Sorry,' Seb says.

She waves a hand and sighs. 'Detective, it's the nature of this job, though if possible I would like the list of where you found these?'

'I've already asked DS Quinn to email it. It may even be with you now.'

Debbie glances at her phone and nods. 'Yes, it's there. Thank you.'

'What will you do with the people who brought them in?'

She sighs. 'God, I don't know. I'd probably send them packing, Barry may have other ideas.' She smiles as she says his name.

'Have you heard from him?'

'No.' She shakes her head. 'This is the longest we haven't spoken for… well, in all the time I've known him.'

'Did you argue?'

She scowls at him. 'What? No.'

'And the last time you saw him was after we saw you in the hospital?'

She nods. 'Yes, he said he needed some space, which was understandable, I felt, given the circumstances.'

'Right.' They know that Barry did indeed go into the hospital that day.

'What time did he message?'

'Early. Sevenish.' Seb nods, Barry had arrived at the hospital at ten; he'd called Seb almost a whole day later. Where the hell was he?

'And you have no idea where he might have gone, or who he might have contacted.'

'No, detective, our whole lives are here.'

'No friends or family elsewhere?'

'No. I think you know about his past. Needless to say he has nothing to do with them.'

'You're both estranged from your families?'

'Yes.'

'Your children must be adults by now.' Seb says the words gently, but judging by the flinch from Debbie he may as well have screamed them in her face.

'They are, yes.'

'Do you keep up with them?' He knows she doesn't. He is in fact due to speak to her son and daughter this evening.

'I know what they are doing.'

'How?'

She smiles. 'Social media is a wonderful thing, detective.'

'That must be upsetting for you.'

'It is, of course, but also motivating.' She sticks her chin out. 'If I can help other people avoid the pain I went through…'

She trails off. Seb smiles. 'That's a good attitude.'

He and Lucy are leaving Hope Springs and driving two towns across to visit Debbie's children when his phone rings. Lucy grabs it and puts it on speaker.

'Hello.'

'Guv, it's Harry.'

'Yes.'

'It's the hospital, where Tiny is.'

'Oh?'

'Security saw someone on camera trying to smother him.'

'What?'

'I know.'

'When?'

'About half an hour ago.'

'Why are we only finding out about this now?'

'Well they called 999. The officer who got the call only realised after he'd arrived that he is linked to an active case.'

Seb swears under his breath as he swerves to avoid a car pulling out of a corner with no warning.

'Guv?'

'Yes. Do they have an ID on the person who went in?'

'Looked like someone who worked there – scrubs, crocs, mask on, hair covered. Probably a male though, tall.'

Seb weighs that up; he's starting to think that whoever has taken Charlie and Laura – whoever took Clare too, he thinks – is trying to get them clean. Someone with a medical background would be an obvious choice. Maybe that someone works at the hospital.

'And why didn't they succeed?'

'The doctor was doing rounds, came in and must have interrupted just in time. The masked person left and they were none the wiser until the security guard came down from his office to warn them.'

'So whoever it was is probably long gone?'
'Yes.'
'Is someone posted to stay outside the door?'
'Yes, and I'll go in with Finn now to take statements?'
'Please. We'll talk in an hour or so.'

CHAPTER FIFTY

CHARLIE

'How are you feeling?' I ask Laura, helping her as she sits up. Her hair is lank and greasy but overall she looks a lot better.

'Not so bad,' she shrugs, 'all things considered.'

I smile. 'If only we weren't being kept prisoners, we may be on the path to living our best lives yet.'

'Am I clean?'

'You're detoxed.' I frown. 'I think they put you through it a lot faster than they did me though.'

'Maybe you were the test.'

'I think I was, yes.'

We sit in silence, my thoughts whirring. *What the hell? Why are we here?* Laura is right, we are detoxed. We are clean, and it is that that is giving me at least a glimmer of hope that we may eventually get out of here. Why bother otherwise? What would the point be? Although, on the other hand, we've been taken, haven't we? Kidnapped. And who would do that but a mad man or woman?

It's unnervingly quiet down here. I've started to suspect that perhaps we are underground. The air when the door is opened seems just as stale as the air in here. At night there is some kind of air conditioning system that kicks in with a faint whir but it never feels or smells quite fresh.

'Laura, you should shower.'

'Is it safe?'

'Well, I did.'

'Are they watching?'

'There's a camera in the bathroom but I think from the way it's angled they can probably only see our feet.'

She nods, stands and heads into the bathroom.

I've seen Laura around and about in some right states before. She'd shown up at the flat to see Sid I think in nothing but a nightdress and flip-flops. But actually, being here with her and getting to know her as the stench of the drugs has worn off, she's not that sort of person at all. I wonder if that's true of her then maybe, just maybe, there's hope for me.

Maybe Charlotte Locke without the drugs is a good mother or a better mother or at the very least able to show up. Even a few months ago when I'd stood and watched my daughter through a windowpane, when I'd seen Seb leave the house with a woman who made him smile... Even then, with all my good intentions, I'd felt that familiar spike. Self-pity... if you had my life, you'd do this too.

Only that's not the case, is it? Seb had my life, and while we hadn't shared a childhood, his had been littered with enough awfulness to make him cross, bitter, resentful. But he was none of those things. He wasn't an excitable man, not when I knew him, and I doubt he is now. He was calm, steady, accepting and dependable. He was young when Tilly came along and he got on with it.

If I get out of here, no, *when*, when I get out of here, I'll spend the rest of my life trying somehow to be more like that.

CHAPTER FIFTY-ONE

SAM

The calls are pretty much pointless, as I'd suspected they would be. By the time I hang up the last call any good coming home to do paperwork might have done me is all but wiped out. It's five in the evening, which is probably not a reasonable drinking hour, but I head into the kitchen anyway, open my fridge and pour myself a small glass of dry white wine. I'm heading back into my sitting room when I see the thin folder of files I'd brought back the other day, including Laura's – that's right, I'd wanted to look up that waiver. I take a sip of wine, savouring not just the flavour but also the immediate easing of tension as my shoulders drop. Alex and I have discussed drink of course, and drugs. Both of us have it ingrained through our work that addiction is a physical illness as much as it is mental. People who have it, people like my mum, are built different. I never saw her have one drink. Even when we were small, when she and Dad were happy, even then, she'd been the life and soul of every party. My dad, who was quiet and reserved, used to shine in her glow.

I don't drink often but I think about it a lot, which leads me to believe that perhaps I have the machinery there, trapped in my DNA somehow. I've always been careful as a result. I limit what I have in the house, I don't drink often in social situations, I sip every drink even when I want to down it.

I put the glass down, worry about Barry clouding my mind. I haven't had a serious relationship since I was at university, have never come close to having anything like Alex has with Caroline. I use my job as an excuse, or so Alex says, but honestly, it would be hard to find someone who would put up with the insane hours I can put in, not to mention the crisis calls from clients. I saw in Barry that same drive I have I suppose, a desire to help that is a need really.

God, I hope he's OK. I don't for a second think he has anything to do with any of this. I've never much liked Owen and Tim, thinking about it, though I like most of the other people linked to Hope Springs. I meant to say so to the detective. I'll call him about that when I find that waiver.

I go through the stack and become more unsettled as I work my way down.

Laura's file isn't here. Nor is Charlie's.

I know I brought them in. I remember putting them in my car, carrying them in, dumping them here on the table, and I've not touched them since.

CHAPTER FIFTY-TWO

'You must be DI Locke?'

'I am. This is Detective Sergeant Quinn. You're James Sanderson?'

'I am, come in.' Seb and Lucy follow him through to a minimalist-style living room. In fact, the whole house is the same. A neat two up two down. There's almost nothing inside that isn't oatmeal.

'This is my sister Isabelle.' She raises a hand but doesn't get up off the beige sofa. On a low pale wooden coffee table is a water jug and glasses. James gestures, adding, 'I can get you something else if you'd prefer?'

'No,' Seb says, 'that's fine.' Time is hurrying on and he has that feeling, as though the answers are just within reach. All the parts of the mad puzzle are working around in his head, so close to clicking into place and giving him the full picture.

'Thank you for seeing us,' he begins. 'I understand that given the circumstances it can't be easy.'

'Ha,' Isabelle says. All eyes turn to her and James sighs.

'Neither of us have anything to do with Debbie.'

'That must be tough,' Lucy says.

'It's not as tough as being in her life.'

'Even after she cleaned her act up?' Seb asks, finding he's genuinely curious. Not least on a personal level. If they find Charlie alive and well, if she improves – how would that look for Tilly and him and Val and Faye?

'If anything she's more insufferable since she cleaned up her act.' Isabelle's words are spiky but her shrug is relaxed. It says – it's shit but it's how it is.

'Oh?'

'The way she tells it,' James chimes in, 'she was downtrodden and abused by my father, who wanted nothing more than to keep her down. The truth is, he paid for multiple rehabs, including the one where she met Owen and allegedly became all born again.'

'Owen?' Seb frowns. 'Not Barry?'

'She met Owen first – they came up with the initial idea for Hope Springs.'

'But they're not, or they weren't… a couple?'

'No, though I suspect Owen wishes they were.'

'OK,' Seb says taking in this information. He was certain Debbie said Barry had brought Owen and Tim in. 'What about Tim Stanton?'

'Don't know who he is,' James says, glancing at Isabelle, who also shakes her head.

'OK, so she met Owen and then…?'

'Left Dad, divorced him, took half the house and as much money as she could get. Inherited an insane amount from her parents shortly after the divorce was finalised.'

'Which she used to set up Hope Springs?'

'Yes, though there would have been some left over. She left Dad short, which is an understatement. And she also told him unless he gave her full custody of us that's the way it was going to be.'

'And he wouldn't?'

'No, he's a good dad. Our needs have always come first. He wanted us to have a good relationship with her and hoped one day they might even share custody, but the courts gave us to him for a reason. Not to mention by this time I was thirteen, Iz was twelve. We started off visiting her and she was all right for maybe a month, and then every single visit was an attack on Dad and a massive guilt trip.' James shakes his head. 'That would have been bad enough, I suppose, but it all came to a head two years later when Owen caught Iz smoking a joint at the back of Hope Springs.'

'Oh?'

'I mean,' Isabelle says, 'probably not the best move, but considering the things we'd seen her doing – lines of coke off the side of our sink at home for example.' She shrugs. 'Not so bad.'

'What did he do?' Seb asks.

James and Isabelle exchange a look. 'He locked me in one of the cellar rooms.'

Seb frowns; they'd just spent the afternoon searching Hope Springs, and he'd not seen a cellar, or any rooms below ground level.

'For how long?' Lucy asks.

'Two days.'

James shakes his head. 'Debbie told me she'd gone back to Dad's; I didn't even think to question it.'

'Isabelle,' Seb leans forward, 'we weren't aware of a basement at Hope Springs.'

'Oh, well you wouldn't be. There's this whole underground bunker sort of thing right on the edge of the property. It's well hidden at the back of what I think is now some kind of dormitory. The entrance is in woodland, so unless you knew where it was...' She shrugs.

Lucy and Seb exchange a look. His heart picks up pace. A bunker wasn't on the plans, so they had no reason to be looking for one.

'What's it like down there, is it habitable?' Seb asks, forcing his voice to remain even.

'It wasn't then, but they had plans for it apparently.'

'What did Debbie say when she found out what Owen had done?'

'That it was for my own good,' Isabelle says, jaw firm, eyes ablaze with anger, 'for smoking a cigarette while I called my boyfriend at fourteen. They also took my phone and went through it.' She shakes her head. 'Genuinely, she's an awful person.'

'This was what, a decade ago?'

'Yes. Maybe a bit more.'

'Did Barry know?'

'I doubt it. I think there has always been a lot that Barry, and most people, don't know about her.' Isabelle says the words with venom.

Seb pulls one of the maps from their search up on his phone and holds it out to Isabelle. 'Could you show me where the entrance is?'

'Yeah, of course.' She scrolls across and points. 'There.' Not far from where Tiny was found but well beyond the extent of the search they'd undertaken today.

'Thank you,' Seb says, standing.

'We wouldn't be surprised if she was involved in all this. Her and Owen,' Isabelle says.

'Two murders and two disappearances?' he says, not mentioning Clare Parker or her ex-partner for now.

'Yup. There's something wrong with her. Izzy was terrified, in a real state. Her own daughter, who she claimed to love so much she'd do anything to get custody.

She was awful to Dad too. Coercive control, which people didn't know about so much back then. It took years for him to even consider that the whole thing wasn't his fault.'

'Some part of him knew though,' Isabelle says. 'Which is why he was willing to be poor to keep us safe.'

'Yes, that's true. Her addiction probably saved us all, which sounds mad but,' James shrugs, 'there it is.'

'Thank you both.'

'No problem – let us know when you get her locked up.'

CHAPTER FIFTY-THREE

CHARLIE

I have made Laura tell me three times the chain of events that led to her being here and she has listened to me tell her everything I remember too.

We'd both been high when we were taken and neither of us has clear memories of it.

'Do you think they gave us something else too?' Laura asks, and I nod.

'Yeah, maybe.'

I'd thought about that, because although blackouts account for large portions of my life, usually I had some scant recollections. I have no memory at all of being taken here, of arriving. I was at the flat, furious at Sid. I used, then I was here.

'I feel better,' Laura says.

I sigh. 'Me too.'

'Maybe whoever has us was just trying to help?' She says it like a question. I have no answer, and it feels confusing to grasp because they have helped. I've wanted to get clean for so long, have tried so many times, that it felt impossibly out of reach.

'They killed Sid,' I say. The one hard truth that makes me think these people aren't on our side. Not really.

Laura opens her mouth to respond but whatever she was going to say gets forgotten as the door opens and a person is shoved in through it.

CHAPTER FIFTY-FOUR

SAM

I get to Alex's, nerves jangled, mind thrumming. Had someone been in my flat? It was possible. Of course it was. I kept myself low key on social media. I didn't even have an active LinkedIn. In my line of work, it's important not to be contactable. Clients can be temperamental and challenging. They can invade your personal space if you let them. I blurred enough boundaries, took calls at odd times, did house visits and other things outside of working hours but I never, ever gave out my address.

Caroline answers with a smile. 'Hello.'

'Hey.'

She frowns. 'Are you all right?'

'Yes. Well, tired. Maybe.' I offer her a smile but it's hard work.

'Of course you are, come in.'

I do so, slipping off my shoes, putting my feet into my slippers, which live here. This place that is my second home, my real home. These thoughts jar with the one unspooling in my mind.

'Where's Jess?'

'Dance and then cinema, a whole gaggle of them, and I will need to go and collect her soonish actually. She said she'd text, though you can wait here of course.' She smiles. We are in the kitchen.

'Where's Alex?'

She frowns, glances at the clock above my head. 'Late, and his phone's off.'

'That's odd,' I mutter.

'I know,' she sighs. 'Whatever it is he's been working on lately has him utterly absorbed, which is great on one hand but...'

'A bit annoying for you?'

She grins. 'A bit sometimes, yes.' Her grin doesn't meet her eyes and that makes me pause.

'Caroline?'

Her eyes fill with tears; she waves a hand in my direction, shaking her head.

'Caroline,' I say again, 'what is it?'

'Oh, god. Nothing? Probably nothing.'

'Talk to me.' I perch at the island; she takes a stool opposite and sighs.

'I don't know what it is.'

'The late nights?'

'Right, that and, he's still cheerful, still saying all the right things but, he's late a lot. When I ask where he's been, he's vague: "Oh god, I don't want to bore you."'

'That's unusual?'

'Yes,' she says. 'We don't keep secrets. Like, we have separate lives: he has his work, I have mine. We both have Jess, although he's brushed her off a few times recently too.'

'That is unlike him.'

'I know. It is. Exactly. He just seems... so... distracted.'

'And do you know for sure that he's at work?'

'Well, here's the thing. One evening, I was worried about him, working so late, you know. I boxed up dinner, drove over to the surgery, and he wasn't there.' Her voice is small.

I reach across the island, take her hand. 'I ended up on this Mumsnet rabbit hole. General consensus – he's having an affair.'

'No,' I say, 'he wouldn't.' My heart is racing. My hands damp. Solid, dependable Alex.

'I know, and I'm sure you're right.'

'Did you ask him where he was?'

'Not exactly. Just said, "How was your evening?"'

'And he said?'

'Dull.'

'You need to talk to him.'

'I know. There will be a reasonable explanation.'

'I'm sure of it,' I agree, squeezing her hand. 'Anyway…'

Her phone beeps and she groans.

'Mum taxi?'

'Right, will you be OK here?'

'Of course.'

I wait until I hear the door click closed behind her and then I slip into his office, palms damp, heart thumping. Trying to push this new and worrying conversation out of mind, which is useless because it just adds to all the other thoughts clamouring for attention. I head over to his desk and I open drawers, nothing unusual, nothing unusual…

My files.

Laura's, Charlie's. I pull them out. Beneath them is Clare's, and underneath that is an agreement of some kind. I scan it; it looks like it's with some pharmaceutical company. I force my eyes down and there is his signature, and Debbie's. I read it. Permission to use facility A. The address given – Hope Springs. Test subjects… no names, but I read height, weight, ages. They match those of Charlie. Laura.

What the hell.

A shadow falls across the desk and the hairs on the back of my neck stand up. I whip round, paperwork clutched to my chest, and we come face to face.

'Hello sis.'

CHAPTER FIFTY-FIVE

The entrance is exactly where Isabelle had said it would be. They'd approached it through the woodland behind Hope Springs, hopefully not alerting Debbie to the fact that they are here.

It's a large locked door but Seb has a team with him who break it in minutes. The door opens and a whumpf of air escapes. A light immediately comes on, exposing a corridor at the end of which is a staircase. Seb looks at his colleagues; Lucy and Harry are here with a team of officers, big ones who Seb had handpicked – just in case.

He presses a finger to his lips; they'd managed not to make too big a racket opening the place up and he hopes they still have the element of surprise. He motions for everyone to follow him.

Down the stairs is another long corridor, what looks like a small office at the end, a tiny room with the door ajar. He swings it open, trolleys, what looks like a plethora of medical supplies, a laundry area.

The next room along looks like it is set up to hold a person – there is a bed and an en-suite – but it's empty. Harry and other officers head to the office at the end of the hall and come back just seconds later with Tim and Owen, hands cuffed behind them.

'Huh,' Seb says.

'This door's locked,' Lucy says.

'Key?' Seb is talking to Owen and Tim.

Tim looks sideways, spits on the floor. With a sigh, Owen says, 'Electronic, there's a remote on the desk in the office.'

Lucy goes for the remote while Owen and Tim are walked out and into a waiting police van.

CHAPTER FIFTY-SIX

SAM

'Alex.' I turn around and look into eyes as familiar as my own. 'Why?'

He sighs, stepping further into the office. I am uncomfortably aware that he is blocking the door. Which my mind immediately dismisses as stupid. This is Alex. I'm not in danger. I step back. He steps forward.

'We've had some success you know.'

'W... what?'

'Tim, and Carly, you know, the girl who works on reception?'

I nod.

'She was a hopeless case. Stuck on the merry-go-round of get slightly better, take up with some idiot, abandon her child. She's thriving now, works at Hope Springs. Liaises with people for Debbie and me.'

'Debbie?'

He smiles. 'A brilliant woman.'

'You're in it together?'

'We shared the same frustrations. The same annoyances. The truth that you always fail to see, Sam, is that many of these people are already dead. We just formalised it.'

'Alex, this isn't you...'

'It absolutely is me.' His voice is hard and steely. 'I tolerate your bleeding heart thing because I know you mean well, but honestly Sam, where does it all end? What ever changes?'

'People have to choose to get well.'

'What, like Mum did? She ought to have been locked up, dried out and she might have stood a chance. It's the only way. Plus drugs have come a long way. We have more choices in treatment than ever.'

'You've been testing various concoctions on people without permission?'

'People who would have died anyway.'

'Like Clare Parker?'

'Clare was hopeful, did well even, but as soon as she was out started making noises about our unfair treatment.' He shakes his head. 'The lack of gratitude.'

'So now what?' I ask, though I'm not entirely sure I want to know.

CHAPTER FIFTY-SEVEN

CHARLIE

Barry, our unexpected plus-one, had looked as shocked as I'd felt.

'What's happening?' I'd asked the second after he was shunted into the room.

'It's Debbie,' he says. 'She's been using this place as some kind of test centre.'

'Where are we?'

'Hope Springs.'

'Really?'

'Really.' He pauses and I watch him grappling to get his emotions under check.

'You knew nothing about this?' I say it like a question, but it's a statement really.

'What, kidnapping and murder?' He meets my eyes.

'You lived with her, you know her.'

'I thought I knew her, Charlie. I guess I was wrong.'

'Why are you here with us?' Laura asks.

'I found some stuff when I was going over old records, and Tiny is in hospital. I don't suppose you know that.'

'Is he all right?' Laura asks, eyes widening, fear for her friend making her already tense body even tighter.

'He's being looked after but...' Barry's eyes are damp. 'It was a very close call. He got the dose wrong for his insulin.'

Laura frowns. 'Tiny would never do that, he's so careful.'

'Exactly what I thought. But Debbie, she was so insistent, which made me suspicious. That and the fact that I might never have found him. None of us come out past the woodland area at the edge of Hope Springs. We never have any need to, but that's where he was found.'

'What's beyond the boundary?' I ask.

'This place. A whole underground facility.'

'That Debbie has kept secret from you?'

'From everyone,' he pauses. 'Actually that's not entirely true – it turns out quite a few people seem to know about this place. Just not me.'

—

Time passes: an hour, maybe two. I tell Barry everything that has happened here. I tell him too that I'm clean.

'Will you stay that way?' he asks. 'If and when we get out of here?'

'Yes,' I say, no doubt in my voice and no doubt in my heart.

'You'd have done it anyway,' he says. 'Eventually.'

'Maybe,' I tell him. Though I'm not sure if that's true, and if it's not, should I be grateful to Debbie?

'No,' he says, 'I had a good feeling and about you Laura.' She nods, but it's a weak movement.

The door opens and Barry immediately stands, putting his body between the door and us. But it's not the people in masks – Owen, Debbie and Tim, he's told us. It's people in uniforms, police uniforms, and they pour in in a stream.

Barry steps forward, Laura and I cling to each other a few steps behind him. He moves aside and I come face to face with Seb.

CHAPTER FIFTY-EIGHT

'Are you OK?' Seb asks Charlie, amazed that upon seeing her the thing he feels most strongly is relief.

She nods.

'There are paramedics on their way.'

She nods again. Seb blinks, and she feels tears sting her eyes. 'Thank you.'

He turns because he's afraid that he too might cry, and he's not even sure what the tears would be for. Lucy steps forward, taking over and helping Laura and Charlie up and out. Charlie looks back once and her eyes catch Seb's. She gives him a small smile which he returns, and in that moment she is hit with a hundred memories, a series of all of the kindnesses he'd shown her, which were too many. Far more than she deserved. And now here he is again, rescuing her from this makeshift prison. Saving not only the day but maybe her life too. She mouths, 'Thank you.' And he nods, heading up behind them.

Barry is a step behind Seb. 'Hey.'

'Barry, I'm glad you're OK.'

'I am. Have you got Debbie?'

'No.'

'She's gone?'

Seb says, 'This is all her doing, isn't it?' He'd realised that Barry had run because he'd suspected her.

Barry nods. 'Hers and Alex Martin's.'
'Dr Alex Martin?' Seb frowns.
'Right.'

CHAPTER FIFTY-NINE

SAM

We hear the sirens. Alex pauses, head tilted, and I think even at this stage, he doesn't for a second think they have come for him. Has he always been so arrogant? So hard and unyielding? I think of Caroline, Jess. I think of the years he'd raised me. The small things I hide from Alex because I know he won't necessarily approve. The way I'd always just thought it was his standards. His high standards, which are a good thing.

I'm crying, sobbing now, my shoulders shaking.

Alex steps forward, concern etching his face. 'Sam, nothing's changed, I'm still me.'

'No,' I step back again, shaking my head. 'Alex, you lied to me. You've been lying to Caroline.'

'Caroline will understand.'

'Will she? That you and Debbie are in cahoots.'

'It's nothing like that,' he scowls. 'I'd never cheat on her.'

'But you'd commit murder?'

'I didn't commit murder.'

'But you sanctioned it?'

'I was part of the decision-making process around removing problems. Those men, the partners, they hinder recovery, they cause children, children like *us*, Sam, to suffer with no mothers.'

'And Amanda?'

He sighs. 'Unfortunate. She saw Tim leaving after Sid was killed. Swore to Tim she wouldn't say anything but,' he shrugs, and I look at him, wondering who the hell he is, 'we couldn't risk it. Look, we're on the verge of something. A breakthrough in the way addicts are treated. It's big, Sam, and important.'

'And illegal and wrong.'

There is a banging at the door. Shouting. Alex looks surprised. Then panicked. The door clicks open. I hear Caroline, who must have just got home, the sound of Jess crying, and then there is a swarm of people.

Alex is cuffed, taken from his own office, his own house and spat out onto the Instagrammable drive, where Jess and Caroline are both standing, mouths agape. Caroline runs to him. My brother; her husband. He avoids looking at her, allows a uniformed police officer to ease him into a car.

They drive away and we are left surrounded by people waiting to question us. I have no idea what comes next.

EPILOGUE

'He's nice,' Faye says, grinning at Seb, who is looking at Tilly and Kai. The two teenagers are settled on the lawn among a gaggle of their other friends currently taking it in turns to photograph themselves holding Mimi. Mimi for her part in it is placid but looks uncomfortable.

'They'll be lucky not to get scratched,' Val sighs.

'Mimi wouldn't hurt them,' Seb says, and it's true. If ever a cat thought she was a person, she is it.

'Classic only child pet.' Faye grins. Seb rolls his eyes and Faye laughs. 'Hey, I know my dog was the brother I never had nor wanted.'

Seb feels a hand on his shoulder. It's Barry. 'We're heading off, man.'

'Yeah, OK. Thanks for coming.'

'Thanks for the invite,' Sam says. It had been a brilliant day celebrating Tilly's sixteenth birthday. It had been almost a full year since the arrests, the rescue and the closure of Hope Springs. Barry had set up a drop-in centre via the council, Sam had gone to help as had Tiny, and Seb supposes one thing had led to another between Sam and Barry as these things tended to. Owen, Alex and Tim were in prison. Debbie was found and detained at Gatwick where she'd been attempting to leave the country on a false passport. None of them would ever get out, though

Debbie had a weird online following and had branded herself as some kind of guru from her prison cell.

Faye had moved in with Seb, Tilly and Val. So after the BBQ was finished, she'd still be here. She'd be here when he woke up tomorrow morning and she'd be here on Monday when he got home from work.

He'd bought a ring, which he is carrying around in his pocket, nervously waiting for the right time. Tilly calls out to her and Faye leaves his side, squeezing his arm and going to his daughter. She is being roped into taking group photos now.

'She's good with her,' Charlie says. He swears she walks silently because he never seems to hear her approach.

'She is, yes.'

'You probably don't want to let that one go, Seb.'

'I think I should marry her.' He looks down at the small woman who looks a million miles from the one he'd rescued in a damp basement almost twelve months ago. Her soft blonde hair shines. Her skin is clear. She looks hardened, harder than she would have, had she chosen a different path, but overall she looks well. And she is. She and Laura rent a flat in the centre of town. Charlie is working in a local cafe and slowly but surely, she is rebuilding the life she once tore down.

Tilly refused to speak to her for almost six months. When she finally did, it was stilted, and while the relationship between mother and daughter isn't exactly smooth, it is getting better. Charlie is in therapy, not just for her addiction but also to come to terms with the kidnapping. It's helping.

'You definitely should,' Charlie says, and he can tell by the way that she says it that she means it. She's not the girl he once knew, and she's not the addict he once hated. She'd come out of some miserable things, mostly self-inflicted. But she is different, better, and Seb is pleased she is here. Today he'd felt a real moment of happiness to see her and Val light the candles on the cake Val had made for Tilly. Mother, daughter, granddaughter, standing side by side. A sight he thought he'd never see.

Tilly comes over now, standing in front of her parents; she shows them the set of images that Faye has just taken.

'They're great,' Charlie says. 'Nice memories of a good day.'

'Yeah.' Tilly smiles and steps between Charlie and Seb, wrapping an arm around each of her parents, carefully turning the phone around by Charlie's shoulder and telling her dad, 'Try not to scowl,' which makes Charlie laugh. Seb attempts a smile, which looks like a grimace. Tilly sticks her tongue out and snaps the photo.

A LETTER FROM NJ MACKAY

This is Sebastian Locke's last story and this one is very personal. Seb is investigating a murder that involves a missing person and the missing person is his ex-wife Charlie. For those who have read books one and two, you'll know that Charlotte Locke (Charlie) is an addict who has made some terrible choices that have had a lasting impact on the family she left behind. Though the book deals with hard topics, and ones that are close to my heart, I think it has some hope in it too.

Thank you for picking up *The Vanished*. I hope you've enjoyed hanging out with Seb, his colleagues and his unconventional family as much as I enjoyed writing them.

ACKNOWLEDGEMENTS

Thank you so much to my fantastic editor, Keshini Naidoo at Hera Books. Also a huge thank you to the wider team at Canelo and Hera, Jennie, Kim, Dan, Deirbhile and Kate. Thank you to Miranda for copy-editing so thoroughly and Vicki for proofreading. I'm delighted to have another fabulous cover, thank you to The Parish.

Thank you to Hattie Grünewald for making the deal and helping me bring Seb to readers. Thanks to the Criminal Minds group for all the usual support, and to my husband and sons.